PREMEDITATED MORTAR

PREHABILITATED MORTAR

A FIXER-UPPER MYSTERY

PREMEDITATED MORTAR

KATE CARLISLE

WHEELER PUBLISHING
A part of Gale, a Cengage Company

GALE
A Cengage Company

Wheeler Publishing® Large Print Softcover Cozy Mysteries.
The text of this Large Print edition is unabridged.
Other aspects of the book may vary from the original edition.
Set in 16 pt. Plantin.

LIBRARY OF CONGRESS CIP DATA ON FILE.
CATALOGUING IN PUBLICATION FOR THIS BOOK
IS AVAILABLE FROM THE LIBRARY OF CONGRESS.

ISBN-13: 978-1-4328-8401-7 (softcover alk. paper)

Published in 2021 by arrangement with Berkley, an imprint of Penguin Publishing Group, a division of Penguin Random House, LLC

Printed in Mexico
Print Number: 01   Print Year: 2021

This book is dedicated to the memory of my brother, Bill Beaver. He had a big heart and a quick, dry wit. He was a character, a raconteur, soft-spoken, complicated, and generous, and he was handsome and oh so charming. He painted houses and read books and walked the streets of his beloved San Francisco every day until the very end. I will always love you and miss you, Billy.

CHAPTER ONE

MacKintyre Sullivan, world-famous crime novelist and former Navy SEAL, had the dark good looks of a movie star, with deep blue eyes, an awesome body, and a sexy smile. The first time I ever saw him, he made a big impression on me. And that was just from staring at his photo on the back cover of his latest Jake Slater thriller. In person, Mac looked even better.

Much like his daredevil fictional protagonist Jake, Mac Sullivan was also kind, courageous, and loyal, with a generous nature and a strong dose of cynical humor. Not to mention, he was brave and strong and — okay, I might be getting carried away.

I met Mac two years ago when my bicycle brakes malfunctioned while I was riding downhill on the highway. Rapidly picking up speed, I frantically struggled to keep the bike straight and avoid crashing into the guardrail. After surviving another hairpin turn, I strategically aimed for a safe-looking meadow. Unfortunately it was riddled with dirt clods, rocks, and slippery slimy mud under the grassy surface.

The bike made it only so far before ejecting me. I flew over the handlebars and skidded across the uneven surface, ending up sprawled facedown in a large puddle of thick mud and brush. Mac happened to be driving along the highway, saw it happen, and rushed to my rescue.

It might've been what you'd call a "meet cute," except for the fact that my face was smeared with mud and weeds and I was pretty sure I had a concussion. I had scrapes and bruises everywhere on my body, along with a twisted ankle. Not such a cute moment for me.

Later, Mac deduced that someone had deliberately tampered with my brakes. As it turned out, that "someone" was a crazed murderer. So, good times.

My name is Shannon Hammer and I'm a building contractor specializing in Victorian home restoration in Lighthouse Cove, a small coastal town in Northern California. Somewhere during those first few months, MacKintyre Sullivan and I became good friends and eventually more than friends, a fact that continued to surprise me and even caused me to pinch myself occasionally.

Like now, for instance. I was in my kitchen making dinner, checking on the baked potatoes, and as I closed the oven door, I glanced across the room — and there he was. The hunky megastar author was standing at the counter slicing cucumbers for our salad. He looked so cheerful and contented. Chopping up veggies, for goodness' sake.

Mac had been out of town for the past few weeks, visiting his agent and his editor and all the people who worked so hard to publish his bestselling thrillers. He and his agent were also working on the next Jake Slater movie deal. He had stopped off in Los Angeles for a few days to visit his adorable niece Callie and had only returned home yesterday. And first thing this morning, he was back at work on his current manuscript.

While he was on the road, Mac and I talked on the phone every night. We exchanged stories and laughed and told each other every little thing that had been going on in our lives. There was just one topic that never came up. We never talked about "us." We were friends, lovers, and always had a great time together. I knew how Mac felt about me and I felt the same way about him, so why would I want to rock the boat?

It might get awkward. It might change everything. Why push it? Why take a chance that the conversation could twist the easygoing, warm, and cozy dynamic we had developed?

On the other hand, I was curious. I had no idea where Mac saw himself in five years. I was pretty sure he was planning to stay in Lighthouse Cove, but did he see me as a part of his future?

It was tempting to just let the topic die a quiet death because the simple truth was, Mac made me happy. As far as I was concerned, we belonged together. And he obviously agreed because, well, there he was, standing in my kitchen, now chopping up a carrot. It almost made me laugh because seriously, the guy was kind of a superstar. Three — and soon to be four — of his ten Jake Slater books had been turned into major motion pictures starring the biggest names in show biz. He would occasionally fly off to exotic locales to watch the filming and he always attended the film premieres in New York, London, and Hollywood. And then there were his yearly book tours around the country.

And me? I was a small-town girl, living and working in the place where I was born. I loved it here, had lots of good friends, owned my own construction company, and wouldn't want to live anywhere else.

So whether we belonged together forever or not, we were doing just fine right now.

At that moment, my adorable Westie, Robbie — short for Rob Roy — came scurrying down the hall, ready to play.

"Hello, you," I murmured. He barked joyously in response and I reached down to pick him up. I gave him some scratches behind his ears and he licked my neck, making me laugh.

Mac set down the knife, put the salad bowl in the refrigerator, and checked his watch. "I'd better go turn on the grill. It'll take about ten minutes to heat up." He gave me a quick look, then frowned. "What? What is it?"

"Nothing," I said lightly. "I was just . . . looking."

"At me?"

I smiled and set Robbie down on the floor. "Yes."

"Everything okay?"

"Couldn't be better."

He crossed the room and pulled me into his arms. "Can I tell you how much I wanted to be here with you tonight?"

"Yes, you may."

"It's true. I had to finish one more chapter

first, but I kept getting distracted, kept procrastinating. I'd stand up, stretch, walk the floor, try to find things to do around the house. Anything but sit down and write." He shook his head. "I managed to find some mindless tasks, like rearranging the bookshelves and fixing the light switch in the kitchen."

"That's not like you."

"No. I tend to attack a book with single-minded determination."

"I know." I smiled. "You forget to eat."

"True." He smirked. "You would know."

I always made it a point to show up with a basket of ready-to-eat food — potato chips, veggies, string cheese, granola bars — whenever Mac was in the middle of a manuscript. He would answer the door, grab the basket, and basically shut the door in my face.

Now he ran his hands up and down my arms. "But today I just wanted to get out of there and be with you."

"But you still finished the chapter."

"Yeah. I had to promise myself a big reward if I buckled down and finished it."

"So what did you reward yourself with?"

He pressed his forehead to mine. "You."

I closed my eyes and savored the moment, then looked up at him, frowning. "What's wrong with the light switch? Do we need to rewire something?"

He laughed out loud. "Always the contractor."

"Hey, my crew and I remodeled your kitchen. If something goes wrong, I want to fix it."

"It was nothing. A loose screw on the light plate."

My eyes widened. "Oh my goodness. And you fixed it all by yourself?"

He grinned. "Can you believe it?"

"You are so awesome," I whispered, and patted my heart.

He gave a bashful shrug. "I know."

With a laugh, I pushed away from him. "Nut."

"That's me." He reached for the wine bottle. "Okay, I'm going to pour us both another glass of wine and go start the grill."

"Perfect. Potatoes will be ready in ten minutes and once the steaks are ready, I'll toss the salad and we'll sit down."

He poured the wine, then planted a kiss on my lips and strolled to the back door. "Oh, and when I get back inside, remind me to ask you about the Gables."

I raised my eyebrows. "Um, okay."

Frowning, he said, "So you know what that is?"

13

"Sure."

He nodded slowly, then walked out to the backyard to start up the grill. I took utensils and napkins into the dining room to set the table. If Mac wanted to talk about the Gables, I figured we'd better use the more formal setting. This was going to get serious.

I was back in the kitchen when he came inside. "So what do you want to know about the Gables?"

"Everything." He picked up his wineglass and leaned against the counter. "It's a place around here, right? I only just heard about it for the first time today when I was approached by someone from a development company. Apparently they're turning some old run-down building into a retail space and they're looking for local investors. My business manager is really upbeat about the project and referred the developer to me. Her name is Rachel Powers. Have you heard of her?"

"Vaguely." My friend Jane Hennessey had mentioned her name, I thought, but I had never met her. "So they want to enlist some big names, I guess."

"That's the impression I got. Not that I'm a big name."

"You're pretty big around here." I picked

14

up my wineglass. "It's smart of them to find someone famous who also lives in the area. Theoretically, you'll talk up the project wherever you go and people will listen. And that might bring in more investors." I angled my head and looked at him. "You look a little wary. Don't you think it's a good investment?"

"I have no idea what to think, but wariness is a natural reaction." But then he grinned. "Especially since I've never heard of the place before today."

I pulled the steaks from the refrigerator. "Did this developer tell you much about the Gables?"

"That's the thing that made me suspicious. She wouldn't tell me anything. Said it would be more exciting if I could see it first. Then she'd give me a tour and point out all the positives."

"In this case, she's probably right. It'll make much more of an impression on you if you see it first." I took a minute to freshen the water in Robbie's and Tiger's bowls before returning to the subject. "I'm still surprised you've never heard of the Gables. You've lived here for at least two years."

"Right, and I'm clueless, which never feels good to me." He sat down at the kitchen table and patted his leg. Robbie gave a

rapturous bark and jumped onto his lap.
"So clue me in."

Was it wrong to be jealous of my dog? I
wondered.

"It's funny," I said, "because you drive
past it all the time. It's about a mile north
of town."

Now he looked baffled. "It is? I've never
noticed a sign or anything."

"There aren't any signs. And it's hard to
see the buildings from the highway. They're
all tucked behind a hill."

Mac lived three miles north of town in
the big house next to the old lighthouse, so
he would've passed the Gables every time
he drove into town. But again, it was well
hidden from the road. If you didn't know
the old place was there, you wouldn't have
a clue.

Robbie hopped down to the floor and was
quickly replaced by Tiger, my marmalade
cat. Mac grinned and agreeably began to
stroke her soft fur. I loved that the man was
so attentive to my little creatures. I could
hear Tiger purring from halfway across the
room. It was hard to blame her.

"So why have I never even heard of this
place before today?" he asked.

I took butter and sour cream out of the
fridge. "Most people around town don't like

16

to talk about it."

"Why not?"

To answer this, I first had to fortify myself with a hearty sip of wine. "Because for over a hundred years, the Gables was an insane asylum."

He blinked, then gaped. "Wait. What?"

"We should put the steaks on."

He shook his head and gave a short laugh. "Way to drop a bombshell, Irish."

I winced. He did look a little shell-shocked. "Sorry."

"That's okay. I'm sure I'll have a few dozen questions for you, but let's get everything on the table before we talk. This sounds like it could get intense."

"Oh, yeah."

He grabbed the plate with the steaks. "I'll get these grilled. Then we can talk while we eat."

Mac managed to make it through the next fifteen minutes of intensive dinner prep without asking any questions. He bided his time, grilling the steaks to perfection while I tossed the salad. He cut open the baked potatoes and heaped on butter, sour cream, and chives. And as soon as we were seated at the dining room table, he pounced. "Now tell me everything you know."

I swallowed a bite of my baked potato and took a quick sip of wine while I tried to recall my local history. "Okay. The Gables was built in the 1870s and back then it was known as the Northern California Asylum for the Insane. They changed the name in the 1960s."

He nodded slowly. "Of course. By then it would've been considered cruel to use the term *insane asylum.*"

"That's right," I said. "And then in the early eighties, the government started cutting off funding, so mental hospitals across the country were closing. But the Gables managed to stay open until around 2002 because they had private funding."

"Do you know where the money came from?"

"From the family of one of the patients."

"So one family paid for the entire facility to stay open?"

"Yes."

"That's awfully generous. But I guess if the place was caring for their loved one, it was worth it to them." He took a forkful of salad, and we both chewed silently for a moment. "So what can you tell me about the place itself?"

"From one angle, your developer is right. You definitely have to see it to believe it.

18

It's massive. The architecture itself is spectacular. Classic Victorian style with a gothic edge. Very dark stone walls, tall towers, ironwork details. There are seven large buildings altogether, and they stretch across the entire hillside." My enthusiasm grew as I talked about the place. "Oh, and there are gargoyles."

He grinned. "Cool."

"The property is beautiful, too. It's situated on a huge piece of land that straddles the ridge at the top of Mount Clausen. The views are amazing."

Mount Clausen had been named after Herman Clausen, one of the founders of Lighthouse Cove. He was a prosperous dairy farmer who had been known as the Butterfat King for obvious reasons.

Mac gazed at me. "Sounds like you've been up there."

"Of course." I took a bite of steak and swallowed it before explaining. "My friends and I used to take field trips up there."

"For real? Field trips to the insane asylum?"

I chuckled. "They weren't really field trips, but we would occasionally drive up and look around. It's beautiful really, but ever since it closed down, it's just plain creepy. It used to be surrounded by a really

19

high, thick concrete wall, but that was torn down. Now it's surrounded by chain-link fencing."

He snorted. "Like that ever stopped anyone."

"Especially high school kids," I agreed. "The exterior is still very impressive, but the inside is a horrific mess. The walls and ceilings are filthy, all the paint is peeling, and there are cracks everywhere. I'm sure there were animals living inside for years, and the ivy that grew on the brick walls managed to slip through the windows and started growing up the walls of the hallways and the rooms. It's dark and forbidding. It kind of looks haunted."

He raised an eyebrow. "Sounds pretty bad. What are the chances of this development project actually succeeding?"

"Don't get me wrong," I rushed to add. "The chances are excellent. The creep factor is really just surface stuff. The development company recently went through and did an intense cleaning and disinfecting of the entire complex. But the individual leaseholders will be responsible for painting and refurbishing and remodeling their spaces, and that'll be extensive. They'll need a lot of landscaping work, too, of course. It's like any big rehab job. Only in this case, it's on a massive scale."

His eyes narrowed, but they still gleamed with humor. "Why do I get the feeling that you're already involved in this?"

"Because, of course I am." I smiled and took another bite of steak. "You were back east all month so you didn't hear the news, but Jane put in a bid for one wing of the old hospital and she won the contract."

He blinked. "Jane? You're kidding me."

"Nope." I grinned. Of all my girlfriends, I'd known Jane Hennessey the longest. We met in first grade and clicked as soon as we looked around and realized we were both taller than all of the boys in class. When you're six years old, that's a truly meaningful basis for friendship.

A few years ago my construction crew and I had refurbished her grandmother's huge Victorian mansion — formerly a brothel — and helped turn it into an elegant inn. A room at Hennessey House was now one of the most sought-after reservations on the northern coast.

And now we hoped to accomplish that same feat up at the Gables.

"What does she have in mind for the space?"

"A hotel," I whispered excitedly.

He paused, then held his hands out. "Well,

why not? Her Hennessey House has been a great success story."

"Exactly. My crew and I are starting work next week," I continued. "We plan on turning the north wing of the Gables into a beautiful new Hennessey Hotel, complete with a restaurant, bar, and spa."

"Wow. I'm really happy to hear it." He set down his wineglass and reached for my hand. I covered his with mine. "It makes me feel a lot better about my decision to invest in the project."

"I'm glad. Are you going to meet with the development people soon?"

"Yeah. Rachel wants to give me a tour this Friday."

I swirled my wine, wondering how soon I could ask Jane more about Rachel. She would've gotten to know her pretty well while going through the leasing process. But Jane was at a hotel conference in San Francisco for a few days, so my questions would have to wait. "If you'd like to take a look at the place, I can drive you up there tomorrow. It might give you a better perspective before you meet with Rachel. A little sneak preview, if you know what I mean."

"You bet I do."

After dinner, both Robbie and Tiger clamored for Mac's attention while I loaded the dishwasher and cleaned and straightened the kitchen.

As Mac gave Robbie's tummy a brisk rub, he asked, "What convinced Jane to take a chance on the Gables project?"

I leaned against the counter and took another fortifying sip of wine. *It wasn't breaking any girlfriend rules to tell him the truth, was it?* I wondered. After a deep sigh, I said, "You'll find out sooner or later, but Jane's mother was a patient at the Gables off and on for years."

"Oh wow. Babe, I had no idea. I'm sorry."

"Yeah, me, too. Jane went through a rough time for a few years. She never knew when her mom might have another breakdown and disappear for a few months or a year."

"Did she ever go up there to visit her mom?"

"She did, and I went with her a few times."

"Really?" He gazed up at me. "So you were actually inside the place? Back when it was a hospital?"

"Yes. It was years ago, of course." But it still brought a rush of melancholy memories, and I had to shake them off. "And then just a few weeks ago, after Jane got the deal, we went up there to survey the interiors and check out the amount of work we'll need to do."

"Was it weird to go back inside?"

"Oh, definitely. But I tried to ignore the vibes and concentrate on the building itself." I sat at the table and pulled Tiger into my arms for a quick hug. "I've been doing a lot of research on the architecture and history of these institutions around the country and on the Gables in particular. It's really helping me get a feel for what the original architects had in mind. And since it's been designated a historical landmark, we'll have to strictly abide by a bunch of construction and demolition rules we normally wouldn't have to consider."

"It sounds like you've done your homework."

"I have. It's fascinating. And I'm totally psyched at the possibility of turning something that was creepy and morbid into a beautiful new place for Jane to expand her hotel empire."

"If it's as creepy as you say, maybe it'll turn out to be haunted after all."

"Oh, don't say haunted . . ." We'd had enough of that already, thanks.

He grinned at that. "I know you'll do an awesome job on the beautification, but I want to see it while it's still creepy and morbid."

"I can make that happen," I said, with a snap of my fingers.

"Fantastic," he said, and winked roguishly. "Creepy and morbid are my stock-in-trade."

CHAPTER TWO

The next morning I turned off the highway and drove up the hill for several hundred yards until I passed Big Hat Rock — so named because the huge boulder resembled a forty-foot-tall solid rock top hat — and turned left onto a narrow, one-lane road. I pulled the truck over to the right as far as I could get without scraping the chain-link fence that bordered the tall, thick hedges.

"You'll have to get out on my side," I said.

"No problem." Mac glanced around. "I still can't see a thing."

"There used to be a thick concrete-block wall along here, but the developers who bought the property took it down and erected this temporary chain-link fence. These trees and hedges have always been here."

"No wonder you can't see anything from the highway."

"Right. And it helps to have Big Hat Rock

standing in the way, too."

"Guess so." He stared up at the rock. "Aptly named."

For years, the bushes that bordered the Gables property had been wildly overgrown. But just recently the landscapers had begun the overwhelming job of trimming it all. Enough so that you could get a tiny peek at the place if you found the right spot between the hedges.

"They plan to cut back most of the brush before it opens."

He nodded. "That's good."

"Let's get out and walk."

"Yeah." Mac climbed down from the truck and walked to the other side of the road. He stretched up on his toes. "Hey, I can see the tops of the towers." He stared for a moment. "Wow. They look like they belong on top of a medieval castle, not a hospital."

"The original designers were really into impressive architecture. They believed it was essential for the security and recovery of the patients."

"Interesting. So how do we get in there and see the rest of it?"

"This way."

We walked farther down the road until I found the gate in the middle of the chain-link fence. "Here we go."

Mac frowned at the black lockbox attached to the gate. "That looks like a serious lock."

"It is." I flipped open a panel and pressed in an elaborate key code. The gate swung open.

He grinned. "Abracadabra."

"Magic." I wiggled my fingers, then grinned back at him. "And Jane gave me the code."

We got through the gate and then pushed our way through the tumble of bushes and tree branches until we reached the edge of a wide green lawn.

"Whoa," Mac whispered reverently, taking in the overwhelming sight of the elegant yet long-dormant Gables. "You weren't kidding, Shannon. This place is mind-blowing."

"Sort of takes your breath away, doesn't it?"

"Uh, yeah."

In the middle of the lawn, a large billboard had been erected that spelled out the plans for the space.

COMING SOON!

THE GABLES!

LUXURY SHOPS * GALLERIES *

RESTAURANTS

WORLD-CLASS HOTEL AND SPA!

CONFERENCE CENTER * WEDDING VENUE

PARK, WALKING TRAILS, BIKE PATHS,
PICNIC AREA!
FOR INFORMATION ON LEASING AND
INVESTMENT OPPORTUNITIES, CALL
THE GABLES DEVELOPMENT COMPANY.

Two phone numbers were listed under the company name.

"That's a pretty ambitious agenda," Mac said, staring up at the sign. "I guess once they've cut back the trees and brush, this billboard will be more visible as you drive up the road."

"That's the plan," I said. "Jane told me the developers signed the lease on the last available space just last week, so they're hoping to make some headlines with their groundbreaking ceremony next week."

We walked a few yards more to get past the billboard so Mac could have an unobstructed view of the rows of buildings. For a few minutes we just stood and stared at the striking Victorian edifice before us.

The Gables consisted of seven separate buildings in one long row across the top of the ridge. The main building — which I understood had once been the administration building and had housed a number of the permanent staff members — was in the center, and its tower stretched up several floors higher than the other buildings' towers. Three identical buildings stood on either side of the central building. Each was set back about twenty feet from the one next to it, so the overall effect was meant to evoke the idea of birds in flight. At least in theory.

All of the buildings were three stories tall but appeared much taller because each of the floors had twenty-foot ceilings. Each building had the same gothic-style tower that speared up into the sky above the rooftops. There were also multiple chimneys, an overabundance of dormers, and row upon row of gabled windows, all classically Victorian touches.

And I knew that along with the fanciful bridges and arched breezeways, there were numerous underground tunnels, all connecting one building to the next.

"And this whole complex is less than a quarter mile from the highway."

"Well, the rock and the wall and the trees have kept it well hidden for a long time."

"Yeah, but still, I can't believe I've never seen it. Never even knew it was here." Mac slowly shook his head. "Mind-blowing," he muttered again.

I was happy that the weather had cooperated with our field trip plans. The early spring day was already starting to warm up as the sun made its daily climb over the eastern hills. A light breeze ruffled the leaves in the surrounding trees. The air was clean and clear and the sky was bright blue, with tufts of white clouds scudding over the ocean.

"Let's take a walk," Mac said finally. "I want to see more of it."

"Okay. And I can show you Building Seven, otherwise known as the future home of Hotel Hennessey."

We followed the dirt path for more than a hundred yards and as we strolled I pointed out some of the highlights of the buildings.

"I know the exterior looks shabby, but the company's going to power-wash it this weekend. They're covering the cost of the outside upgrades so all the buildings will be uniform. The shutters will all be straightened and painted, and they've already started adding new windows and doors."

"That's smart."

"And I think I told you that they've already cleaned up a lot of the interior. They had to. It was nasty."

"I can imagine. It was abandoned for years, right?"

I pointed. "Those three buildings on the south end were closed down in the seventies and boarded up, so those will need some serious rehab work. These four buildings over here remained open until the very end, so they've only been abandoned for about twenty years." I made a face. "But twenty years is plenty of time for rodents and reptiles and insects and plants to do a lot of interior damage."

He smiled at me. "You would know."

"Yeah. I've chased some of the creepiest animals out of the oddest places."

We walked for another few yards and Mac had to crane his neck to take in the entire length of the place. "I can see why they chose to name it the Gables."

I nodded. "It suits, doesn't it?"

There were literally dozens of gables across the long expanse, and following in the Victorian tradition, hardly any two were alike. Some were more steeply pitched than others; some had decorative moldings along the roof edges; some formed a fancy parapet or a low wall along the edge of the roof; many had dormer windows extending out from the exterior walls. It was quirky and beautiful at the same time. And then there were the gargoyles. Not exactly a Victorian touch, but gothic, for sure.

"It's huge," he marveled again, and as we continued our walk, he began to take in the surrounding land. Eucalyptus trees formed a barrier along the northern edge of the property and there were ancient redwoods and pine trees lining the eastern ridge. To the west was an unobstructed view of the ocean and miles of coastline. "I can't believe I never noticed this place when I was out on the water. How is that possible?"

"The view used to be entirely blocked by the wall and by all those trees and hedges. You couldn't even see it from the water."

"Do you know how much of this land belongs to the Gables?"

"Three hundred and twelve acres," I said promptly, then grinned. "To be honest, I just read that number this morning. I wanted to get a little more information about the place before we came out here."

"That's a substantial piece of land. What are they going to do with all of it?"

"You saw the billboard, right?"

"Yeah." He frowned. "But my natural skepticism is bubbling up. Do you really think they can deliver?"

"I do. At least, I hope so, especially for Jane's sake. But I'm pretty optimistic. As I said, the entire place has been leased out so it's already a success from that standpoint."

He raised an eyebrow. "That fact definitely makes it easier to attract investors."

"Doesn't it?" I smiled at him. "And according to Jane, they've contracted a major landscaping company to come up from San Francisco to design a park with walking paths and a place to ride bikes, and they're planning to add a pretty little stream that'll meander through the property, along with fountains and little ponds and lots of flower gardens. She said they'll have a couple of interesting bridges that will go over the stream and link up to the walking path. Jane promises it'll be gorgeous."

"If Jane says so, I believe it."

I beamed at him. "And along the north side of her hotel they've plotted out a big vegetable garden that will supply her hotel restaurant as well as several food vendors that will be moving into the other buildings. And they'll have fruit trees, too. Possibly an entire orchard."

He gazed around. "There's plenty of room for that."

"According to Jane, there were gardens all over the property. They not only yielded lots of fresh produce for the kitchens but also provided some occupational therapy for the patients."

The wind picked up and I held my wavy mop of red hair back off my face. "And I know you'll love this detail, even though it's a sad note. The hospital had its own cemetery." I glanced up to catch his reaction.

His eyes widened. "That really is sad. But you're right, I do love it. In fact, this just gets better and better."

I shook my head, chuckling. "Have I mentioned that you've got a dark side?"

"You only just noticed?"

Amused, I slipped my arm through his and we strolled north toward the trees. "You'll be relieved to know that the graves will not be disturbed during the rehab."

"That's a relief. We don't want any ghostly activity."

I shivered involuntarily. "There's a problem, though, because some of the deceased were buried in unmarked graves and a lot of the flat grave markers only have a number. No names. So the development company is trying to track down the families whose relatives died while in the asylum."

"Now that really is awful."

"I know. But they do have a bunch of gravestones that are still standing and those have full names. Jane says that the landscapers are experienced with issues like this and have promised to respect that area of the property."

"And they've agreed," Mac said, "because they've all seen the movie *Poltergeist.*"

"Exactly," I said with a quick grin. "They plan to fence in the cemetery, lay down sod, and plant a few trees. They'll add some flower beds and little benches. It'll be nice. There are people around town who have relatives that lived and died here, so the hope is that they will appreciate the effort and feel welcome here."

His forehead furrowed. "Did Jane's mom die up here?"

"No. But she died way too young, in her thirties. And it was the same year Jane's father died. That's why she only had her uncle Jesse."

Jane's uncle Jesse had been my neighbor for as long as I could remember, but about two years ago I had discovered his body and Jane and I solved the mystery of his death. At the time, Mac had only recently moved to Lighthouse Cove, but he had quickly become friends with Jesse and was able to help me and Jane find justice for him.

"I remember Jesse," Mac murmured. "He was a great guy. Jane's had a lot of tragedy in her life."

I nodded. "One of the reasons she decided to get involved in the Gables project was to try to turn around the negative memories a lot of us have. She wants to bring some goodness and light to this place."

"That sounds like Jane, for sure." Mac smiled. "And I mean that in the best possible way."

"I know you do." There was nobody more thoughtful than Jane. She had a kind, generous heart and only wanted the best for everyone.

Mac shook his head and muttered, "I have to write about all of this."

Pulling out his phone, he started taking pictures of the buildings from every angle. Then he turned and stared out at the ocean. "Wow, look at this view." He pointed north. "Hey, you can see the lighthouse from here." He turned around to look at the building behind him, then back over his shoulder at the lighthouse. "I guess from the lighthouse, you can see the land, but the view of the buildings is blocked by the trees."

"Exactly." I slipped my arm through his. "Jane's mom used to say that she was lucky to be here because she had the best view of anyone in the country."

He considered it for a long moment. "That's a glass-half-full way to look at it, I guess."

"Kind of like Jane," I murmured.

We continued walking in silence for another minute.

"It's so peaceful up here, I almost hate to see them develop it," he mused. "There'll be hundreds of people driving up here every month causing traffic jams on the highway and marring the view of the buildings." He scowled. "And I would really hate to see it turned into a glorified strip mall."

"God forbid. I don't think the investors and the development company will let that happen."

"*This* investor definitely won't," he declared.

I sighed. "I like to think that visitors will respect the place and see it as something beautiful and different."

Mac shrugged. "I guess it's better to have people come and enjoy it rather than tear it all down or leave it to crumble to dust."

"There's always that trade-off," I said.

"True." He crossed his arms and stared at the buildings.

"There won't be any parking here in front," I assured him. "Jane said they're building a big parking lot around the back so the cars and trucks and RVs coming up here won't spoil this lovely sight." I spread my arms out to indicate the building complex as well as the entire hilltop.

Mac scratched the side of his jaw contemplatively. "I guess that's okay, then. Makes me feel a little better."

"You'll get a clearer idea of everything they have in mind when Rachel takes you on the tour."

"I think I'd better call her this afternoon. I want to schedule the tour for tomorrow instead of waiting until Friday. I'm anxious to see the inside."

We reached the north end of the property and I pointed at the last building. "This will be the new Hotel Hennessey."

Mac gazed at it for a long moment. He turned to take in the views from every angle. "It's beautiful. It's going to be fantastic." He nodded and added softly, "Way to go, Jane."

I pointed. "And look, you can barely see the other end of the complex from here."

"It's impressive, for sure," Mac said.

We followed the fence line around the north side and took a look at the back of the property. The eucalyptus trees lining this area were tall and graceful.

I took in a deep breath of eucalyptus scent. "It's so pretty up here. And it smells so clean."

After a few minutes, we headed back around to the front of Building Seven, Jane's future hotel, and stopped for another minute to study it.

Mac said, "I don't want to be a downer, but there are seven separate buildings with three floors each. I imagine they were usually filled to capacity. That adds up to a whole lot of mental disorders."

"You're right, I'm sorry to say. Back in the day they didn't always understand the different ways that mental illness shows itself, so there were a lot of people who were wrongly diagnosed and shouldn't have been admitted here. Women with postpartum depression, for instance, or anyone suffering from alcoholism. Some men even had their suffragette wives committed."

"Because you must be crazy to want to vote?" Mac shook his head.

"Right?" I smiled, but it faded quickly. "I read of one so-called insane asylum that housed prisoners exclusively. It didn't matter the crime, they were all just sent off to the insane asylum."

"That's bizarre," he muttered. "Sadly, these days it's the opposite. A lot of mentally ill people are put in prison for want of a better option."

I looked up at him. "We should probably leave before we both get more depressed."

He threw his arm around my shoulder. "Good idea."

We turned and began the long walk back

to the truck.

"What's with the towers on each building?" he asked. "Are they an elevator shaft or something?"

"I don't think so, but I didn't get a good look at them when I took the tour with Jane."

"They're dramatic, for sure."

"Yeah. I haven't figured out if they were simply a decorative architectural feature or if they actually had a practical purpose. You could be right about the elevator shaft, or maybe there are rooms up there. You know, apartments for the head doctor and his family or a dormitory for the nurses. Or they might've used the space as a chapel, or a place for occupational therapy."

He gave me a light nudge with his elbow. "You must love that classic Victorian touch."

I gazed up at the towers. "They're great, aren't they?"

"They're amazing. Definitely add to the gothic atmosphere. And how many chimneys do you count?"

"A few dozen, at least," I said. "That's typical of the Victorian style, too."

"I dig the gargoyles, but they're not Victorian, are they? And wouldn't they scare the patients?"

"Good point," I said, beaming. "According to the history I read, they only used the ones with sympathetic features. No scary, ugly ones."

"Seriously?" He glanced up and studied the nearest stone creature. "They might not be scary, but those are all really ugly. Not sure I'm buying that theory."

I chuckled and we continued to walk in silence for a minute or two, enjoying the sounds of the birds and the rustling of the leaves. Then Mac shook his head. "I'm still baffled as to why I never saw all of this before."

"If it makes you feel better, there was a practical reason why it couldn't be seen from the highway."

"Yeah? What is it?"

"Well, I mentioned that the original doctor of this facility envisioned a place where air and light circulation would be key aspects of a patient's treatment. Part of that philosophy included the daily practice of bringing the patients outside to the lawns where they would have a planned activity of some kind. Either a game or an exercise program, or even dancing. And gardening."

"So let me guess," Mac said. "With all those people cavorting outside, the doctor didn't want some nosy passersby gawking at them."

"Exactly. He knew it would be detrimental to their progress if they realized they were being watched."

Mac nodded. "He was probably right."

"So the doctor — his name was Dr. Jones, by the way, and he was a contemporary of the great Dr. Kilbride, who first championed these theories back east. Anyway, our Dr. Jones instructed the architects and contractors to build the hospital behind that hill."

"Makes sense," he admitted. "And it's compassionate as well."

Mac reached for my hand and as we continued our walk, I shared some more of what I'd learned in my research.

"Dr. Jones thought the best way to heal insanity, as they called it back then, was to provide a beautiful, quiet, comfortable, and safe environment."

"It sounds almost holistic, but I'm not sure if that concept existed back in the 1870s."

"I'll have to get back to you on that," I said.

"I've done some research myself since I occasionally deal with these issues in my books. The doctor sounds like he was a very kind and thoughtful man, but whether or not these architectural niceties could actually 'cure' someone? Seems like a reach, don't you think?"

"I suppose so, but it was a long time ago. Doctors today know so much more about all the different levels and types of mental illness, like bipolar disorder or dissociative identity disorder, the different forms of psychosis, severe depression. And with all the types of medications and treatments available these days, it seems that if you can actually name the specific disorder, you can begin to treat it. In theory."

"I agree."

"But back when Dr. Jones was running things, he believed very strongly that the architecture of the place would help cure the disease. He was adamant that his builders follow his specifications, right down to the desired width of the hallways and the height of the ceilings."

"Sort of early feng shui," Mac said.

I laughed. "That's a really good way to look at it."

"It's pretty fascinating stuff."

"Yeah, it is. I'm just happy to know that the doctor took a more humane approach rather than some of the awful methods we've heard so much about."

"You mean, where they would lock someone up in the attic or throw them into a pit?"

I took a deep breath. "Something like that."

He stopped walking and wrapped his arms around me. "Sorry. I tend to get cynical sometimes, in case you never noticed."

I gazed up at him. "I'll bet you've seen a lot of inhumanity during your military years."

"Yeah, and you don't forget it."

"Of course you don't."

He rubbed his hands up and down my back. "Thanks for coming up here with me. I want to soak up the atmosphere for another few minutes, and then we can go."

Holding me, he swayed gently. I wondered if he was a million miles away, but then he gazed down at me and smiled. Hoping to lighten the mood, I said, "I know that look in your eyes. You're going to use all of this in your next book."

He sighed. "I've become transparent."

"Only to me," I said easily.

He beamed at me. "In *my* book, though, the good doctor will turn out to be a mad scientist."

I nodded solemnly. "You've got to go with your strengths."

"Always," he said with a short laugh. Staring at the buildings, he added, "Now that I've seen the outside, I'm anxious to get a look inside."

I glanced around. Only half-kidding, I said, "We could always sneak in."

His grin was mischievous. "Don't tempt me. But let's take a closer look." He grabbed my hand and we ran over to the central building. Cupping his hands over his eyes, he peered through the first-floor windows.

Stepping back, he grumbled, "They're covered in some kind of blue paper."

"It's because the windows are all brand-new. The sticky paper protects the glass while they're being transported."

"Well, that's a drag." He looked around, then knocked lightly on the windowpane. "I could probably break in without doing too much damage."

"You're going to get us into trouble, aren't you?"

He gave me a lopsided smile. "Sometimes it's worth it. For research purposes only, of course."

I rolled my eyes. "Right."

"Besides, we won't get in any trouble. I know the police chief."

"So do I." The chief was never happy when I got into trouble. "He gets cranky."

Mac laughed. "He's lightened up a little since he met your sister."

I smiled. "True." My sister Chloe was a

46

good influence on our occasionally grumpy chief of police. "That reminds me, she's coming up here next week and staying for a while. Her show is going on hiatus for a month."

"Cool. Is she going to help you with Jane's hotel project?"

"I doubt I'll be able to keep her away." Chloe was the star of a hit DIY show on the Home Builders Network. She had lived and worked in Hollywood for the past ten years, but on a visit home to Lighthouse Cove a few months ago, she met and fell in love with our very own police chief, Eric Jensen. And Mac was right; the chief really had mellowed since then.

We walked toward the hedges, then stopped and gazed at the buildings again. "You should definitely call and move your tour to tomorrow," I said. "Otherwise . . ." I stopped. From the corner of my eye, I caught a blur of movement. Chills rushed across my shoulders and I clutched Mac's arm. "Did you see that?"

"See what? What is it?"

I pointed. "I thought I saw someone sneaking between those two buildings."

Mac was immediately on alert. He stared at the area I'd pointed toward. "Which way did he go?"

"He went north."

Mac took off running toward the north end, staring at the buildings as he moved, trying to catch a look at the guy in between the structures. At the end of the row of buildings, he stopped, looked around, then shook his head and jogged back. "Sorry, love. I didn't see anyone."

I took a deep breath and let it out. "Pretty sure I wasn't imagining it."

"Of course not, but he's probably hiding now. Can you describe him?"

I shut my eyes to bring back the fleeting image. "Baseball cap. Orange, I think. Giants. Or Oregon Beavers, maybe?" I glanced up at him. "We've got a lot of Beaver fans around here. They had a good season last year."

"Remember anything else?"

"Yeah. Dark hoodie. Black or navy blue, I think. And blue jeans."

He nodded pensively. "Okay."

"I guess it could've been a woman." I scowled and shook my head. "Or heck, maybe I imagined it after all."

He scoffed. "Orange hat? Blue hoodie? You wouldn't have imagined such a specific outfit."

I set my teeth, certain of what I'd seen. "No, I didn't imagine it. I saw him."

The question now was, who was he and why was he sneaking around?

CHAPTER THREE

On the drive back to town Mac pulled out his cell phone to call the developer.

"Hey, Rachel," he said. "It's Mac Sullivan. How are you?"

He listened to the woman for a quick moment, then said, "I'm good. Listen, I'd like to move my tour of the Gables to tomorrow. Are you available?"

She had one of those bright, assertively loud voices that could be heard without benefit of the speaker. She was saying how much she would love to meet him up there tomorrow morning.

"Great," Mac said. "I'll see you at ten o'clock. Hey, by the way, do you have anyone working up there right now?"

"Oh no, Mac," Rachel insisted. "We opened up the grounds and buildings a few weeks ago to allow our new lessees to do an assessment of all the work to be done and the equipment they would need. But then

50

we locked it up tight because our own people still have a lot to do before the lessees can get started on their individual spaces. We don't plan to open it again until the day of the groundbreaking next week."

Mac grinned at me while he spoke to Rachel. "But you'll let me go in there, right?"

I heard her trilling laughter. The woman sounded overjoyed. And why not? She was talking to Mac Sullivan. Who could blame her for getting all giggly?

"As an investor," Rachel explained, "you will always be allowed to come and go whenever you want. Just be sure to give me a call first and I'll meet you anytime."

"Sounds reasonable."

"Oh, and Mac," she continued. "I must caution that it's not safe to wander around alone up there. Not just yet. By the time we open it up to the tenants and their construction crews next week, everything should be perfectly safe and wonderful."

"Good to hear. Thanks, Rachel. See you tomorrow."

He ended the call and looked at me. "No workers are up there, according to Rachel."

"I heard her." I huffed out a breath. "But I saw someone. If Rachel doesn't know anything about it, then the guy must've broken in."

He grabbed my hand and held it. "Look, it could be perfectly harmless. Maybe some guy wanted to get a head start on cleaning and prepping his space."

"Maybe." I nodded. "Okay, yeah, I'm sure it's completely innocent. Why wouldn't it be?"

"You don't sound any more certain of that than I am."

"Because I'm not. I guess it's because he was trying really hard not to be seen." I pictured the guy again. "He was running, but he looked, I don't know. Furtive, I guess. Sneaky. Like he knew we were there and he didn't want us to see him. You know what I mean?"

"I know exactly what you mean."

I worried about it for another moment, but I had to wonder *why* I was worried. Was it because of my tendency to stumble onto murders? Boy, I hoped not. Finally, I waved the worries away. "I'm making too much of this."

But Mac wasn't ready to let it go. "Your instincts are usually right on. And look, it's not like the place is very secure. Anyone can climb a chain-link fence."

"And we didn't go all the way around the property. Maybe there's a spot where the fence has been pulled down."

"Totally possible. But look, instead of dwelling on it, let's just assume the guy you saw was a new tenant who wanted to get in there for some reason. But he knows he's not supposed to, so when he saw your truck drive up and saw us walking around, he thought he'd better be careful. He thought he had to sneak around instead of just walking over and saying hello to us."

"That's probably all it was." But I decided right then to call Eric as soon as we got home and ask if he had assigned anyone to patrol the Gables property. Enough strange things had happened in Lighthouse Cove over the last few years that I didn't want to take a chance on something going wrong with this huge new project.

Mac stayed over that night, and the next morning as he scrambled some eggs and buttered two pieces of toast, we talked about his expectations for the meeting with the Gables developer later that morning.

I poured more coffee for both of us. "It sounds like you've made up your mind to invest in the project."

"After we went up there, I thought about it all afternoon. It's a fabulous location and even though I haven't seen the inside, I'm really interested. So I talked to my business manager and my agent, and then called my broker. They're all for it. But you're the one who ultimately convinced me. And the fact that Jane is involved is one more reason to go for it."

"You're going to make Rachel's day," I said. "She sounded positively giddy over the phone yesterday."

"Well, let's not forget I'm giving her a boatload of cash."

"Boatloads of cash always make me giddy."

He laughed. "I won't make my final-final decision until I meet her and actually see inside the place. If I get a good feeling about the whole deal, I'll pull the trigger."

"Okay." I took a sip of coffee, then considered. "You're going to need a hard hat for the tour."

With a grin he asked, "You got one I can borrow?"

"I might have one or two hanging around."

"Great." Then his eyes narrowed. "Are they pink?"

I was well known for using pink tools on my construction sites, along with pink hard hats and tool belts. My pink tools were just as rugged and strong as the usual ones, but for some reason my guys never mistook them for their own.

"I do have a pink hat," I said, "but you can use the manly blue one if you prefer."

"Definitely," he said, his voice going deeper than normal.

I chuckled. "I'll get it for you." At the back door, I turned. "Hey, you should see if Rachel will give you a tour of Jane's hotel space. Then we can compare notes."

He shot me an appreciative look. "Great idea."

As I walked out to the garage, I wondered if one building inside the Gables was pretty much the same as another. Since I had only seen inside Building Seven, I didn't know if it was in worse or better condition than the others. It didn't matter, I thought, but I was hoping Mac would be able to tour a couple of the buildings and give me his impressions.

An hour later I stood in the driveway and waved good-bye to Mac, just as Jane pulled up in front of my house. The two of them waved to each other and Jane walked up the drive.

"Hey, kiddo," I said. "What are you doing here?"

"I just got home from the conference last night so I thought I'd come by and say hello. And also talk to you about the Gables project."

"Well then, hello." I gave her a hug. "Let's go inside."

She glanced over her shoulder. "How's Mac?"

"He's wonderful. He's going up to tour the Gables this morning."

"Really? With Rachel?"

"Yeah. He's thinking of investing."

"That would be fantastic."

"I think he's almost convinced. I'm hoping Rachel does a good job of selling it to him."

"Oh, she will. She's gaga over the place."

"Good." I pushed open the kitchen door. "Come on in."

We were greeted at the door by Robbie, who barked joyfully. I shook my head. "You'd think I'd been gone for a year."

"Oh, but he's such a good boy," Jane said, and knelt down to play with the frisky dog. "Yes, you are."

Tiger was her usual aloof self, although she did finally stroll over to rub up against Jane's legs. Jane reached down and gave the cat's soft furry back a few long strokes.

"Do you want coffee?" I asked.

She stood. "Sure. Thanks."

I poured two mugs and set them on the table. Jane sat down and I joined her.

56

"So, Mac spent the night." It wasn't a question.

"Yes."

She looked at me through narrowed eyes. "Is he moving in?"

"No." I smiled at her and placed a pitcher of half-and-half on the table. "He just likes to spend time with me and it makes me happy to have him here."

Jane gave me a cockeyed look. "Why doesn't he just move in?"

"Because he has his own beautiful home just up the highway. And I should know how beautiful it is because I did the full rehab, remember?"

"You're skirting the issue, Shannon."

"Maybe." I gave a light shrug.

"He's here most of the time and he wants to be with you. So why haven't you invited him to move in?"

"I've told him he's welcome to stay with me anytime he wants."

"That's not the same thing."

I sighed. "Do you want sugar?"

"Yes, please."

I jumped up and grabbed the sugar bowl from the counter. "I just don't want to push it."

"No, you wouldn't," she murmured. "But

57

you should because you deserve to be happy."

"I am happy," I insisted, sitting down and sliding the sugar bowl over to her. "Heck, most days I'm practically ecstatic."

She eyed me with suspicion. "The fact that you don't want to push it makes me think you're *afraid* to push it."

Up to this point, the conversation was a familiar one, but I was about to delve into new territory.

"I'm not afraid," I insisted. "Well, not exactly. Okay, maybe I'm a little afraid, but it's not the kind of fear that has me shrieking at a bug or freaking out in a dark basement."

"Of course not. You're the bravest person I know." She grimaced. "I'm the one who's afraid of bugs."

I smiled at her. It was true. "It's just that I feel like Mac and I have gotten to the point in our relationship where I just want to know what the next step is. But it's hard to ask that question without sounding pathetic."

"I totally get that." She clutched her collar and whined, "Don't you want to marry me?"

I laughed. "Yeah. Sounds pretty lame."

"But you still want to know."

I sighed. "I guess I'm worried that things between us will change if I *go* there."

Jane nodded slowly, then shrugged. "So for now, don't go there. And maybe one of these days when you least expect it, *he'll* go there."

"So just wait for him to make the move." I winced. "Does that make me a complete chicken?"

"Not at all," she said stoutly, then thought about it. "Well, maybe half a chicken."

I chuckled. "Your unflinching support makes me feel all warm and snuggly."

She smacked my arm. "You know I love you."

"I love you, too."

She took a sip of coffee. "I actually stopped by to see you for another reason."

"To bolster me with your love and support?"

"Naturally. But also, I wanted to ask if you'd come over to the B and B sometime this week and take a look at the crown molding you did for the Ophelia Suite."

Jane had named each room of Hennessey House after one of Shakespeare's heroines. Ophelia was an exquisite jewel box of a room on the second floor with an extra-high ceiling and a tiny balcony overlooking the garden.

59

"Why?" I frowned. "Is it cracked? Is it falling down?"

"No. It's perfect. I love the twelve-inch moldings and the way you edged them with the sunflower ceiling frieze and the step-up at the inside corners. I want you to do that for the rooms at the Gables."

"Okay. But I don't have to look at it. I know what I did."

"I know, but I'm just concerned that the rounded corners near the ceilings will be a problem. I'd like to talk it through, if you have time."

I gazed at her. "You're nervous."

"Of course I'm nervous," she said. "I'm scared to death. What was I thinking, opening a brand-new hotel?"

"You were thinking that this is a once-in-a-lifetime opportunity to expand your business while also giving you a chance to transform a dark moment from your past into lightness and joy."

She sniffled. "You nailed it."

"It's a gift." I handed her a tissue.

"Thanks." Jane blew her nose and then took a deep breath. "It's going to be great, right?"

I grinned. "It's going to be super great."

"Okay." She shook her head back and

forth as if to readjust her brain cells. "I'm good."

"Of course you are, and so am I."

She took another sip of coffee. "I also want to show you this old architectural magazine that I ordered online. It came in the mail while I was gone and I should've brought it with me, but I was out running errands and didn't think. And then I just decided to come by and take a chance that you might be home."

"So tell me about the magazine."

"There's an article that features a couple of institutions that were built around the same time as the Gables. There's a reference to one of the doctors who played a role in the design of the buildings and some of his theories. Anyway, I thought you might want to take a look at it."

"Do you remember the doctor's name?"

"No, sorry. But there are some great photographs of the rooms and the hallways and stuff. It might be helpful."

"Absolutely." I checked my wristwatch. "I can come over now if you're up for it."

"Oh, that's great." She waved her hands rapidly, as if she were nervous about making a speech. "But first, I need to make one more comment about you and Mac."

I steadied myself in my chair. "Okay."

"He loves you, Shannon. It's so obvious. And he would be a fool to ever leave you."

My friend Jane was a true romantic who saw love and devotion everywhere she turned.

"And Mac is no fool," I said lightly.

"That's right."

"So what am I worried about?"

"Nothing, I hope."

I stood and wrapped my arms around her. "Thank you." Then I picked up her empty coffee mug and set it in the sink. "Let's go check out your crown moldings."

I followed Jane toward Main Street and turned, then drove a few blocks and turned on Olive Street. In front of the beautiful old Victorian mansion, I pulled up to the curb. Jane continued until she reached the driveway and parked in the renovated garage behind the property.

We met on the sidewalk in front of Hennessey House and walked up the steps to the wide, wraparound porch. I took a moment to bask in the glow of pride I always felt when gazing at this elegant Queen Anne Victorian with its three-story circular tower, its six chimneys, its quirky roofline, and its multiple mini-balconies.

"We did good work here," I murmured.

"Yeah, we did." Jane slipped her arm through mine and gave me a light squeeze. "Let's go inside."

We walked into the comfortable front room, where Jane greeted two guests who were sitting on the wide sofa reading books.

After a moment, I followed Jane into the hall and up the stairs to the second floor, then down the hall to the Ophelia Suite. As she unlocked the door, she said, "I'm expecting a guest to arrive in a few minutes so I don't want to take too much time."

"I don't need much time." I was already staring up at the elegant white crown molding that contrasted so beautifully with the blue walls. For some reason, I could still recall the name of the paint we'd used. "Stone blue," because of the touch of gray mixed in with the blue. It gave the room a calmness that I imagined the guests appreciated.

"What do you think about duplicating this pattern in the Gables rooms?" Jane asked.

"It's fabulous, isn't it?" I pulled my phone out and took some photographs.

"I thought you remembered exactly what you did."

"I do, but I still want to have some pictures to refer to when I'm up at the Gables."

I stared at the fancy embellishments for

another long moment. "Now that I'm seeing it again on this fourteen-foot-high ceiling, I'm not sure the style will work for those twenty-foot ceilings at the Gables. But we'll see how it goes."

"Why wouldn't it work?"

I shrugged. "You might not want something this fancy. The Gables' ceilings are so ridiculously tall that it might be interesting to go more minimalist and put the emphasis on the floor-to-ceiling windows, maybe hang some really awesome long drapes. Maybe give it a whole monochromatic effect. Or not. I don't know. Let's see how we feel when we get up there."

Jane smiled at me. "That's a really good idea. The drapes, the minimalism. I like it."

"Think about it."

"I will. Thanks."

We headed downstairs and as we stepped into the hallway, we heard someone speaking loudly at the front desk.

"I don't know why everything has to change so much," a woman griped. "Why are there so many cars? I used to live here and I don't remember taking that turnoff from the highway. And now there are so many stop lights."

Sandra Larsen, Jane's unflappable assistant manager, spoke in a friendly tone.

64

"Lighthouse Cove has grown a bit since the last time you were here, Ms. Baxter. But I think you'll find that we still have the same small-town sensibility and friendliness we've always had."

"I don't know about that," the older woman said. "I noticed they put angle parking on Main Street. In my day, people knew how to parallel park."

Jane walked quickly toward the front desk. "Is everything all right here, Sandra?"

"Just dandy. I was just helping Ms. Baxter check in."

"Yes, of course. Hello, Ms. Baxter. I'm Jane Hennessey."

"Hello. I'm Prudence Baxter." She sounded a little paranoid, as though she might've thought Jane was lying about her name. Or maybe she thought Jane was faking that whole "nice" act. The woman was a pain! While Jane was the personification of grace under fire.

The woman was thin and probably about fifty years old, but her style of dress made her look much older. A starched, white, long-sleeved blouse was tucked into a prim, pleated navy skirt that came down well below her knees. The chunky black shoes she wore added to the spinster look. Her hair was long and gray and she had it pulled back tightly in a single braid down her back. She looked like a really strict schoolmarm.

"It's wonderful to meet you," Jane said. "You'll be staying in our Ophelia Suite and I hope you enjoy it. It's a lovely room with a small balcony overlooking the gardens. Do you have any luggage I can carry upstairs for you?"

And just like that, Ms. Baxter was mollified. Or as mollified as she would ever be, I thought. The woman seemed genetically incapable of saying anything pleasant.

"It'll just take another minute," Sandra said.

"Then I'll be right back after I see Shannon to the door." She nudged her chin to indicate which way to go and we walked quickly in that direction.

"I want to show you that magazine," she murmured, "but I think Ms. Baxter might require some hand holding."

"That's okay. Why don't I take the magazine with me and we can talk about it later?"

"Good idea." She dashed back upstairs to her suite and I wandered into the kitchen, naturally, and greeted Paige, Jane's talented chef.

"Hey, Shannon," Paige said. "I just finished baking these red velvet cookies and I need a guinea pig for a taste test. Can you help me?"

"If I must." I picked up one of the cookies — they really were red and looked as soft as velvet — and took a small bite. "Oh my God. They're heavenly. And they're filled with something wonderful." I took another bite and couldn't speak for a long moment as I savored the delicious tastes.

"It's a cream cheese filling." She frowned. "Your opinion?"

"Fantastic."

"Oh, good. So they don't suck."

I laughed. "Nothing you do sucks. This is just divine. I'll stop talking before I turn into a gushing fool."

"I'll give you another one if you gush a little more."

"You're the devil. But wow, they're really good." I took the last tiny bite. "So good. I've got to get out of here before you force me to eat another one."

"Coward." She grinned, but she was already putting another cookie inside a small white bag.

"Yes, I am." But I took the little bag and started to back out, just as Jane walked into the kitchen.

"Here's the magazine," she said.

"Thanks," I said, slipping the magazine under my arm. "I'll call you later to talk about it."

"Good," she said. "Oh, Paige, the cookies look gorgeous."

"They taste gorgeous, too," I whispered.

Jane frowned. "You have crumbs on your shirt."

"No, I don't." I brushed away the one tiny measly crumb and gave her a quick hug. "I've got to go. Thanks, Paige. You're a genius." Then I lowered my voice and said to Jane, "Good luck with the battle-ax."

"Oh, she's not so bad." Somehow she knew I was talking about Ms. Baxter. "Just set in her ways."

I smiled at her as I moved toward the door. "I don't know how you do it, but you're really good at this."

She waved me off. "Talk to you soon."

Less than ten minutes later, I parked in my driveway and called Jane back.

"What's wrong?" she asked.

"Nothing. I just realized I spent so much time talking about me that I forgot to ask how you and Niall are doing."

Her voice softened. "He's wonderful."

I smiled. "I love that you sound so happy."

"It's strange, isn't it, Shannon? Who would've guessed that Emily's brother would move to town and fall in love with me?"

"Why wouldn't he?"

"It's just so weird." She paused. "It's in the air, I think."

"It must be."

"He asked me to marry him."

I blinked. "He what?"

She laughed. "Yeah."

"Oh, Jane, I'm so happy for you. But why didn't you say something earlier? You let me whine on about my problems and never said a word."

"I was on a mission to interrogate you and my plan worked."

I chuckled. "It worked a little too well. Okay, I'm giving you a virtual hug, which I will give you in person as soon as I see you again."

"Aren't you going to say that we're moving too fast?"

"Why would I say that? He's lived here for, what, eight months? Ten? It doesn't matter. You're old enough and wise enough to know what you want."

"Thanks for making me sound so old."

I laughed. "You know what I mean."

"I do. And it's true, I know what I want." She gave a dreamy sigh. "And I want him."

"I got that," I said. "From day one."

69

"Isn't it funny that our whole gang seems to be pairing up and settling down? Even Chloe."

"It's funny, but wonderful." Mac and I were definitely a part of that happy group, but I just wasn't sure how settled we were or for how long. I didn't say it out loud, though, because Jane would worry. We ended the call shortly after that and I climbed out of the truck and went inside.

In the kitchen, Robbie clamored for a hug and I couldn't refuse. "Come here, little dude." He jumped into my arms and I carried him with me into the living room where I sat down on the couch to call Police Chief Eric Jensen. I had forgotten to call him yesterday but figured it wasn't too late to tell him about the Gables intruder. "Hi, Chief."

"Shannon. How are you?"

"I'm great. I called to talk to you about the Gables."

"What about it?"

"I was up there yesterday and saw someone sneaking around inside the perimeter fence. He looked suspicious to me, so I was wondering if you'd be willing to have someone drive up to check on the area."

"We usually patrol the Gables twice a day. But I'll send a squad car up there this

70

afternoon to check for signs of a break-in."

"That would be great. Thanks, Chief."

"Hey, I just heard from Chloe. She'll be here next week."

"Wonderful," I said, with genuine affection. I loved seeing the chief and my little sister so happy together. "I hope we can all get together while she's visiting."

"I'm sure she's hoping the same. You should expect a call any minute now to set things up."

"I'm sure," I said with a laugh. "I'll see you soon."

As soon as I finished the call with Eric, Mac phoned to give me an update. "It's a done deal."

"With the Gables?"

"Yup."

"Yay!" I jumped and raised my hands in victory. Robbie whipped around in a circle, clearly as thrilled as I was. "You gave Rachel a boatload of money?"

He chuckled. "You bet I did."

That made me happy for a couple of reasons. For the community and the project, sure. But also, if Mac was making a substantial investment in a local business, that meant he was here to stay, right? Sure, it did.

"Was she giddy with excitement?" I asked.

"You bet she was," Mac said dryly. "But seriously, aside from the giddiness she comes across as a savvy businesswoman. And boy, she knows everything about the project. I asked her all kinds of questions and couldn't stump her. I've got to admit I was impressed."

"That's great, Mac," I said. "And you got the grand tour?"

"Yeah, and I'd be lying if I didn't admit that the interior damage and neglect is horrific."

"I know what you mean." As a contractor I'd seen some properties that would give civilians nightmares. But the Gables was even worse from my perspective.

"I got to see a lot of Jane's building. We also walked through the main building. And like I said, it's horrific, for sure, but Shannon, the possibilities are amazing." He paused as if picturing everything he'd seen. "The ceilings in the patients' rooms are twenty feet tall, just like you said." He paused. "I assume the patient rooms will become the hotel rooms."

"Yes."

"So I remembered how you said that the doctor believed that patients needed lots of air and light and space."

"Right. He didn't want them to feel as if

the walls were closing in on them."

"Claustrophobia," Mac murmured. "I believe it."

I sighed. "It's sad when you think of the people who suffered."

"It really hits you as you walk through the buildings."

"Oh, yeah. Loud and clear. But thanks to Dr. Jones and his architectural principles, the patients at the Gables might've been a little better off than others were back in the day."

"I'd like to think so. Anyway, once you're done with the rehab and people have a chance to see how beautiful it is, it's going to be amazing. Shannon, I know I keep talking about it, but those high ceilings are fantastic. They're going to be a great feature in Jane's hotel rooms."

I smiled at his enthusiasm. I would have to thank Rachel Powers for sealing the deal.

"I was impressed with the whole place," he said, then chuckled. "But you nailed it when you called it creepy, Irish."

"Disturbing, isn't it?"

"For sure," he said. "Doesn't matter. I can totally see how you and Jane will make it look fantastic."

"You know we will."

"Rachel says that the groundbreaking is

next Monday," Mac said.

"Right. My crew and I will be ready to get started right after they wrap up the speeches."

"And Rachel said that the estimated grand opening is one year from now. Do you really think you'll be finished with the job by then?"

I grinned because here, I was on solid ground. "I absolutely do. I've gone over timelines and schedules countless times with Jane and Wade and Carla. We're determined to have the place finished by then. But on the off chance that something disastrous happens to make us fall behind, Jane says that she'll do an incremental opening."

"You mean, just open part of it?"

"Right. We'll definitely be finished with the lobby and front offices and all the public areas like the bar, the restaurant, and the spa. And we'll have at least the first- and second-floor hotel rooms completed. That's forty rooms."

"Whenever you finish, I know it's going to be awesome."

"It will be finished on time," I said with absolute certainty.

"You're going to be busy, babe."

"For sure. But I've got a solid crew and

I'll be hiring at least five more guys to cover the other jobs we've got going around town. And I've got specialists whenever we need them."

"What kind of specialists?"

"I found this fantastic tile guy who's a whiz with granite and quartz. He's got a whole team that'll help my guys finish off all the new bathrooms, along with the main kitchen and the spa." The more I talked about this job, the more my excitement grew. "And Amanda is a genius with wood paneling details. And Niall, of course, will be working with the interior brick walls and he'll also build a large terraced patio in back for the spa."

"I can personally verify that Niall and Amanda do great work. I have complete confidence that you'll get the job done."

"Thanks."

He paused for a second, and then he nearly gushed, "Damn, Shannon. This is going to be the hottest place on the West Coast."

I grinned. "It sounds like you've got the bug."

"I'm completely bitten."

CHAPTER FOUR

The day of the groundbreaking arrived at last. Mac drove his car and followed me in my truck up the hill. I was surprised to see that the chain-link fence was gone, the trees had been skillfully pruned, and most of the old hedges had been torn out. It was amazing what a difference that small bit of landscaping had made.

There were clearly marked signs instructing visitors to park around the back of the complex. I spotted a large crowd of people already spread out across the front lawn awaiting the start of the groundbreaking ceremony. We drove around the back and parked close to the double doors that were the rear entrance to Jane's Building Seven. Dozens of trucks and cars were already parked back there, a good sign that the tenants were eager to get started on the project.

We trekked around Jane's side of the complex and over to the south end of the

Gables lawn, where the billboard stood as backdrop to an elaborately decorated and elevated stage. I spotted my two foremen, Wade Chambers and Carla Harrison, standing on the outer edge of the crowd facing the stage. I waved to Sean Brogan, my head carpenter, and took a mental head count of every crew member I had assigned to the project this first day. There was Todd, Billy, Johnny, Amanda, and my newest crew member, Lacey, who was a virtuoso with drywall. I picked out the five new additions I'd hired after working with them on other job sites. They were all seasoned and talented construction guys — and that included two more women. They were all my "guys."

I had also asked my structural engineer and my architect to meet me here, and I saw them drive up with their own crew.

Niall, my genius stonemason, stood a few yards away, holding Jane's hand. The assistant manager and chef from her Inn were here, too, ready for a tour of their new spaces. Everyone was present and accounted for, I thought. At least for today.

I planned to bring on a lot more help once Jane, Wade, Carla, and I got inside the building and were able to conduct a more thorough survey of the work that had to be done. We were fairly clear on the work itself and knew that we could have it finished within the year we'd been given, but we still needed to set up a more precise timeline with schedules for our individual crew members. We would have to place an order for supplies: lumber, bricks, hardware, and paint, along with equipment to stock a working hotel kitchen.

Each of Jane's hotel rooms would have a brand-new private bathroom installed, which meant choosing all the deluxe hardware, accessories, and ventilation systems that went with it. The original patients had been forced to use several large group bathrooms, and those spaces would be turned into laundry and utility rooms. Over the next few days we would need to pin down all of the other obstacles we'd have to overcome in order to complete the job in plenty of time for the grand opening next year.

Wade and Carla approached me.

"Hey, boss," Carla said. "Beautiful day, huh?"

"It sure is." The air was still cool but the sun was already shining. A good sign.

Wade said, "Rather than wasting time listening to speeches, Carla and I thought we would take our crew over to Jane's and get a head start."

"Yeah," Carla said. "We can scope out the place, find some good spots to set up our utility tables and equipment, ladders, storage areas, and all that stuff."

"That's a great idea," I said. "I'll join you in a little while, but I want to meet this developer and then talk to some of the other contractors, see if they've run into any problems or issues with the powers that be."

"Good to be aware of those things from the get-go," Wade agreed.

Niall and Jane joined us. "What's going on?" she asked.

I told her the plan.

"I'll go with the crew." She pulled a key ring from her jacket pocket. "I've got the keys and I'm anxious to see the place again."

"Don't you want to hear the speeches?" I asked.

She gazed at me for a long moment. "Seriously?"

Niall laughed. "See you later, Shannon. I'm with Jane."

They had a point. And Jane had probably heard the developer's spiel more than once before. "Okay, I'll join you in a few minutes."

I watched with fondness as my intrepid friends and crew members walked away. I totally expected them to be working at close to full strength by the time I got there.

"You've got a good group there," Mac said.

"I know." They really were the best in the business.

I turned and faced the stage area and that was when I noticed a statuesque blonde approach the stage and walk the three steps up to the platform. She crossed to the lectern that had been set up in front of the big cheery Gables billboard, tapped on the microphone, and said, "Can everybody hear me?"

"Yes!" a bunch of people shouted.

"That's Rachel Powers," Mac murmured in my ear.

"I figured it had to be."

"I'll introduce you later."

"Okay." I studied Rachel Powers as she gazed out at the crowd of fellow developers, investors, tenants, and workers. She was at least five or six years older than me, maybe in her early forties. She was lovely, successful, and high-powered in an attractive dark red suit that showed off her long legs and shapely figure. Her shoes, black sky-high patent leather heels, helped emphasize the look. And just as Mac had said, she came across as a savvy, take-charge businesswoman. And she was gorgeous, in case I hadn't mentioned it before.

But I had to wonder, how did she walk across the grass in those heels? I studied my own well-worn, steel-toed work boots, faded jeans, sage henley, and down vest. There was no way I could compete with the woman based on our wardrobes, but at least I wouldn't be the one to stumble over a dirt clod.

To be fair, I knew that I looked good and cleaned up well, but this woman was very impressive.

Was it petty of me to pray that Rachel Powers was a bitch? I wanted her to have at least one flaw I could point to and feel good about.

My guilt lasted about a nanosecond as I watched Rachel's gaze focus in on Mac and saw her mouth curve in a coy smile. The little twist in my heart — or was it my stomach? — had me wondering what that was all about.

Of course, I didn't have to wonder too hard because Mac had that effect on all women. I sighed. But right then Mac looked down and smiled at me as though we were sharing a lovely secret all our own. And any worries I might have felt about Rachel quickly faded away.

I tuned in to her welcoming speech, which she smartly kept brief. She started with a quick bit of Gables history and then zoomed into the future to emphasize all of the wonderful shops, restaurants, and high-end businesses that would occupy these buildings. She praised the fabulous artwork they planned to display, the beautiful park that would completely surround the complex, and finally, the exquisite new Hennessey House Hotel that would ultimately bring thousands of visitors to the magnificently redesigned Gables.

I appreciated her glowing words for Jane's hotel and wondered if maybe the woman would turn out to be a friend.

When she wrapped up her speech there was lots of applause and cheers. She stepped away from the lectern but remained on the stage as she greeted the many people who rushed over to say hello.

Glancing around, I recognized some local folks in the crowd who must have come to check out the exciting new project up the hill. There were a surprising number of reporters and camera crews here, too, looking for a story. But the rest of the people were dressed in outfits similar to mine and I decided they had to be the other tenants here with their work crews, ready to get down to business.

Before Mac and I could move through the crowd and meet Rachel, I heard loud shouts coming from behind us. Turning, I saw a group of people stalking up the road, holding signs and posters and chanting something unintelligible. One guy marched right out in front with a sign that was so big, it completely hid his face. Whenever he yelled something, the crowd behind him answered. As they got closer, I could make out their words.

"Burn down the Gables!" the lead guy shouted.

"Gables must die!" his followers chanted in answer.

That was hostile, I thought uneasily, then winced. If these folks or their relatives had been forced to live at the Gables, maybe they had a right to feel that way.

The guy in front lowered his poster in order to talk to someone behind him and I finally got a good look at him. His baseball cap was orange and he wore a dark blue hoodie.

I sucked in a deep breath. This was surely the same guy who'd been sneaking around up here last week. So he wasn't a curious tenant anxious to get to work. He wanted to burn the place down! Instantly I wondered if the Gables interior was safe now for my crew. What if Orange Cap had set up traps or something?

He looked younger than I had expected, and he was thin, with a short, scruffy brown beard. I couldn't see his hair color under the cap but figured it was brown, too. He was shouting and waving his sign and looked really angry.

Whipping around to Mac, I whispered loudly. "Do you see what I'm seeing?"

"Yeah," he said flatly. "Call the cops."

Before I could answer, Mac took off, effortlessly maneuvering his way through the crowd of people standing nearby. When he reached the Gables billboard, he ducked behind it and disappeared from sight. What was his plan? Some kind of secret ninja attack?

The chanting and shouting from the protesters grew louder and more threatening as they got closer. I pulled my phone from my pocket and quickly called 911 to report the unrest.

"911, what's your emergency?"

"There's a protest going on up here at the Gables and I think it could turn violent. Can you send the police here right away?"

The dispatcher paused and I heard the sound of her fingers hitting the keyboard.

Then she said, "I've dispatched a squad car and I've also alerted the chief."

"Thank you."

"You're welcome, Shannon," the woman said. "Are you okay?"

I sighed. "Hi, Ginny." The dispatcher and I had gone through twelve years of school together, but I had talked to her more in the past two years than in all those school years combined. It was all because of my alarming tendency to call and report a dead body on a regular basis. "Please ask the chief to come up if he can. It's getting scary around here."

"Cops are on their way, kiddo. Hang tight."

"I will. Thanks." I ended the call and shouted to the whole crowd, "The police are on their way!"

The guy in the orange baseball cap moved inexorably toward us, waving his sign and shouting, "Burn it down!" He and his gang of close to two dozen rabble-rousers were now less than thirty yards away and were still shouting and waving their signs in protest. I could see a few of them shaking their fists, but they didn't appear to be carrying anything that could be used as a weapon. Like rocks or baseball bats. Thank goodness for that, anyway.

I scanned the protesters' faces and wondered who they were. None of them looked familiar, but then some of them had their faces partially hidden with bandanas or scarves. So what were they doing here and why were they so opposed to the Gables project?

And where had Mac disappeared to?

Watching Orange Cap warily, I had to wonder what he was up to. He was clearly the same man I'd seen skulking around the Gables last week, but who was he? And what had he been doing here? Had he simply been looking around, checking things out? It had to be more sinister than that. Otherwise, why was he here with a bunch of protesters, making trouble? Was I right about the traps? Or was it worse than that?

Burn it down!

Who was this guy? Why did he want to destroy the Gables?

"The police will be here shortly," Rachel shouted into the microphone. She must've heard me yelling. "Our cameras are filming this disturbance and all of your faces will be on record. You are trespassing on private property and if you don't immediately disperse, you will be arrested and prosecuted."

Rachel sounded professional, tough, and

concise. It made me wonder if she'd had to deal with this sort of thing before. Or maybe she just had a knack for calming down angry mobs.

Not that her approach was working in this case. Orange Cap and his followers continued their march across the long stretch of grass, obviously aiming to torment our well-behaved group of investors, new tenants, construction workers, and cleanup crews.

What would happen if they got close enough to actually hurt someone? And why hadn't the development company hired a private security firm to guard this place?

Maybe they'd hired security but they were only assigned to patrol at night. I decided to cut her some slack. Still, it was annoying and frightening to have this loud, angry group heading straight for us.

Rachel grabbed the microphone again. "Stay back! This is not an idle threat. You will be arrested if you don't leave immediately."

Again, her words had no visible effect on the agitators, who continued to shout and threaten and relentlessly move forward.

"We see you!" one of the women protesters shouted at Rachel, and the others cheered and howled in support.

The shouting woman had to lower her

bandana to be heard and I almost choked when I saw her face. It was Jane's odd new hotel guest. Ms. Prudence Baxter. The complainer. What in the world was she doing here?

All of a sudden Orange Cap dropped his sign and took off running right toward our group. He was followed closely behind by a good-looking, slightly older man with hair the color of carrots. It was probably rude of me, but since I didn't know his name I instantly named him Carrot Head. Hey, I have red hair, too, so I figured that gave me some leeway.

The rest of the crowd ran behind them, keeping up their shouting and fist waving. Carrot Head clutched a big brown shopping bag to his chest and the two men were running straight for my group.

And suddenly I felt myself cringe inwardly. I was honestly scared to death. What was in that brown bag? I wondered. Was he carrying a bomb?

There was nowhere to hide.

Others must've had the same thought because the people around me began to scream in panic and run off in every direction.

"Oh my God, no," I whispered. The thought of a bomb was so disturbing that I had to shake it off. No way would someone try to blow up a group of innocent people. Not in Lighthouse Cove of all places. Not in my town.

And where was Mac? I wondered.

With our people dashing every which way, the two main protesters had a clear path. They were headed straight up to the stage where Rachel Powers was still standing. But before they could get there, I took a step forward and stuck out my leg.

Carrot Head stumbled but he didn't fall down and he didn't drop his big brown bag. He turned and glared at me with disgust.

What was in that bag?

"Get out of here!" another woman yelled at him. She was a big woman and she shook her fist at him.

He scrambled to get away from us and continued toward the stage.

Rachel valiantly grabbed the microphone and held it out like a sword, but it was useless for warding off the threat of the two men headed right for her.

Without warning, Mac appeared from behind the billboard and plowed headfirst into Orange Cap's stomach, knocking him to the ground.

My hero, I thought with a sigh. I figured he had to have been waiting, biding his time, watching those two. Mac had Orange Cap pinned on the ground. The protester tried to flip over to get on top of Mac, but he wasn't strong enough.

Still, I was panicked at the possibility that Mac could get hurt and I prayed that the police would show up soon.

While everyone's attention was on Mac, Carrot Head inched closer to the stage, followed by Prudence Baxter, who kept turning around to ward off anyone else who got close.

When Carrot Head pulled something heavy from the brown bag, my heart almost stopped. Was it a bomb? It actually looked like a paint can. I wasn't sure what his plan was, but I knew it couldn't be good.

"Stop him!" I shouted, and tried to get close enough to knock him down, but Prudence elbowed me. I pushed her away and she tripped, but caught herself. She turned to run away and bumped into Carrot Head, who flung the can and its contents toward Rachel and the stage. The can itself flew by without hitting her, but the stuff inside splashed all over Rachel and the cheerful billboard behind her.

The poor woman was now drenched in a viscous, dark red liquid that looked very much like blood. The billboard was also

90

covered with the gooey crimson fluid.

I looked at Prudence and noticed her smirk. As she melted into the crowd of protesters, I turned back around to make sure Rachel was all right.

Clearly in shock, Rachel blinked, saw the red liquid dripping from her hair and down her face, and gasped.

Was it blood?

Shoulders shuddering visibly, Rachel squeezed her eyes shut. Her hands began to shake uncontrollably and that was when the true screaming began.

CHAPTER FIVE

The sound of Rachel's high-pitched shrieks was almost as frightening as anything I'd ever heard. It conjured up images of screaming banshees — not that I'd ever heard a banshee screaming, since they were mythical creatures, after all. Or were they?

I didn't blame Rachel one bit. After being taunted by those protesters and then getting personally attacked and saturated with some icky sticky red liquid that definitely looked like blood? It would make anyone scream. But at least she was alive, thank goodness. And it wasn't *her* blood. That had to count for something.

She had to be terrified, and I didn't blame her. I ran up to the stage. "Are you all right?"

She was trying to catch her breath. "I'm . . . yes, I'll be fine. I was just frightened for a moment." She touched the red slime dripping down her arm. "It's not real blood." She took a few more breaths. "Thank you."

I nodded. I still didn't know the woman and I wasn't sure I would like her if I did. But nobody deserved this.

Someone in the crowd yelled, "He's getting away!"

I whipped around and saw Carrot Head trying to make his escape. Without another thought, I took off running and with a flying leap, I grabbed him from behind. I figured I was just as surprised as he was and we went down, landing with a hard thud.

Now this was why I didn't wear fancy suits to construction sites, I thought.

Carrot Head immediately tried to push me off and get away, but the big woman who'd yelled at him a minute ago trotted over and plopped right down on his butt.

"You're not going anywhere, sonny," said the woman, and grinned at me.

He continued to squirm and wiggle under her, but she was a formidable opponent who had retained her sense of humor. She wasn't really hurting him, just making sure he didn't go anywhere.

"Are you good here?" I asked her. "I need to go check on my crew."

"You bet," the woman said, still cheerful.

I got up and limped over to join the crowd. Most of the protesters had scurried off, unwilling to get caught and arrested with Carrot Head and Orange Cap. I scanned the area to find Prudence Baxter. I wanted to talk to her. What the heck was she doing here? Whatever it was, I didn't want her staying at Jane's place another day.

Several of the men approached Mac and offered to keep an eye on Carrot Head. Mac nodded curtly and stood. He came over and wrapped his arm around my shoulders.

"Nice tackle."

"Thanks." I chuckled, but it was half-hearted. I was already worried and exhausted, and the workday hadn't even begun.

"So when do we get to stop having fun?" he wondered aloud.

The sound of approaching sirens announced the arrival of several police cars and I couldn't have been happier.

"About damn time," I muttered.

Ten minutes later, Orange Cap and Carrot Head were in handcuffs. I would need to find out their real names eventually, I thought, as police officers led them over to one of the squad cars. The two of them were clearly the main agitators while the rest of

their group had been protesting more peace-
fully.

I watched the action from the edge of the
lawn a few dozen feet away. Mac walked
over to check on Rachel and I watched him
sit down on the stage with her to commiser-
ate. As developer and investor, they probably had a lot to discuss. Such as hiring
private security immediately.

Four uniformed officers rounded up the
stragglers that had failed to disappear as
quickly as the other protesters. They secured
the scene and began taking each of the
protesters' statements before either holding
them for more questioning or letting them
go.

Two other cops came over to corral my
group. They took our phone numbers and
let us go with a promise to call us later to
get our versions of what happened.

Earlier, while we were waiting for the
cops, I had texted Wade to ask him for some
of the thin muslin work cloths we used to
wipe off our hands and clean up spills. Now
he jogged over with a short stack of cloths.

"Thanks," I said, and carried them over
to Rachel. She was still sitting on the edge
of the stage with Mac. She seemed grateful
for the cloths, but still traumatized.

Once she had wiped most of the red liquid

off her face, Mac officially introduced me to her. We nodded to each other and Mac explained, "Shannon's construction company is working on Jane Hennessey's hotel."

Rachel managed a smile. "It's so nice to meet you. Jane is a delight and her hotel is going to be the crowning glory of this project."

"Once we're done, it's going to look incredible. And with Jane running things, it will be spectacular." It was a point in Rachel's favor that she appreciated Jane's contribution to the project. I smiled with complete sincerity. "I want to compliment you on your valiant attempt at crowd control."

"Didn't exactly control them," she muttered, using another cloth to scrape and scrub the red liquid out of her hair.

"But you didn't cower or run away, either," I pointed out. "You stood your ground and that was really brave of you."

She stared at me and slowly nodded. "Thanks for that. Maybe we'll have a chance to talk later."

"I'd like that." But I got the feeling I was being dismissed. Mac must've caught the vibe because he stood and took my hand. "I'll catch up with you in a minute."

"Okay. I'll be inside working." I casually

waved good-bye, but instead of heading for Building Seven, I walked over to the edge of the lawn where the hedges had once stood. The cops were still working the scene and I was just nosy enough to want an unobstructed view of the action. Most importantly I hoped to have a word with Chief Jensen before he left.

I was glad that Mac was taking his role of investor seriously, but that didn't mean I needed to watch him sitting at Rachel's side, consoling her. I knew I was being ridiculous, so I focused instead on Assistant Police Chief Tommy Gallagher as he talked to Carrot Head, who leaned against the cop car looking sullen and defensive. His attitude didn't seem to bother Tommy, who chatted cheerfully with the paint-throwing agitator. Didn't it just figure? Tommy was the most upbeat person I knew, even at a crime scene.

Tommy had been my high school boyfriend and even though he had broken up with me in the worst way possible — by going out with my sworn enemy and getting her pregnant — we had managed to remain friends. I simply couldn't stay angry with him and besides, I blamed the girl. Whitney Reid had gone out of her way to make my life miserable in high school, and her greatest achievement had been to steal my adorable boyfriend away from me.

I was long over it, but she wasn't. Which made it imperative that I never pass up a chance to annoy her. As if on cue, Tommy saw me, grinned boyishly, and waved. "Hey, Shannon."

I smiled and waved back. "Hi, Tommy." I knew that if anyone up here mentioned our brief exchange to Whitney, it would cause her to throw a fit. And that possibility was enough to cheer me up again.

After a few minutes, Police Chief Eric Jensen strolled over to join me. "Why am I not shocked to find you at a crime scene, Shannon?"

"It's always a thrill for me, Chief."

"I'll bet."

He had been finding me at crime scenes ever since he first moved to Lighthouse Cove two years ago. Thankfully he no longer suspected me of the crimes that had been committed. But it was always disconcerting to look up and find the police chief staring at me in complete dismay. There was often a dead body nearby, adding to the misery.

Eric folded his muscular arms across his wide chest. The move reminded me of the first time we met and I had secretly nick-named him "Thor." Not that I would ever reveal it to Eric, but the name suited him.

98

He was ridiculously good-looking, big, blond, tough, and powerful, very much like the Nordic god his appearance called to mind. And he rarely smiled, which added to his mythic quality. Although ever since he met my sister, I had caught him smiling a lot more often.

"What the heck is going on around here?" he asked.

I gazed up at him. "It's all about the Gables project."

"I still don't get it. These buildings are fantastic, by the way, even without the rehab." He gave an approving look at the long row of Victorian structures in front of us. "I know when it's finished it'll bring a lot of visitors and revenue to town, but I'm not crazy about the way it's starting out."

"I'm not, either," I agreed. "To tell the truth, it was just a small group of protesters that showed up, but they succeeded in making a lot of noise and freaking us out by hurling what looked like blood on the woman sitting over there with Mac."

He gazed across the grassy expanse where Mac still sat with Rachel Powers. Eric's frown reappeared. "Do you think she was their intended target?"

"Probably. She represents the Gables Development Company, so who better to target?" But then I remembered Prudence Baxter bumping into Carrot Head. Had that affected his aim? Had Rachel been the actual target? If not, who or what was the real target?

Eric stared at Mac and the developer for a few more seconds, then frowned at me. "I haven't seen her around. Do you know anything about her?"

"Absolutely nothing, except that she represents the development company. Mac is a new investor in the project, by the way."

"I see," he said slowly, in a way that had me thinking he would do some investigating of the whole Gables project.

And that made me think of something. "Hey, you're not going to close us down over this, are you?"

"Nah, don't worry. It's not like we found a dead body or something."

I blinked, then looked around for some wood to knock on. There was nothing nearby so I surreptitiously knocked on my head. Good grief, why would he tempt fate like that?

Oblivious, Eric pulled a small leather-bound notepad and a pen from the pocket of his bomber jacket and flipped to a blank page. "My officers are taking everyone's statements, so why don't you give me your version of what happened?"

I wondered briefly if he was trying to distract me. If so, I appreciated it. I told him exactly what I had seen and the sequence of events. I told him about Orange Cap, explaining that he was the same guy I'd seen creeping around here last week. I told him how Mac had wrestled Orange Cap and how I had tackled Carrot Head to the ground.

"Pretty heroic of you two."

"It didn't stop the jerk from throwing that red goop at Rachel." I glanced up at Eric. "Do we even know what the liquid is?"

"Likely it's some kind of animal blood. Or it's just plain fake. Tommy had Lilah collect a vial of the stuff and run it over to Leo. We'll know more in a few hours."

"Good." Leo Stringer was our town's lone crime scene investigator. Lilah O'Neil was a police officer whose science background gave her enough knowledge to help Leo when he needed assistance.

I scowled. "I just hope those protesters didn't kill a bunch of animals to collect enough blood for their stupid prank."

"The possibility of that alone should have them cooling their jets in my jail for a long time."

"I sure hope so." I sighed. "I know it

might not sound like a big deal, but those two terrorized everyone here, especially Rachel." I frowned and glanced around again. "There was another woman here, but she must've disappeared before you guys showed up. Her name is Prudence Baxter and she's staying at Hennessey House. She was marching with the protesters and she kept up with those two guys."

"She's marching with protesters, but staying at Jane's place?"

"Yeah. Pretty nervy, right?"

He nodded as he wrote it down. "I'd say so."

"In fact, she was the one who bumped into the red-headed guy holding the brown bag. I wonder if she did it on purpose."

"Was she trying to make him miss his real target?"

I shrugged. "I have no idea what the story is there, but you might want to talk to her."

"I'll do that." He wrote it down in his notepad.

I rubbed the side of my head, hoping to ward off the headache that was threatening to erupt. "I'll admit that for a minute there, I truly thought the redheaded guy might be carrying a bomb in that stupid brown bag."

"Jeez, Shannon. Come here." He pulled me into his arms for a hug, rubbing my back for a minute. "For that, I'll gladly throw the book at both of them."

"Thank you, Eric." I stepped away, anxious to change the subject from bombs and animal blood. "So, Chloe arrives tomorrow."

His expression softened at my sister's name. "Yeah."

"Is she staying with you or with me?"

He gave me a look. "Seriously?"

"Just wondering," I said, biting back a smile.

"She's staying with me," he said.

I almost laughed at the tone of feral possessiveness in his voice. A few months ago the two of them had met and fallen hard for each other. It had all happened in the span of a week and I couldn't be happier. It meant that Chloe was visiting us more often now, especially during these monthlong hiatuses, but she still had her television show in Hollywood so the two of them couldn't be together as often as they wanted to be.

"Once she gets here," I said, "I want to talk to her about planning a dinner with Dad and Uncle Pete and all of us."

"I'll remind her to call you. Not that she needs reminding. She'll probably be on the phone with you as soon as she gets to town."

I grinned. "True. Anyway, I'll text everyone and we can compare schedules and choose the best night."

"Sounds good." His forehead wrinkled as he frowned and glanced around. "So back to the incident. I understand that most of the protesters managed to escape before we got here."

"Yeah." In the chaos that followed the blood tossing, I had watched the other rabble-rousers scatter and run down the road. "But there were a couple of television camera crews filming the groundbreaking ceremony. You should talk to them. I'm sure they got plenty of shots of the protesters so you might be able to post their pictures on the local news and identify them that way."

"Good idea. Did you recognize any of the protesters?"

It was my turn to frown. "Just that one woman staying at Jane's place. I don't think any of the protesters actually live in Lighthouse Cove."

"If anyone would know, it would be you."

I smiled. "Yeah, I kind of know everyone around here."

Eric pointed to the squad car in which the two main perpetrators were now occupying the backseat. "The redhead over there told Tommy that the protesters are all members of an online chat group dedicated to shutting down the Gables project."

I nodded slowly. "Huh. That answers one of my questions. So they could've come from anywhere in Northern California or even farther away. I wonder if they're all as fanatical as those two men."

"What do you mean?"

I had to take a minute to put my thoughts together. "First of all, they all sounded really hostile to me. They weren't talking about shutting down the Gables. They were shouting to *burn* it down. 'Burn down the Gables. Gables must die,' they said. So that makes me think this is deeply personal and that the Gables is a real sore point for them. I wonder if they all have someone in their life, a friend or a relative, who was committed to the insane asylum back in the day."

He gritted his teeth. "Very possible."

"Yeah, it is. And all the announcements about this project could've triggered some bad memories of the times their loved ones were taken away to the asylum."

"Possible," he mused. "Also possible they're just a bunch of weirdos looking for a cause. I'll dig some more, have one of my IT guys go online, check out that group."

"Good. I'm afraid the Gables rehab might be a grim reminder of a really traumatic time for their families."

He jerked his chin toward the squad car. "Are you giving those two an excuse for doing what they did?"

I frowned. "No. I don't excuse their behavior. They frightened everyone and they terrified Rachel Powers. But I want to know specifically why they did it. It obviously has something to do with the insane asylum connection. I mean, I doubt they're riled up over the thought of having some old buildings repurposed."

He snorted. "Not likely."

"On the other hand, it could happen." I shrugged. "People get radicalized over a lot of things these days."

He studied my expression. "You've given this some thought."

I smiled. "I had to do a lot of research in preparation for this project. From one angle, we could be trespassing on sacred ground. You know, how dare we cover up the past by trying to make this place beautiful? Why don't we just leave it alone and let the whole place crumble to dust and blow away in the wind?"

He gazed at the row of magnificent Victorian buildings before us. "That would be a real shame."

"I think so, too. And Jane agrees. She has

a personal connection to this place, too. And it's not a happy one. But you know Jane. Her goal is to take a moment in her life that was ugly and sad and turn it into something beautiful as a way of celebrating the loved ones who suffered here." In spite of everything I had to smile, thinking of my best friend. "She doesn't want to erase their memories, she just wants to make them accessible to more people."

"Jane has a beautiful soul," he murmured.

"Yes, she does. But someone out there might not agree with her commitment to this cause."

His eyes narrowed. "Do you think she could be a target, too?"

"Oh God." The thought had chills threatening to overwhelm me. "I really hope not."

His expression turned to stone. "That settles it. I'm going to assign two officers to patrol this area during working hours. And we'll schedule drive-bys every hour all night long."

I felt a wave of relief pass through me. "Thank you. That's a really good idea and I'm grateful. But you do know that this project is estimated to take a full year to complete."

He held up a hand. "We'll have someone on the property for as long as it takes."

"Thanks, Eric." I patted his arm. "Makes me feel better."

"That's what I'm here for."

I laughed. "I hope you interrogate the heck out of those two."

He glanced at the squad car. "That's the plan." Closing his notepad, he slipped it back into his pocket. "Be careful up here, Shannon. Call me if you see anything suspicious."

"I will. See you later, Chief."

But I really hoped I wouldn't see anything more suspicious around here. Weren't rabble-rousers and animal blood enough for one day?

CHAPTER SIX

I waited until the police drove off before I looked around for Mac. I found him chatting with another tenant, who was refurbishing part of another wing to turn into artists' studios.

"Hey, you," he said, slinging his arm around my shoulder. "I'm off to write for a few hours but I'll try to make it back here later. I want to check on your progress."

"You know where I'll be."

After kissing me good-bye at the front doorway of Building Seven, he jogged away to the back parking lot.

I stepped inside the grand foyer of Jane's building and had to stop, breathe, and take in the sight of my crew already hard at work. Ladders were erected everywhere along the main hallway and inside several of the rooms. The caustic odor of bleach permeated the air and caused my nose to twitch, so that meant the guys had discovered some patches of mold that they had effectively wiped out. I hoped.

The electricity was working and every ceiling light and wall sconce was turned on. Still, two dozen light trees stood in various spots around the interior to help brighten up any dark corners. My guys had been busy.

Wade came walking up the hall with his tablet in his hand, as always. "Hey, there you are. You ready to look around?"

"Let's do it."

"Good," he said. "Carla and I gave out the initial assignments and all the guys jumped right in."

"That's nice to hear."

We walked slowly down the hall and I took a look at the rooms as we passed each door. Most of these rooms would be for public use, such as meeting rooms for conferences. The guest rooms would be farther back, away from the front business area.

"All of the guys opted to wear masks," Wade continued. "Just in case there's any residual odors from the fumigating and such."

"Did you find more mold? I can smell the bleach."

"A few small patches. And you'll probably catch a whiff of vinegar in some of the

110

wallpapered rooms."

"Whatever works," I said. Vinegar was more effective with porous materials, like wallpaper, drywall, and some types of wood.

"Right. My point is, everyone wears a mask for now."

When Jane and I had visited a couple of weeks ago to survey for the first time, it had been dark and empty and eerie. Now, even with lots of light and clean smells and hard work going on, the place was still unsettling. There were all kinds of wonderful possibilities of course, but remembering what this place had once been was sobering. The feeling of utter abandonment was still palpable and heartbreaking. I knew we could change that, but it would take time and a lot of hard work.

I had been renovating Victorian homes for years and had seen the devastation that occurred when a venerable old building was left abandoned. Mold and mildew were the least of the problems my crew and I had encountered.

Happily, the entire Gables complex had already been fumigated so we wouldn't have to deal with termites or wasps' nests and beehives inside the walls. Before the fumigation, the rats and other rodents burrowing in the cracks or running loose in the halls had been trapped and collected by a humane catch-and-release service, so we wouldn't have any trouble with animals.

There was nothing we could do about the ghosts. All I could do was hope they liked the makeover.

The development company had also done us the favor of conducting mold and mildew remediation throughout the complex. That was a big relief. We had dealt with the dreaded black mold issue in the past and it wasn't an easy fix.

Still, I expected to continue to run into small pockets of mold here and there, especially in places where the ventilation was poor. For now, we would learn to live with the delightful scents of bleach and vinegar.

The company had also hired experts to go through the entire place and check for asbestos. Unfortunately they found some ceiling tiles and other materials that had been added on during some minor remodeling work in the 1970s. The asbestos abatement experts had taken care of that problem, so as far as I was concerned, my guys were good to go with our part of the cleanup and rehab.

Wade, Carla, and I had prioritized the most immediate jobs. One team would have to sweep away hundreds of old tiles, chunks of plaster, dead insects, and dirt off the floors of the hallways and all the rooms. Next would come the scraping of walls and ceilings throughout the place. After so many years of neglect, the old paint was cracked and peeling so badly that the hallways resembled odd-looking forests with large, ugly flakes of paint wafting like leaves on the trees. Carla had commented that many of the flakes were bigger than Wade's hands, and Wade had really big hands.

Of course, after the scraping we would have to repeat the floor-sweeping round, but it was still better to have the place swept down first thing. Always good to have as tidy a work space as you could manage, if only for the morale factor.

Now as I gazed around, I was pleased to see that the guys had already started clearing away the main hallway floor. It made me think that we could have the entire hotel swept clean within a week or so, thus keeping to our timeline.

In the main hall, Wade had assigned six workers to start the job of scraping the loose paint off the walls and ceilings. They were already busy, using extension ladders to reach the ceilings and the tops of the twenty-foot-high walls.

The main hall was twenty feet wide as well, room enough for ten people to walk side by side. It was amazing — or it would be when we were finished. The wide hall stretched from the front doorway all the way to the grand stairway at the far end, which led to the upper floors. Once it was all cleaned up and the wood was sanded and painted, it was going to be sensational.

I was pleased to be able to confirm that this part of my research was factual: Dr. Jones really had wanted these wide open spaces on the inside of his hospital.

"So, everything okay out there on the lawn?" Wade asked.

I knew he was talking about the protesters. "It got rowdy," I said. "But no one was really hurt. The woman in charge, Rachel, was drenched in some kind of bloody liquid, which was disgusting but not life-threatening. Two protesters were taken to police headquarters for questioning. I tackled one of them and another woman sat on him to hold him down."

"Way to go, boss!" Wade high-fived me. "I'd rather not have to deal with that kind of trouble every day."

"You and me both."

Together we watched the activity in the main hall for a few minutes. "We're going to have to expand our workforce for this job."

Wade nodded. "Even with extra crew, it's going to take longer than we had scheduled."

"We didn't really take into consideration how massive this space is," I said, turning in a slow circle to take it in.

"No, we had to get inside and look it over. Now that we know it, we'll be able to schedule accordingly." Wade tapped his tablet and then swiped to another page. "We've got three more guys starting tomorrow so we'll see how it goes for a few days. If we decide we need to go faster, I can always add more workers to this team."

"Good." I observed the work for one more minute. "The walls are so high we might have to put up scaffolding sooner than we'd planned."

"We scheduled it to go up next week because we first wanted to see if the ladders alone would be enough." He glanced at me and shrugged. "Yeah, we'll need scaffolding."

I watched him make notes on his tablet screen, then folded my arms across my chest and stared up at the flaking ceiling. "Is there any way to attach one of those paint scrapers to a long pole so the guys don't have to keep climbing up and down the ladders and stretching out over the side rails?"

Wade stared at me for a few seconds. "Not a bad idea. I'll talk to Arnie."

Arnie was our painting expert. He had spent years painting hundreds of those old beautiful Victorian homes in San Francisco before moving to Lighthouse Cove. We were lucky to get him.

Five minutes later Wade came back wearing a grin and carrying a pole with a tool attached at one end. "Check it out. Arnie had this in with his supplies. Calls it a scraper extender."

"Ingenious name," I said with a laugh. "Because that's exactly what it is." I studied the homemade contraption. The large handle of the paint scraper was soldered and bolted into the hollow end of the pole. "It's smart. And it feels strong enough. Did Arnie make it himself?"

"Yeah. And see, the pole itself extends like a tripod." Wade demonstrated. "You loosen or tighten these interlocking doohickeys and you can extend it up to ten feet. He says you don't want it much longer than that because it starts to lose stability, especially since the guys will have to push the scraper pretty hard to get all this old paint off."

I gazed at him. "Doohickeys?"

116

He grinned. "Technical term."

"So they'll still have to use the ladders, but they won't have to strain quite so hard and move the ladders so often."

"And risk falling," he added.

"Exactly." The thought of anyone falling made my stomach twist into a knot. "Any chance Arnie can make a few more of these?"

"He's got a couple more in his truck. I'll ask if he can rig four or five more."

"That would be great. If he needs cash to buy the parts, tell him to see me."

"Okay." Wade stared again at his tablet screen and swiped to another page. "I think you're right about the scaffolding. It'll have to go up sooner than we planned. And it'll stay up for the duration because the guys will need to get up close in order to sand the ceiling surfaces and then brush them down, then patch, prime, and paint."

I blew out a breath. "Jeez, does it feel like this project will take forever?"

"A little bit." He shrugged. "But we've done it all before. And we have a full year to finish the job."

"And it's only the first day." I glanced up at him and chuckled ruefully. "Don't worry, I'll get rid of my downer attitude before tomorrow."

He studied my face. "You do seem a little down. What's up?"

"Those protesters showing up really bummed me out. I sympathize with them, but I hope they don't come back."

"I'm sorry we weren't out there to help you all face them down."

"Mac took care of one of the main troublemakers. And let's not forget, I brought down the other one — with a little help."

He gave me a pat on the back. "Mac can handle himself, but I would've liked to see you in action."

I grimaced. "It wasn't pretty. I kind of wish you guys had been out there."

He chuckled. "I'd like to watch those punks try to intimidate Sean."

That made me smile. "Sean Brogan never took grief from anyone." Sean was one of my oldest friends and a real sweetheart. And he was built like a linebacker.

"You shouldn't have to worry about protesters after today," Wade said. "Now that Chief Jensen has assigned the cops to patrol the area, we won't have any more trouble."

I really hoped we hadn't just jinxed ourselves.

At the end of the day after my crew had gone home, Jane and I took a stroll through the hotel to get a better feeling for the space and for the amount of work we would have to get done over the next few days. Jane had a rough idea of what each room would be used for and how she would furnish them, but her plans would change and grow as we got to know the place better.

From the foyer we walked down the main hallway, stopping at each of the eight large rooms that opened onto the hall. We guessed that these had once been used as reception areas, staff rooms, doctors' offices, and business offices for this wing of the asylum. Jane stepped inside the first room on the left, closest to the front doorway.

It was a large square room with a big picture window that faced west. Thin blue film still adhered to the window glass to protect it from dirt, smudges, fingerprints, and paint spatter during the rehab process.

"Do you remember going into this room when we visited my mother?" Jane asked.

"No." I stared at the walls and ceiling, intrigued. "Did they bring us in here?"

Jane sighed. "Yes, this is where Uncle Jesse had to sign in whenever we came to visit."

"Oh God, Jane. I'm so sorry I forgot."

"Don't worry. It's just . . ." Her eyes clouded up. "I remember everything."

I slipped my arm through hers and pulled

her close. "With all the emotional trauma you went through during those years, your awareness must've been heightened to the max. Even though you were so young."

"I was eight years old the first time I came here to see her."

"So young," I murmured, repeating myself.

"Yeah." But she smiled. "Honestly, I'm thrilled for the chance to transform it into a beautiful space for her and for everyone who was here. Even so, once in a while it hits me."

"I know what you mean. There are a lot of ghosts in here."

She looked at me. "You're seeing ghosts?"

I chuckled. "No, just feeling the vibes. They're heavy."

"Yeah, they are." She turned in a circle. "But this room will be really lovely when it's finished. I'll use it as our registration office. It should be as close to the front entrance as possible, don't you think?"

"Definitely. We can knock out part of this wall, too, if you want, so the room itself will be even more accessible to the front entrance. How do you see it set up?"

She walked around, thinking for a minute, then pointing. "We'll have an elegant wooden counter here. Maybe Amanda can do a design of wood inlays."

"She absolutely could."

"And then a couple of nice chairs on this side for guests who are waiting to check in. The rest of the area behind the counter will be taken up with desks for other personnel."

"I can see it," I said.

"A computer and credit card machine at the counter. Then four or five desks spread out on this side, with computers, copier, fax machine, space for a reservations clerk or two and a few clerical workers. Maybe an onsite web designer? An IT guy? Who knows?"

She was mostly talking to herself, already picturing it, so I quickly opened my tablet and began making notes. Jane might change her mind later, but at least this would give me a rough idea of what she had in mind with the rooms off this hallway. We hadn't been able to go into this much detail when we'd been given the tour last month. We had spent that visit mainly trying to figure out how much time and manpower it would take to simply clean up the place.

The room on the opposite side of the hall had the same layout and the same wonderful picture window. Jane suggested that it might make a nice sitting area or lobby, with comfortable couches and chairs, a coffee service, maybe a wide-screen television mounted on the wall. It could be a place where guests could relax while they planned their day trips, and it would be nice to have a concierge desk with information about tours and whatnot. And with the picture window it would be a lovely spot for guests to gaze at the view while they waited to be picked up and taken to the airport.

We walked farther down the main hall and found the elevator — an ancient one, but still functional and larger than most. I pushed the call button and it lit up. "I don't want to go for a ride, but I'd like to see what the elevator's interior looks like."

"I'm just glad there is an elevator," she said, and when the door opened, she stared inside. "Wow, it's so big."

"It had to be big enough to transport gurneys up and down to the other floors."

She gazed at me. "You're right. How do you know that?"

"I've done some research," I said with a shrug.

"Of course you have." She just smiled and we continued walking. "The elevator interior will look as classy as the rest of the place. Maybe we'll put a plush little bench in there."

"To rest your weary legs while you're transported all the way up to the third floor."

"Exactly," she said, laughing.

"How are you feeling after this first day?" I asked.

"I'm totally psyched," she said, wrapping her arms around her chest. "This was such a good idea. I didn't always think so, as you know, but now I do. It's a sound investment and it's going to be an incredibly popular place to vacation."

"I agree. And it'll be so fresh and elegant and beautifully furnished, and the view is so fantastic that people will love it."

She grabbed my arm and squeezed excitedly. "It's really happening, Shannon. I honestly wasn't sure this day would ever come, but now I'm so happy."

"I'm happy for you."

We reached the impressive stairway and looked up. Like the hallway, the stairs themselves were twenty feet wide, with thick mahogany railings and heavy, highly polished newel posts. Halfway up was a landing that stretched forty feet across with a floor-to-ceiling window that was covered in blue paper but would eventually reveal a totally breathtaking view of the coastline.

"This is so grand," I said. We climbed the

stairs to the landing, then stared up at the remaining set of stairs that would take us to the second floor.

"I didn't remember that front room from before," I said. "But I remember these stairs."

"They made an impression."

"Your mom was in this building." It wasn't a question. I knew her mother had lived here, on the top floor.

"Yes."

"I only came inside once and they made me stay in some other room while you and Jesse went upstairs. It must've been that front room."

"Probably."

"But I did get a look at this stairway from all the way down the hall. It's memorable."

"That was the time Mom was too sick to come downstairs. But even so, they had her sitting out in the hall. They didn't allow any patients to stay in their rooms during the day, so even when someone was sick they were carted out to sit in the hall or out on the lawn if the weather was good enough."

I had read about the practice of making patients leave their rooms during the day. This was one of the reasons why the halls were so wide. They had chairs lined up along the walls and insisted that patients sit out there, even when they had nothing to do. It made sense for security purposes so the staff could more easily keep an eye on everyone and limit the possibility of self-harm if someone was left alone in the room.

"The other two times I came with you," I said, "your mom was resting outside on the lawn."

"She loved it out on the lawn," Jane murmured.

"Did you ever get the chance to see inside her room?"

"That one time Uncle Jesse and I were allowed upstairs, I sneaked a peek. Mom told me it was okay as long as I didn't get caught. All I remember is that the windows were so big and the ceiling was so high, it was almost overwhelming. The next time we came to visit, one of the doctors said they didn't allow kids on the upper floors, so Jesse and I didn't mention that I'd been allowed to go up there a few weeks before."

"Someone would've been punished."

"Probably. Anyway, we were sitting on the lawn and Mom pointed out her room to me. She said she knew which room was hers because she had taped a little picture of me on the window and sure enough, you could see the little square of paper all the way from the lawn."

"That's a sweet memory."

"Yeah." She shrugged. "That's what she said, anyway."

"Then it must be true." Again I slipped my arm through hers and we continued walking leisurely up the stairs. "It's going to be beautiful, Jane."

"I'm sorry it wasn't so beautiful back then, just utilitarian. And sad." Her eyes clouded up again. "My mom deserved to have pretty things. She deserved to be happy."

I squeezed her arm. "She would be happy to know you're doing this for her."

She sniffled once, then smiled. "I think so. You'll probably think it's strange, but I'm happy when I'm here. I'm happy knowing that Mom would've loved the changes we're making."

"I'm sure you're right." I gave her a sideways glance. "Maybe another reason you're happy here is because Niall is here, too, working with you every day."

She grinned impishly. "That might have a little something to do with it."

"I plan to have enough work to keep him busy for most of the year."

"Yay!" She waved her hands in a cheer.

I laughed. "He might not have the same level of enthusiasm for all the work I'm giving him."

"He loves his job."

"And I love having him on the crew." We reached the second floor and I glanced around. "It's pretty dark up here."

"And it looks like it gets darker the farther up we go."

"We can turn on the lights. No problem."

But she was staring up toward the third floor. "I was thinking we might try to find my mom's room, but I'd rather wait and do it in the daytime."

"Okay. The guys are still cleaning up the first floor so you might want to wait until they've reached the third floor before going up there."

"Good idea."

We turned around and headed downstairs. "Oh, maybe while I have you here, I can show you what Niall was working on today. I think you'll find it intriguing."

"I happen to think that everything around here is intriguing." She continued looking every which way, studying each little nook and cranny.

"I do, too. But this is more like an actual mystery. I wanted Niall to figure out what that odd wall in the back hallway is all about."

"Which odd wall?"

"I'll show it to you. You weren't around when Wade and Carla and I checked it out earlier."

"No." She thought for a second. "Where was I?"

"I don't know. I couldn't find you and neither could Niall, so we went on our own."

"Oh, wait," she said, suddenly remembering. "Sorry. I had to leave for an hour or so. It's been such a busy day, I completely forgot."

"Where'd you go?"

"Sandra called, said she needed me to help with some guest issues at the Inn."

"Everything okay?"

Jane grinned. "Oh, yeah. Turns out, this couple just wanted to meet me and tell me how wonderful everything was."

"You're kidding. They couldn't tell Sandra?"

She sighed. "Hennessey House was recommended to them by some big-deal friends of theirs who apparently gushed about me. So these people wanted to be able to tell their friends that they actually met me."

"Because you're . . . a celebrity?"

"I know, right?" She rolled her eyes. "You'd probably consider it a waste of my time and I was a little annoyed at first. But

128

you know, I was glad I went. They were thrilled to pieces and now they have bragging rights with their friends and have promised to come back as a foursome. So hey, I improved our customer relations, and that's always a good thing."

"Definitely. And they'll recommend you to all their other friends, too."

"But it's weird, right? I don't get it."

"It's a little weird that they insisted," I agreed. "But you should probably get used to it. You've developed a reputation as a fabulous hotelier and everyone wants to meet you."

Jane's expression was dripping with skepticism. "Okay, whatever."

I just laughed. "Wait until this hotel is up and running. They'll put you on the cover of *People* or something."

Jane laughed out loud and I smiled at the sound. But then I suddenly remembered something. "I completely forgot to tell you. Speaking of your guests, one of them was out protesting this morning."

She stopped halfway down the stairs. "What are you talking about?"

"Your grumpy guest, Prudence Baxter, was one of those rowdy protesters. In fact, she deliberately elbowed me and I had to shove her away."

She stared in disbelief. "Are you kidding?"

"I wish I was. Then she bumped into the guy carrying the can of blood and almost knocked him down."

"This is unbelievable."

"I know. I thought it was pretty rude of her to be staying at your B and B while protesting against your future hotel."

"That's so insulting. I should kick her out." She shook her head. "But I won't."

"But you should. But no, you won't, because you're too polite."

"That's usually a good thing," she said, and scowled. "I'll have to figure out what to do about her."

I patted her shoulder. "Let me know if you need backup."

"Thanks."

We reached the bottom of the stairs and circled around the side of the staircase until we found the door in the middle of the heavily paneled wall.

"I've never seen this," she said. "Where does it lead?"

"I'll show you." I pulled the door open and we stepped inside a dark passage. "We have to go under the stairway through here."

Jane was right behind me and I could hear surprise in her voice. "Wow, I didn't realize there was a passageway through here."

"I just found it this morning." We got to a door on the other side of the passage and I pushed it open.

Jane grabbed my arm. "There's a whole other hallway."

"Right. Wade and I had seen it on the blueprints when we went over them with the architect. So this morning, Wade brought Niall back here and apparently he's already started working on one of the brick walls. I want to take a look at what he's done."

She sniffed the air. "Musty."

"Yeah. They must have closed off this section years before the rest of the Gables was shut down. It still has the old carpeting while the rest of the floors are hardwood or tile."

"I want to turn on some lights." Jane searched the walls for a switch and found one. The hallway filled with light. "That window at the end of the hall needs to be bigger."

She was right. A sliver of late-afternoon sunlight streamed in, but it wasn't enough for us to see any of the details of the hall.

"We'll enlarge it if you want."

"Let me think about it."

I noticed that leaning against the wall beneath the small window was a thick stack of discarded glass from other windows around the site. I wondered if any of them could be recycled and made a mental note to ask Wade to look into it.

Jane glanced around. "So Niall was working back here today?"

"Yeah," I said. "And I really wish he was still here. I could use his expertise with this little puzzle."

"He had to leave early today," Jane explained. "Our shipment of flagstone for the spa and patio was ready to pick up. But look, you and I can check it out ourselves and if we have questions, we can ask him about it tomorrow."

"True. After all, we're both professionals."

She gave a firm nod. "Yes, we are."

I stopped halfway down the hall, found one of the light trees nearby, and flipped the switch. The space was instantly filled with even more light. "That's better."

Niall must've used the light tree while he was working here earlier. There was also a ladder leaning against the wall next to a pile of neatly stacked bricks.

"What's with all these bricks?" Jane asked. "Is he bricking up this wall?"

"No, he's taking them down."

"Did they come loose?"

"No. Niall has been removing them row

by row. See?" I pointed to the top of the wall where eight or ten rows of bricks had been carefully removed from a ten-foot-wide section.

"But why?"

"That's why I wanted you to see this hallway."

"This is the mystery you were talking about?"

"Yes. So do me a favor."

"Sure."

"Check out the wall." I pointed to the section in front of us at eye level. "Let me know if you notice anything odd about it."

Jane took her time examining the wall, brick by brick. She got up close and touched them, then skimmed her hands over the edges where one section didn't quite match up with the rest of the wall. Then she walked to the other side of the hallway and ran her palm across the plaster. It was cracked and peeling, but it had once been pale and smooth.

She said, "I really like how this side of the hall is smooth plaster and painted this nice light color, while the other side is all dark exposed brick. I love that contrasting look, don't you?"

I nodded. "Yeah, I do."

"I know that has nothing to do with the

mystery," she said, grinning. "I just wanted to say how much I like this effect."

"Good to know."

"Okay, back to the odd wall you were talking about." Jane splayed her hand across the different sections of brick. "This part here is definitely much newer. The bricks here are redder, not so aged. They're smoother, not so pitted. They were definitely added more recently than the rest of it."

"Exactly," I said brightly. "Thank you."

She folded her arms. "That was too easy."

"I know. But here's a tougher one. *Why* exactly was this part of the wall replaced?"

"There's probably a simple answer."

My eyebrows went up. "I'm dying to hear it."

"Well, there could have been an earthquake," Jane said. "A section of the wall collapsed and they had to fill in that part of it with new brick."

That made perfect sense. Here on the northern coast of California we experienced earthquakes on a regular basis.

"That's possible," I admitted. "But here's the problem. The old blueprints show a doorway that opens to another hallway leading away from this one. It's right around this section."

"Wait." Her eyes widened. "Are you serious? A hidden doorway?"

I should've been as excited as Jane, but instead the idea freaked me out. And frankly I was a little surprised that Jane wasn't just as freaked. I rubbed my arms to get rid of the goose bumps that had suddenly erupted all over me. A mystery in a plain old house was one thing, but a mystery in a former insane asylum? I had to confess, it gave me the willies.

"Oh, I know!" Jane continued, with tongue in cheek. "Maybe they bricked it off to hide a body."

I shivered. " 'The Tell-Tale Heart.' "

"Cool, right?"

"No. Creepy."

"Oh, come on," she said.

"Sorry, but I'm the one finding dead bodies all the time, remember? And I don't like the thought of an Edgar Allan Poe story coming to life on this particular construction site."

"Yeah, I guess it is a little ghoulish." She grinned. "But hey, talk about a PR coup."

"PR? Really?" I couldn't help it, I started to laugh. "You're seriously starting to scare me."

"They always say, any PR is good PR." She was still smiling as she gazed up at the ceiling. "I wonder why they built this whole place out of brick and stone. Especially given the fact that we're in earthquake country. Most of the Victorians around here are built out of wood. All this stone had to have been a lot more expensive than lumber."

"I actually know the answer to that," I said with a smile.

"You do? Does it have to do with your Dr. Jones?"

"Yes." I smiled sheepishly. I had obviously overshared my research stories with anyone I could get to pay attention. "Anyway, the story is that back in the early Victorian era a lot of mentally ill people were sent to almshouses, which were the poorhouses built by churches and charitable groups. Naturally they used the cheapest materials for construction, so it's not surprising that many of them burned to the ground."

"That's horrible."

"Yes. And while some of the destruction was suspicious, they mostly burned down because the buildings were old and built out of cheap wood."

"So Dr. Jones had a different plan," Jane said, biting back a smile.

"Yes, grasshopper." I beamed at her. "His philosophy was to build with brick and stone so the patients would feel safer. He was all about providing safety and comfort for his patients because he thought that was the best way to cure them."

"That's good to know," Jane said. "I personally feel safer already. And I'm so happy that you've turned into the official Gables historian."

"Hey, I want to do this rehab the right way. That research really helps."

"I know it does. And I appreciate it."

"Thank you," I said, mollified.

"We'd better get going. Oh, I almost forgot to tell you. I'm meeting Niall at the pub tonight. Do you and Mac want to join us?"

"Um, sure. I'll have to call him. But wait." I hefted the ladder that was lying against the wall and pulled it over in front of the spot where Niall had been working. "This will only take a minute, but I want to check out what's on the other side of this wall. It might be the passageway I saw on the blueprints."

"Are you sure you don't want to wait for tomorrow when Niall will be here? He can help you figure out what's back there."

"This'll be quick, I promise."

"Okay, then. Let me help."

We set up the ladder and adjusted it so

that it leaned against the middle of the new wall.

"Do you want to go first?" I asked.

"No, you go ahead. This is your adventure."

I laughed, but quickly stepped onto the ladder and climbed to the top where Niall had removed several rows of bricks. I refused to think about the fact that I was now sixteen feet off the ground and poking my head inside a pitch-black space. What was I thinking?

"Can't see a thing," I muttered.

"Use your flashlight app."

"Good idea." I pulled my cell phone out and stared at the screen. "I can't believe it, my battery is dead. Can I use your phone?"

"Sure."

I scrambled halfway down and she handed it up to me. "Thanks." I climbed back to the top and leaned in close to the wall. Sticking my head inside the opening, I tapped the flashlight icon. I had to stretch up to get a better look. "Oh wow. Okay, this is cool."

"What is it?" Jane sounded impatient and I didn't blame her. "Can you see the door?"

"Yes. There's a few steps going down before you get to it." I squinted into the chamber. "At least, I think so. It's hard to see clearly."

"I want to see," Jane said.

"Okay, one more look and I'll be right down." I gripped one side of the ladder and leaned over, closer to the wall, clutching the row of bricks with my other hand.

"Shannon, that looks dangerous."

"I'm fine. This is so great." But the row of bricks I was holding on to began to give a little. They were no longer supported by the other bricks and suddenly felt loose. Was the mortar starting to disintegrate? "Oh, shoot. This wall is . . . not so solid."

I tried to back away, but my movement pressed the ladder more heavily against the wall.

I reached blindly for the nearest rung to steady myself, but I couldn't get hold of one.

How could a solid brick wall move like this? It almost felt like an earthquake.

"Shannon, come down right now."

The wall began to cave inward and I felt myself moving forward with it. "Jane?"

"Shannon!" Jane screamed.

I screamed, too, and struggled to hold on to the ladder as the wall collapsed beneath me. At the last second I felt my feet slip off the rung and barely managed to grasp the ladder rail with one hand as all the newly

loosened bricks tumbled down into the
empty space.

CHAPTER SEVEN

"Oh my God!" Jane cried. "Hold on!"

"I'm trying to." I could hardly hear myself over the clatter of falling bricks, not to mention the pounding of my heart.

"You're scaring me to death."

I was scaring myself to death. I tried to breathe, but I was afraid to move even that much. I was clinging by one hand to the side rail, dangling like a circus monkey at the top end of a really tall extension ladder.

The top of the fly rail had caught on the edge of the still-solid old wall, but it was so close to the hole that I knew it could slide off at any minute and go down. And take me with it.

I began to tremble with equal parts relief and terror. Relief that I hadn't yet fallen. Terror that I would drop any second now. It wasn't a long fall, maybe twelve or thirteen feet. But if I dropped down from here, I would plummet onto a pile of hard, unforgiving bricks. At the very least, I would break some bones.

"Hold on, please," Jane whimpered.

"That's the plan," I whispered.

"Should I run and get someone?"

"No time. Besides, I might need your help here."

"Okay. If you can get down a few more rungs, I can grab your feet and plant them on the rung. Will that help?"

"Yeah, that'll help." Except that I was hanging off one side with only one hand and I couldn't maneuver it over to grip a rung. "First I have to get both hands on the rail. And then I've got to slide down a few inches at a time."

"Can you swing yourself around and grab the other rail?"

"I can try."

"Should I hold the ladder steady for you?"

"Yes, do that." I took stock of my position. "Let me work on this." I knew as I was fighting for my life that it was taking far less time to experience it than it would when I finally told the story. If I survived to tell it. Actually, I felt like I was on fast-forward and pause all at the same time.

"Shannon, you're bleeding."

I already knew that, could see blood trickling down my arm. "It's just my knuckles. They scraped against the brick." And they were hurting like crazy, but Jane didn't need to know that. And I didn't have the presence of mind to both hold on and hold a conversation.

"Oh God," she said, then, "Okay, you can do this."

"Yes, I can. Give me a second or two." I hoped I would only need a second or two.

I had worked in construction most of my life, so my arms were pretty strong. I had somehow forgotten that fact while hanging so perilously above the abyss, so it took me a few serious deep breaths to take stock, then start solving my problem. Slowly and very deliberately, I raised my other arm up toward the rail, being careful to distribute my weight in a way that wouldn't cause the ladder to jerk and fall. When I finally got hold of the rail with both hands, I blew out a heavy breath.

"Okay, that's a start at least." If only I had worn my gloves, I thought. I could've gone sliding down the rail without too much effort. But even that movement might've caused the ladder to collapse, I realized, so I would take each small victory as it came.

Inch by cautious inch, I placed one hand under the other and descended the ladder. My fingers were aching from gripping the rail so tightly.

"You're almost close enough for me to grab you," Jane announced. "Just another couple yards or so."

That sounded really far away.

"Jane, step back so I don't hit you with my boots."

"You won't."

"Good, because I have no idea what I stepped in today."

She stifled a laugh. "Shut up, will you?"

"Just trying to keep it light." Besides, I realized that talking was actually helping.

"I'm not ready to laugh yet."

"But I've got more jokes."

"Stop it, you goofball."

I was out of breath from the exertion and the fear, but kept going. A couple of inches at a time, I told myself, in spite of the ache in my arms and fingers.

"Shannon?" a deep voice yelled from the front hall. I jolted from the unexpected sound of another person in the building, then cursed under my breath when the ladder shook.

"In here, Mac!" Jane shouted.

"Coming," he called.

"Mac," I whispered. "Thank God," I added in complete and utter relief. I had to steady myself and keep breathing.

"Hurry!" Jane's shout echoed what I was feeling.

"Damn," I said in a loud whisper. "I look like a complete fool." Oh well, it could've been worse. I could've been sprawled on a pile of bricks.

Paying no attention to my momentary attack of vanity, thank goodness, Jane raised her voice and shouted, "We're back here, Mac. Go past the stairway and look for the door in the wood panel."

It took a few long seconds before he answered, "Found it."

We could hear the sound of his boots thudding against the wood floor of the passageway, and then it was quiet as he stepped onto the ancient carpeting.

"There you are," he said, then gaped. "What the hell is going on?"

"Help her, Mac," Jane said.

"Wait," I cried. "Don't get too close to the ladder. It feels like it could fall away at any second."

Mac moved right up next to the ladder without touching it. He raised his arms and I realized he was close enough to catch me if I fell.

"Easy, babe."

I continued moving one hand and then the other, slowly down the ladder rail. With

145

each inch, I prayed the ladder wouldn't slip off its precarious perch.

"You've got this," Mac murmured.

Jane added, "Shannon, you're so close."

I wanted to stop and rest my head against my hands, but I couldn't lose whatever momentum I'd built up. I just kept moving.

"Keep going, sweetheart," Mac said, his voice a little shaky. "I can almost reach you."

I smiled at his words. Even facing certain death, he could turn me real sappy.

"Come on, baby," Mac said. "Just a few more inches."

"Am I there yet?"

"Yeah, you're there," he said, and grabbed me around the upper thighs, pulling me away from the ladder and letting me slide to my feet before wrapping his arms around me.

"Jeez, Irish." He buried his face in my hair. "You scared the hell out of me."

"And me," Jane said tightly.

"Right there with you both, but I'm okay." It was probably due to the rush of adrenaline from almost plunging down into the abyss of darkness, but I really did feel okay. I would start shaking any minute and I knew I would want to cry, but on the outside I was totally cool and mellow to the max.

146

My beloved friends were not fooled.

"You are never going near this wall again," Jane scolded, then grabbed me in a hug. "God. I was so scared."

"Me, too." I held on to her for a long moment. "You're right. I'll be careful."

"You *will* be careful," she warned. "Because I'm going to be watching your every move."

I didn't remind her that she had been just as excited as I was to look inside the brick hole. But that would come later. In private.

"I dropped your phone," I confessed. "I'm sorry."

"Oh, shoot." She glanced at the floor until she found it a few yards away. Glancing at the screen, she let out a relieved breath. "It landed on the carpet, so it's fine. No worries."

"I'm so glad."

"Let's get out of here," Mac said.

"I've got to put the ladder back first."

"I'll take care of it." He easily pulled the ladder away from its position and moved it a few feet away where the wall was more stable. After expertly using the rope and pulley to bring in the fly section, he laid the ladder on the floor against the wall.

I took one quick look at the dangerous pile of bricks and decided I would have to check it all out more closely tomorrow. For now, though, I kept that thought to myself, knowing that Jane might not handle it well.

"What are you doing here?" I asked when Mac was finished.

"You weren't at home," he said. "And you weren't answering your phone. I called Wade and then Sean and they both told me you were still here when they left. So I took a chance and drove up here." He grinned. "It's right on my way into town."

"The battery died on my phone, but I didn't realize it until a couple of minutes ago. Jane and I were walking around talking and surveying some of the work we've got to do over the next few days. And I wanted to show her this wall."

"The wall that is no longer a wall?" he said, glancing at Jane before turning to study the piles of bricks that had fallen down beneath me and were now scattered and broken inside the small antechamber. Even though most of the wall was gone, about three feet of brick wall remained at the bottom. Niall would be able to demo that section in an hour or so.

I glanced from Mac to Jane. "Yeah, that wall."

He smoothed my hair back from my face. "Shannon, are you sure you're all right?"

148

"I'm fine," I insisted. "More frazzled than hurt. It was just a little mishap."

Jane snorted. "A little near-death experience, she means."

I watched her give Mac a serious side glance and then roll her eyes. I decided not to take it personally.

"We can go now," I said brightly. "We'll deal with this mess tomorrow when Niall's here."

"Now that's a great idea," Jane said with a genuine smile at last. "Let's get out of here."

I switched off the light tree and grabbed Mac's hand. "I'm ready."

Mac glanced back over his shoulder at the space in the wall. "So what's with all those bricks?"

I started to explain as we walked through the under-stairs passage and down to the front entryway. Once outside, I held the phone for Jane as she locked the doors and entered a security code on the keypad nearby.

In the parking area, Jane said, "So do you guys want to meet Niall and me at the pub in a little while?"

"Sure," Mac said.

"Great," she said. "I could use a drink. We'll see you there about seven thirty."

We waited until she got in her car and

149

took off, and then Mac followed me to my house. He parked behind me in the driveway and met me by the back gate. I could hear Robbie barking like a wild dog and it warmed my heart.

He chuckled. "Let's get inside before he claws through the door."

Mac played outside with Robbie while Tiger waited in the kitchen, watching as I changed the water bowls and filled their food dishes.

"It's been quite a day," I said, plugging in my phone to charge it. "Do you mind if I take a quick shower? I'm not going to wash my hair so it won't take me too long."

"I don't mind at all. I'll make a few calls and watch the ball game."

"Perfect."

But first, he leaned in close and kissed me. "I've been wanting to do that all day."

"Me, too. I guess we were all pretty busy."

"After the blood-throwing incident this morning, I hung out with Rachel for a full hour."

"That was nice."

"Yeah, but she was so freaked-out, I stayed longer than I wanted to."

"You probably helped calm her down a lot."

He chuckled. "Trust me, I would rather

have been scraping paint with you."

It was my turn to laugh. "Said *nobody* in the history of construction ever."

"Oh, come on. I'll bet you and your guys were having a good old time."

"We always do." I gave him another quick kiss. "I'll only be a few minutes." Dashing upstairs, I wrapped my long, curly hair in a thin towel to keep it dry. I was in and out of the shower in seven minutes and felt one hundred percent better, except for the constant images flashing through my mind of me, hanging unsteadily from that ladder. I popped two ibuprofens because my shoulder was giving me some grief after stretching to reach for the ladder rail. And holding on, getting myself back to the ground, was the longest five minutes of my life. I rubbed some topical pain relief cream into the joint and my shoulder began to feel slightly better.

I bent over and fluffed my hair out, moisturized my face, and added a touch of lipstick and mascara. I dressed in my standard black jeans, a dark turtleneck, and short black boots. I grabbed my black leather jacket and jogged downstairs.

Mac's eyes lit up. "Wow, you are beautiful. Sexy and dangerous."

I couldn't help but laugh. I might've spent

time wondering about our future lately, but there was no question that right here and now, Mac Sullivan was pretty close to perfect. "I love you."

"And I love you right back." And he kissed me again.

Strolling into the pub, I spied Eric and Tommy standing at the bar. I would've walked over to say hello, but sadly Tommy's wife Whitney was with him, along with her best friend Jennifer Bailey, another of the mean girls from high school.

Instead I turned and waved at Jane, who was already sitting in a booth with Niall.

Mac pointed toward the bar. "I want to talk to Eric for a minute."

"Oh, I want to talk to him, too. But I'm going to join Jane first."

"Okay. I'll order you a glass of wine and be right there."

"Thanks." I turned and headed for the booth. "Hi, guys."

"Hello, Shannon," Niall said, reaching over to pat my back when I slid into the booth. "Did the work go well today?"

I could listen to him talk in his Scottish brogue for hours. He was wearing his kilt tonight, as he often did when he came to the pub, and I was certain that every woman in the room had been eyeing him as he walked from the door to the booth. There was something magical about a big strong man in a kilt.

"The work went really well," I said. "It's only been one day, but I'd say we're right on schedule."

He grinned. "Aye, because you keep a tight rein on all of us hooligans." His eyes narrowed. "But I understand you put yourself in a wee bit of danger tonight."

I scowled at Jane. "You had to tell him?"

"Of course I told him," Jane said, and gave me a look that said she clearly thought I was crazy for even asking the question.

"Don't blame Jane," Niall said calmly.

"I don't," I said, with an apologetic smile. "It's my own fault anyway. I shouldn't have gone up on my own, but we were just so curious." It sounded like a lame excuse, even to me.

"We'll have a look tomorrow," he said.

"Sounds good."

His smile faded. "I'm truly glad you weren't hurt."

"Me, too." Without thinking I rubbed my shoulder.

He frowned. "Ach, you didn't escape pain-free, I see."

"Are you okay, Shannon?" Jane asked.

"I'm fine." I waved away their concern. "Just a little soreness. On a bright note, you won't have to remove all those bricks from the wall, Niall."

"So I heard." He chuckled. "I'll clear the rest of them away tomorrow."

"Thanks. And when you're finished we can get a better look at that chamber and see what's behind that door."

"I'm weel chuffed to do it, but I'll be arriving late in the morning." As he glanced at Jane, I tried to translate some of the words he'd just used. But then he turned and gave me a somber look. "So you're to wait for me. Promise."

"I'll make sure she waits," Jane said firmly.

"Good," he said. "I've got a couple of fellows coming first thing to help me unload the flagstone from my truck."

"No worries," I said lightly. "I'll just take a peek at the damage and then when you get there we can —"

"No," Jane said, scowling. "I don't want you going near that brick wall without Niall around."

"Nor do I," the man himself intoned with a hard look at me.

"Fine, okay, I get it," I said, then gave them a weak smile. "But really, what's the worst that could happen? Most of the bricks have already fallen down."

"There's still a third of a wall standing," Jane said. "And I don't want you trying to jump over it by yourself."

"All right." Silently I admitted that she might have a point. "But I recall a certain hotelier was just as excited to explore the hidden doorway as I was."

Jane sniffed. "I was only there to support you."

I laughed. "Yeah, right. Okay, Niall. I'll wait for you to get there and we'll explore together."

"I want to be there, too," Jane said.

"Aha!"

She lifted her nose in the air. "As the new owner of Hotel Hennessey, I feel a responsibility to my staff and crew."

I gave Niall a look. "Oh, we're *her* crew now."

Niall kissed Jane soundly. "I'm fine with that."

I laughed again. "Okay. But Jane, if you're not around, we're going ahead without you."

Jane leaned in close and jabbed her finger at me. "I've got three little words for you. 'The Tell-Tale Heart.' "

"Ooh." I frowned. "That's cruel."

She just grinned.

Mac joined us then, setting down my glass

of wine and his bottle of beer on the table before sliding into the booth next to me. Eric followed him over.

"Hi, Chief," Jane said. "I hear you took care of those rabble-rousers this morning. Thank you."

He gave me a steady look. "We had to release one of them earlier today, but we held the other one up until a half hour ago."

"Which one did you release earlier?" I demanded.

"The one wearing the orange ball cap." Before I could protest, he held up his hand. "He didn't do anything but yell out some protests. I had a uniformed officer drive him home, so we know where he lives now."

"Well, that's something." I took a quick sip of wine. "What about the other one? The skinny redhead?"

"That guy actually caused some real damage."

"But he was still released?"

"Yes. He got in touch with a lawyer this afternoon and he'll have to appear in court next week, but he was free to go for now."

"Darn it." I scowled. "So I guess they didn't kill any animals to get that bucket of blood?"

"No, it was a homemade concoction. Something we call Halloween blood. Basically corn syrup, chocolate sauce, and red food coloring."

Jane made a squinchy face. "Yuck."

My shoulders fell. "That's disappointing. I mean, I'm glad they didn't kill any animals, but I'm sorry they're free to cause us more problems."

"Let me remind you that we'll have a couple of officers assigned to your construction site, so if there's any more trouble, just yell for them. And I might try to swing by tomorrow, too."

"That's a great idea," Mac said. "I think it'll help calm down Rachel, the woman in charge of the project."

"She's the one who got slimed?" Eric said.

"Yeah. She was pretty shaken."

"Tommy took her statement today," Eric said. "But I'll be sure to pay a call on her tomorrow."

Mac nodded. "That's probably a good idea, if you can make the time."

"Would you mind telling me those two protesters' names?" I asked. "I've been calling them Orange Cap and Carrot Head."

"Creative," he murmured. Pulling out his notepad, he flipped to a page. "I assume Carrot Head is the red-haired fellow. His name is Judson Killian. The other guy in the orange cap is Ricky Patterson."

"Okay, good to know." I pulled out my phone and made a note of the two names.

"I'm going to take off," Eric said. "Shannon, if Chloe doesn't call you on the way into town from the airport in the morning, I'll be sure to remind her to get in touch about that dinner."

"I appreciate it. See you tomorrow, Chief."

As soon as Eric left, we ordered food and another round of drinks. We tried to avoid talking about the Gables project and concentrated instead on personal stuff, like Chloe's impending visit and Mac's new book. We had to gush about Niall's sister — our good friend Emily — getting engaged to our friend Gus Peratti. And then Niall showed us pictures of his adorable new niece back in Scotland and we all oohed and ahhed over her cuteness.

We were halfway through our dinners — cheeseburger and fries for me, chopped salad for Jane, fish and chips for Mac and Niall — when I glanced up and almost dropped my wineglass. Whitney Reid Gallagher was actually standing at the bar talking to Orange Cap. What was his name? Ricky Patterson.

"Unbelievable," I muttered, and scanned the room for Tommy but didn't see him anywhere. I figured Jennifer must have gone home, otherwise she'd be right there with her BFF.

"What is it?" Mac asked, sipping his beer.

"Check out who Whitney's talking to."

Mac swung around to see who it was. He whistled as he turned back to me. "Now that takes some brass ones."

I smiled at him. "Are you referring to Whitney's or the protester's?"

He chuckled. "The protester. He spent the morning being interrogated and now he's drinking a beer and chatting up the wife of the assistant police chief."

Jane took another quick look back at Whitney. "I'm willing to bet that Whitney was the one who initiated the conversation."

"That's probably true," I said, glad that Jane had brought it up first. "She's naturally attracted to all the worst people."

"Shannon speaks the truth," she insisted. "We've both known her since high school."

"But what about Tommy?" Niall asked. "He's a good man. Friendly, too. How did he and his wife get together?"

"A question for the ages," I muttered.

"Long story," Jane whispered loudly. "I'll tell you later."

I just rolled my eyes and sipped my wine.

It was true that except for Tommy, Whitney always seemed to attract the jerks. Even her girlfriends were jerks.

I didn't know Ricky so I couldn't say whether he was really a jerk, but he sure was angry. I would hold my final judgment because he could have a personal reason why he was so outraged with the Gables renovation.

Now that I got a good look at him, he looked like a regular guy, hanging out and having a beer. He had lost the orange baseball cap and I saw that his hair was light brown and wispy thin, matching his beard. He had seemed young when he was protesting, but now I could see that he was probably in his midthirties. He would've been too young to be a patient at the Gables, but maybe one of his parents had been stuck there for a while. Knowing what Jane had been through with her mom, it couldn't have been easy for anyone.

Mac frowned at the two of them by the bar. "Do you really think Whitney knows that guy? Maybe they just happened to meet here tonight."

"I'll call Eric and ask," I said. "It could be important."

"Let me do it," Mac offered, knowing how Whitney might react if she found out I was checking up on her. "That way you won't get stuck in the middle of things. I'll ask

160

him to talk to Whitney about the guy."

I breathed a sigh of relief. "That would be great."

"Why does it matter if she knows him?" Niall asked as he dipped a chunk of his fish in tartar sauce.

"If she knows him she might be able to share some useful information about him," I explained. "I want to find out his connection to the Gables."

Mac shrugged. "I could go over there and ask him myself."

"Mac, no," I said, grabbing his arm. "I don't want him to see you."

He grinned. "Worried I can't defend myself?"

"Of course not. You can obviously kick his butt." I gazed across the bar at the guy in question. "But he was so angry this morning. I'm concerned that he'll do something stupid, like come after you with a knife. Or worse."

He squeezed my hand. "He won't come after me."

"I hope not, but think about it. Here's this guy who shows up out of nowhere. We've never seen him before. And all we know is that he wants to burn down an important historical landmark. A landmark, by the way, that we're all planning to be working

161

on for the next year, at least. I would really like to know who he is and what he's thinking."

"Maybe he'll go away if we can just ignore him," Jane said, always the optimist.

"Ignore him?" I frowned into my wine-glass. "I doubt he'll let us do that."

If he had wanted to be ignored, he wouldn't have been making trouble at the Gables earlier. And it made me wonder when he'd be coming back.

CHAPTER EIGHT

The next morning I arrived at the Gables ready to go to work. My shoulder pain was almost gone and I had vowed to stay out of trouble. I had added a whole slew of new items to my list of things to do and texted Carla and Wade to meet me first thing to discuss their own plans for the day.

More than anything else, I was looking forward to checking out that pile of bricks that had almost wiped me out the night before. But I would have to wait until Niall showed up, if only to keep Jane from giving me more grief.

And along with that, I was anxious to explore the small antechamber and find out if that door led to someplace interesting.

After meeting with my foremen, I planned to get down to work myself. I would start in Jane's future registration office, scraping all that ugly paint off the walls. That would keep me busy and out of harm's way, I thought.

I parked my truck, grabbed my toolbox, and was rounding the front corner of Building Seven when I saw a pack of at least twenty people, mostly reporters and several camera operators, hanging out right in front of Jane's doorway. Someone had set up a lectern on the flat grass nearby. I could tell it was the same lectern, minus the raised stage, that Rachel Powers had used the day before.

A thick cable snaked down from the microphone to the grass, then across and up the steps and through the doorway. From there it disappeared inside Building Seven, where, I assumed, it had been plugged in.

Obviously, they were expecting someone to speak. But why here, in front of Jane's hotel? Maybe it was far enough out of the way that it wouldn't interrupt the work of everyone else in the complex. Just ours, I thought grumpily.

I glanced around and realized that some of the protesters were here, too. I recognized them from the day before. Some stood alone and a few others chatted with the reporters. Happily, none of them were shouting to burn it down. Not yet, anyway.

"Shannon," someone called.

I looked around and saw Palmer Tripley, owner, editor, and chief reporter for the *Lighthouse Standard,* our local newspaper, walking toward me. "What's going on, Palmer?"

"How are you, Shannon?" he asked jovially. Nudging his chin toward the front entrance of Building Seven, he said, "This is Jane's new place, right? Maybe I can wangle a tour with you later."

"Absolutely," I said. "But next week would be better, after we've swept away some of the cobwebs."

"I'll give you a call and set it up."

"Sounds good."

"I understand I missed all the action yesterday," he said. "I was stuck down at the Whale Watch festival."

"I was wondering where you were. I saw Brandi, but didn't get a chance to talk to her." Brandi was Palmer's daughter and I'd known her since she was a baby.

"Ever since she came home from college she's been working at the paper." He smiled fondly. "She's turning out to be a good little reporter."

I winced. "You're making me feel really old. I remember when she started first grade."

He chuckled. "She's only a few years

165

younger than you."

I smiled. "I'm glad to hear she's doing well."

And that was enough small talk, I thought. Glancing around at the crowd, I asked, "So what's happening out here?"

He pulled a folded press release from his back pocket. "The Gables' last chief physician has called a news conference."

"Chief physician? Really?" I hoped my expression didn't reflect the shock I felt at the news. I grabbed the press release and skimmed it. "Lorraine Fairchild?"

"Yeah," Palmer said. "She was the one in charge of the place when they finally shut it down."

"A woman?" I murmured. "That's interesting."

He took the press release back from me and checked it again. "Yeah, Dr. Lorraine Fairchild is pleased to discuss her years of work at the Gables."

"They shut it down over twenty years ago," I mused. "Wonder where she's been all this time. And I wonder what she wants to say now."

"Whatever she says, it'll be news. Especially with all the protesters carrying on yesterday. Brandi interviewed a couple of those guys and they had plenty to say."

"So the doctor wants equal time?"

"That's my guess," Palmer said.

I told myself to remember to read Brandi's interviews from yesterday when I got home tonight.

At that moment, Rachel Powers walked up to the microphone followed by a sturdy-looking older woman. She wore her platinum hair in a sophisticated French twist, and her charcoal business suit matched her sensible heels. This had to be the chief physician, I thought. She appeared to be in her midsixties and attractive in a no-nonsense sort of way. She must have been awfully young when she first came to work here.

"That's the doctor," Palmer whispered, after comparing the press release photo to the real-life woman.

I happened to glance around and to my shock, Prudence Baxter appeared at the edge of the crowd.

"Oh, Pru, there you are," Dr. Fairchild said. "Hold my pocketbook."

I blinked at her command. But sure enough, Prudence rushed right over to the doctor and proudly took hold of her purse. Then she backed away, clutching the purse strap with both hands.

Rachel spoke first. "With so much attention focused on the Gables transformation project, I would like to ask you not to forget the contributions of the many doctors, nurses, and staff of our Gables family who worked for years giving comfort and care to our friends and loved ones."

"Dr. Lorraine Fairchild is one of those special people. She was chief physician and head psychiatrist of the Gables for ten years, and today we are honored to have her say a few words and then take your questions. Please welcome Dr. Lorraine Fairchild."

There was polite applause. Rachel moved quickly away from the lectern as Dr. Fairchild walked up and tapped the microphone. She glanced around at the faces in the audience, taking her time, making eye contact. It almost felt like a power play. *You WILL pay attention to me.*

I wanted to admire her for that ability, but instead I thought she was kind of scary. Some doctors could really carry off the "God complex" vibe. She seemed to be one of them.

Once she had scanned the entire audience, she spoke in a clear, commanding voice. "Good morning, everyone, and thank you for being here. As Ms. Powers said, my name is Lorraine Fairchild. For ten years I was head physician and chief of psychiatry at the Gables until it was closed down in 2002. I've come here today to answer your questions, but first I will make a brief personal statement."

There was a respectful silence in the crowd but I could hear the distant hum and buzz of power drills and sanders at work inside the nearby buildings.

She had to hate that, I thought.

"I started as a staff psychiatrist and quickly rose in the ranks until I became chief physician. My psychiatric practice continued concurrently. I consider those ten years to be the most rewarding and enjoyable time of my professional career. I'm very proud of the work I did and the breakthroughs we made."

"After ten years, sadly, the Gables was closed. It was not a choice I would have made. I wanted my work to continue. It was important work. Lifesaving work. I wanted my patients to thrive. But alas, that was not to be."

"I can recall the faces of every single one of my patients and I am proud to say, in all modesty, that they loved me. I helped them. I was responsible for their safety and welfare. In many cases, I literally brought them back to life. They are leading active and healthy lives now and it's all because of the time they spent with me and my staff at the Gables."

Wow.

I hated to be cynical, but I really had to wonder whether those same patients would agree with her. She seemed so full of herself, but maybe it was just a "doctor thing."

Dr. Fairchild straightened her shoulders imperiously. "Now I will be happy to take your questions."

"Doctor! Dr. Fairchild! Over here!" A half dozen reporters shouted her name.

I gazed at the faces in the crowd. Most of the reporters were in a frenzy to get their questions asked, but I noticed that some of the protesters had also gathered to hear the doctor speak. I recognized one or two of them from the day before. One of the older women looked slightly dazed and not in a good way. I watched one man shake his head and then turn and walk away. He stopped to talk to another woman whose hands covered her face. After a few words, he wrapped his arm around her.

It made me sad and I chalked up my emotional reaction to my being a little fragile from last night's mishap. I really needed to get to work. But I wanted to hear some of the questions first.

The reporter said, "I imagine you're here

because you've heard that the Gables is being renovated and will soon house an art gallery, shops, and a hotel. How do you feel about that?"

Dr. Fairchild sniffed. "I think it's frankly pathetic that a fine institution, one dedicated to health and wellness, is being replaced by crass commercial enterprises. It's sickening, but I suppose it all comes down to money. Doesn't everything?" She tossed her hair back. "That's why I've come back. I'm here to remind you people that when I was in charge, some very important work was taking place." She held her arms out. "You are all standing on hallowed ground because of me. Because of my work. My methods. My vision."

Whew. Was she completely self-absorbed? Or just a whiny old crab? Both seemed to apply. Maybe I was being harsh, but the woman's ego was exhausting to me.

I managed to lean over to Palmer and whisper, "I have to go, but give me a call next week about the tour."

"Thanks, Shannon. See you later."

I walked quickly toward the entryway to Building Seven, stomping on Dr. Fairchild's hallowed ground all the way. I had a sudden thought that she must have considered Dr. Jones ridiculous with his notions of safety and caring and his use of architecture as an essential tool in the treatment of mental illness.

I doubted she would be impressed with anyone's notions but her own. I mentally shook myself. I had to stop thinking about Fairchild and get to work.

I reached the steps of Jane's building but stopped when I saw Rachel standing on the top step. She was staring out at the audience, looking as if she'd swallowed a big, nasty potato bug. I couldn't blame her after hearing the doctor's scathing critique of our renovations.

"Are you okay?" I asked.

"What? Oh. Hi. It's Shannon, right?"

"Yeah. Is everything all right?"

She exhaled heavily, then flashed me a big, bright, fake smile. "I'm fine. Just thought I saw someone I knew."

I glanced back at the audience, but everyone was facing away from where we stood. Except for Dr. Fairchild and Prudence. They were both looking this way.

"Okay, then. Have a good day." I brushed past her and walked inside.

I thought about it for a few seconds, then stopped, turned around, and took another look through the half-open door, just to be sure. The doctor had been distracted by another question, but good old Prudence was still staring in this direction.

Was Dr. Fairchild or Prudence the one who'd put that look on Rachel's face? Did Rachel know these people? Her glowing introduction of the doctor and her reference to "our Gables family" had made it sound as if there might be a connection there. Did they know her? All I knew was that she wasn't glowing now. She looked really unhappy and a little bit fearful.

Who could blame her? I thought. Dr. Fairchild was scary! And Prudence was just odd.

I shook my head, closed the front door, and walked down the hallway, away from that totally weird scene. It was time to go bury myself in work.

I spent the first hour inside with Wade and Carla, checking out the rooms on the second and third floors. Because of all the flaky old paint and cracked plaster on every surface, we all wore lightweight surgical masks. But the mask couldn't hide the grimace on Wade's face as he looked around. "These upper floors are in even worse shape than the first floor."

"They might've been closed off for years,"

I guessed. "Even longer than the rest of the place."

"I wonder if all the other buildings are in the same condition," Carla said.

Wade took some photos with his tablet. "At some point it would be interesting to go around and check out those other buildings."

"Mac went through the main building and this one when he went on the tour. He didn't say there was much of a difference between them, but I'll ask him what he thought." I made a note on my tablet.

Wade frowned. "Don't you think it would've made more sense to close down some of these outer buildings and concentrate the patient population in just one or two buildings?"

"That's what I was thinking," Carla said. "Seems more practical, but then, I freely admit that I don't think like a doctor."

I shrugged. "Maybe they felt that the closer they were to the ground, the better it would be for the patients' well-being. So they moved everyone to the first floors of all the buildings and sealed off the upper floors."

Wade nodded. "That goes along with your theory about airflow and stuff."

I shook my head. "It's not exactly *my*

theory, and it has to do with a lot more than just airflow."

Wade grinned. "You know what I mean."

"Yeah, I know." Clearly everyone involved in this project had received an earful of what I'd learned in my research.

None of us were willing to say out loud that maybe the people in charge had just stopped caring about the patients' environment. Federal funding was drying up and they might've been expecting to be shut down at any minute anyway. And the place had been shut up for twenty years, after all. Abandoning these buildings for that long a period could've easily caused plenty of this deterioration.

"And let's not forget," Carla added. "Being so close to the ocean can cause a lot of damage as well. The aforementioned mold, for one thing."

"Humidity is a killer," Wade agreed.

With all of those depressing possibilities to think about, we headed downstairs and went our separate ways. I was standing on the landing between the first and second floors when my cell phone rang. It was almost ten o'clock and I saw Niall's name pop up on my screen.

"Hi. What's up?" I sat right there on the top stair and gazed down the long hallway toward the foyer. Even in its present shabby condition I could see that it was really going to be fabulous someday.

"I'm sorry, Shannon," Niall said, "but I won't make it back there before noon."

That was two hours away. I was disappointed but didn't want to make him feel bad. "That's okay. I've got plenty to do until you get here."

"Is everything going well?"

"Yes," I said. "The work is coming along fine. But the big news is that one of the original doctors from the Gables actually showed up and held a news conference."

"A news conference, you say. He must be quite old."

"It's a woman and she's probably in her sixties, I'd guess. There were also some protesters here, but they weren't yelling, thank goodness. Maybe the police were able to discourage them."

"I hope you've the right of it."

After another minute, we ended the call and I pulled up my schedule to see what I needed to deal with next. I sat on the stairs for ten minutes adding to my ongoing list. Now that we'd gotten a good look at the problems of the upper floors and that back hallway, I had a lot more items that would require attention.

I made a note to have a couple of guys carry utility tables up to the second and third floors. We would need to set out some more bleach, vinegar, and spray bottles because the three of us had come across more stubborn pockets of mildew in the upstairs bathrooms that had been closed off for so many years.

"Shannon, do you have another minute?"

I glanced up and saw Carla walking up the stairs. "Sure."

She sat down next to me. "I know I always mention this on other job sites, but I'm concerned that with this project stretching out for a year, some of the guys might get stuck doing the same jobs for a long period of time. We know how that goes. A few of them will get bored and start goofing off, and others could develop some sort of repetitive motion injury. So we should think about shaking things up every few weeks or so."

This was a regular concern of Carla's since her husband had been treated for carpal tunnel syndrome a few years ago. I nodded. "You're right. We've had that issue come up on other jobs so it's worth discussing."

"What are you two up to?" Wade stood at the bottom of the stairs looking up at us.

"We're discussing repetitive motion injuries," I said.

"We need to switch up jobs and workers," Carla said. "This hotel project is going to go on for a full year, so we don't want to take a chance that any of our guys will burn out."

"Good point," he said, swiping at his tablet screen. "I can set up a spreadsheet, lay out all the guys' names and the different jobs and we can play with it, figure it all out tomorrow."

"The spreadsheet king rocks," Carla teased.

"Okay, king," I said. "This is in your hands. Now, I want both of your opinions on something."

"What's up, boss?" Wade asked.

"It's just a personal thing, but I would love to be able to take the protective film off some of the windows. You've noticed it can get really dark in parts of this building, right?"

"We'd be taking a chance on damaging the glass," Carla said with a frown.

"That's the downside," I agreed. "But we can always replace the glass."

Wade narrowed his eyes. "You afraid we'll all get depressed from not seeing the sunshine?"

"Yeah, that seasonal depression thing," Carla said.

"Seasonal affective disorder." I smiled and shook my head at her. "It's not really about that specifically since we're heading into spring. But I just think the view is so spectacular from up here."

Carla raised one eyebrow. "So this is more about enjoying the view than actually lighting up the place."

I gave her a meaningful look. "I know you're just teasing me."

"Of course I am," she said with a grin.

"Okay, good," I said. "I'm thinking that we should uncover all the windows and when we get to the point where we're spackling and painting, we hang tarps over the windows to protect them."

"We would have to mask off the window frames anyway, so hanging tarps is probably a good idea."

"You guys are both right," Carla said. "And with the natural light coming in, we'll be better able to judge paint colors and trim."

"There you go," I said, smiling at her.

"And then you'll be able to see the ocean," Wade said. "And the blue skies, the clouds, the coastline, and the surfers."

"Wait, there are surfers?" Carla said.

"Yeah." I smiled. "Who doesn't like surfers?"

Wade opened his tablet. "Okay, I'm writing all this down. Just to be clear, we've agreed to take the protective film off the windows and if we damage a window, we buy it. But even with the natural light, we should probably rent or buy a dozen more light trees to brighten up the darker spots we'll be working in."

"Good idea," I said. "We'll need them all year for this job."

Carla nodded. "And we'll be able to use them on other jobs, too."

Our impromptu meeting broke up and I found myself wandering the building on my own, noting more trouble spots. The wood paneling along the staircase would need to be sanded down and refinished. I put Amanda's name next to that item. She was our expert when it came to anything wood-related. I retraced my steps going back toward the foyer, then thought about working by myself in Jane's future reception office. But when I reached the doorway, I thought again about that back hall.

Niall wouldn't be here for a while so I didn't dare check out that brick wall and the hidden antechamber on my own. But I wanted to.

I glanced at my wristwatch and saw that I still had an hour to wait before Niall got here. "Patience, girl," I muttered, taking a deep breath. I headed for the reception space when I saw a woman hurrying down the hall toward the main stairway. She wore jeans, work boots, and a black hoodie. She passed the stairway and stopped at the door to the passageway under the stairs. I didn't recognize her. Or *him,* I added. It could be a short, thin man. *Like Orange Cap,* I thought, scowling.

"Hello?" I called. "Wait." She didn't hear me — or she ignored me because she ducked into the passageway and disappeared.

"What the heck?" I took off down the hall. This was my job site and I insisted on knowing everyone who was working here. It wasn't just me being nosy. There were liability issues involved. But yeah, sometimes I was just plain nosy.

I picked up speed and made it to the passageway in less than ten seconds. I pulled the door open and walked through the dark to the second door. Pushing it open, I stepped into the carpeted hallway, making sure the door didn't shut behind me.

And didn't see another person.

"Hello?" I called again.

Nothing.

I stared down the hall and counted eight doors — all closed — on the wall opposite the crumbling brick wall. Whoever had just walked in here had to have gone into one of those rooms. How else could they have disappeared so quickly?

But was I really going to try to search each of those rooms by myself? Absolutely not. But I knew without a doubt that the stranger who came this way was hiding behind one of those doors. Where else would they be? I would simply have to wait for Niall before I took off searching on my own.

I thought that was a pretty grown-up decision on my part and mentally patted my back.

I started to head back to the passageway but stopped at the three-foot-high brick wall for a moment. It wasn't as if I were going to throw myself over that wall. Mainly because Jane would have a fit, but also because I didn't want to go near that pile of bricks until I had someone — Niall, Jane, or maybe Mac — with me. And I wasn't going to climb any ladders, either. So I was safe. Everything would be fine.

Now that I had won my own argument, I stared around the hallway. Everything was exactly where we'd left it last night. The ladder was on the floor leaning against the wall, the light tree was still nearby, and the piles of bricks were, well, everywhere.

I didn't know what I had expected, but there was much more of a mess than I'd thought there would be. I suppose after the mishap last night we had walked out of here without cleaning up. That rarely happened. My crew and I always straightened things up at the end of the day.

I pulled the light tree over and turned it on, then stared at what was left of the wall. Not even three feet, I thought. The bricks barely came up to my knees so it was more like two feet.

Taking a step closer, I gazed down at the large pile of bricks scattered on the other side of the wall. It looked like a small mountain. Niall and his two helpers would need a few days to clear these away, I thought, and decided I would line up two more guys to help him out.

I stepped back and gazed up at the few remaining rows of bricks closest to the ceiling. I realized that this was where the top edge of my ladder had caught, thank God. And that had probably saved my life. I shuddered briefly at the realization.

"How in the world did this wall collapse?" I wondered aloud for the hundredth time. I

183

reached down and gave the two-foot wall a quick shove. It didn't budge. I tried it again and it remained firm. So how had those middle rows of bricks collapsed so completely?

I had worked in construction long enough to know the answer. The bricks and mortar in this new section had been stacked in one thin column with nothing to hold them erect and keep them stable. When the mortar began to deteriorate, as it had after so many years of neglect, the wall had come tumbling down with almost no effort.

I stared again into the antechamber and all those bricks. This area had been closed off by a brick wall for so many years and I wondered again . . . why?

Why had this section been bricked up and hidden from the world?

Naturally I first thought of Jane's theory, that this was where they had hidden the bodies. Here in the light of day the thought made me smile, remembering how tickled Jane had been by the idea. But off the top of my head I could come up with several other innocent reasons, such as the possibility that there was unfinished construction behind that door that could be dangerous to patients. Or maybe that part of the building was no longer up to code. Either the stairs were too steep, for instance, or the doors were too narrow. Maybe that was where they stored old hospital equipment that was rusted or broken and could hurt someone.

I shivered and wondered where the sudden draft of air had come from. I turned to look toward the passageway and saw that the door I'd come through was closed now. Did the wind do that?

I heard a quick intake of breath behind me.

"What the —"

Before I could finish the thought, I was shoved forward with alarming brute force and fell headfirst into the abyss.

I woke up to hammers pounding in my head and a giant table saw buzzing in my ears. My cheek was pressed up against something rough and hard and I knew I had scraped it badly. Was it bleeding? Was anything broken? All I knew was that I ached all over, especially the top of my head, and I realized that I must've hit it hard. And that scared me. I knew I had passed out. But I was alive. Good news.

My head was still foggy so it took me a few more seconds of blinking and trying to see in front of me before I could remember where I was and how I got here. Someone had pushed me, hard, over the wall. I had landed on a pile of bricks, the very thing I had been so worried about last night.

Was the pusher still here? Was it the woman in the black hoodie? Who else could it be? At this moment was she waiting for me to get up so she could hurt me even worse?

Just in case she — or he? — was still nearby waiting and watching me, I remained perfectly still. It wasn't too hard to do since I could barely move. I was lying at an awkward angle on the bricks, with my head near the bottom of the pile and my feet farther up. The downward angle worried me because if enough blood rushed to my head, it might cause me to faint.

I shook that unpleasant thought away and silently surveyed each part of my body, taking stock of any pain or injuries. Especially injuries. I could live with the pain, but I dreaded being badly injured.

I started with my toes. I could move them, so at least I wasn't paralyzed. I almost cried in relief. Then I tried to flex the muscles in my legs. Good to go, but I could feel my knees stinging and figured I had scraped them on the top of the brick wall.

My hips were okay. I hadn't landed on my

back so that was a good thing. My stomach felt empty and I realized I was hungry. It made me wonder how long I had been unconscious.

My arms and fingers were still working, hallelujah. My shoulders and my neck were okay. My head was pounding, but I looked on the bright side: it meant I was alive.

Whoever had pushed me hadn't killed me. Had that been their plan? If so, they had failed. It gave me a chill to realize that they were obviously insane, whoever they were. Why would any normal person do that?

I waited another few minutes until I thought I might be alone. I couldn't hear anything now, but then, I hadn't heard anything earlier — except that quick intake of breath just before the push. Whoever it was that had tried to hurt me — kill me? — had moved with the stillness of a sylph.

I tried to push myself up and that was when I felt the pain rush from my hands and wrists all the way up to my shoulders. I slowly collapsed, taking care to avoid having my head hit the bricks. Again. This was crazy, but I couldn't gather enough strength to raise myself up from this stupid brick heap. I was sprawled upside down and too weak to move. It was sad, but I knew I was going to need some help.

Once I made my decision, it took another few minutes to get myself into a position where I could pull my cell phone out of my vest pocket. Exhausted, I took another long minute to maneuver it in front of my face. The first thing I saw was the time of day and realized I had been completely out of it for at least five minutes. That couldn't be good. But I'd been awake and conscious for a while now, just trying to figure out how to get out of here, so that was something. Still, I kind of figured I was lucky to be alive.

I awkwardly pressed Mac's number and waited.

His face appeared on the screen and I realized too late that I had hit video. Big mistake.

"Shannon." He smiled. He was so handsome, I wanted to curl up in his arms and stay there forever.

"Hi." I tried to smile, tried to look normal, but knew I was blowing it.

His smile faded and his eyes narrowed. "What's wrong? What happened?"

"Can you . . . help me?" It was hard to get the words out. Maybe my mind was more scrambled than I thought.

"Where are you?" he demanded.

"I'm . . . at work. Gables. The back hallway . . . where we were last night."

"Oh, hell."

"I'm . . . okay. But if you could just . . . come soon."

"Stay where you are. I'm on my way."

I stayed where I was, mainly because it was too painful to move. I knew I hadn't broken anything, but I was stiff and aching and had landed on a steep brick incline with my head facing downward. It was mortifying. Or it would be as soon as Mac got here.

I had time to think about my position. With everything hurting and my muscles aching, it would be hard enough to push up from a flat surface. But sprawled at this weird angle, it was impossible. Gravity was not my friend.

It even hurt to think too much, but I wanted to. I had to figure out who had done this to me. Someone had deliberately tried to hurt me. Someone vicious and disturbed. I wasn't ready to deal with that cold reality just now, but I would, and soon. For now, I closed my eyes and waited for Mac.

He didn't make me wait long. It was less than ten minutes when I heard the sound of someone running toward the area.

"Shannon!" Mac shouted, and I had a little moment of déjà vu. It was just like he had shouted my name last night.

"In here," I said, but I wasn't sure my voice carried.

"Oh my God," he whispered.

"How'd you get here so fast?"

"I was already in my car on my way here."

"Lucky me."

He frowned. "I'm not so sure about that."

"I'll be okay. I just need some help getting out of here."

"I'll help you."

"It's just . . . a little awkward, trying to get up."

"Is she here?" a woman cried out.

I groaned out loud. That was Jane. She was going to kill me.

"Tell her I'm not here," I muttered.

Mac laughed. "Sorry, babe. You'll have to tell her that yourself."

"Damn it," I grumbled.

"Shannon! Oh my God, she's not moving." She sobbed. "Is she alive?"

"Of course I'm alive," I groused.

"Good," Jane said. "Because I'm going to kill you."

I sighed. "I know."

CHAPTER NINE

Getting me out of that stupid pit of bricks was harder than any of us thought it would be. It was because of the way I was positioned — basically, upside down — that made it tricky. I'm no petite flower like my friend Lizzie, but I'm in really good shape and my arms are especially strong. And yet I couldn't push myself up from this angle and it was darn frustrating. I felt like an idiot.

Mac finally solved the problem by climbing over the wall and scrambling down the mountain of bricks like a seasoned rock climber — which he probably was. He caused a few tiny brick avalanches, but made it down far enough that he was able to plant his feet near my head. Bracing himself, he leaned over and slipped his arms under my shoulders, then lifted me up as though I were lighter than air. He hefted me over his shoulder in a fireman's hold and carefully hiked up the brick pile until he reached the wall.

"I'll take her," Niall said, reaching out. "Then when you're over the wall, I'll hand her back to you."

I said nothing, just let them work it out. I was simply relieved to have escaped from Brick Mountain.

Mac was strong and tough, but Niall was huge, with muscles on top of muscles. He'd spent his youth playing rugby and tossing cabers with his mates. Caber tossing was a true Scottish sport, somewhat akin to tossing a telephone pole as far as it would go. Happily, this meant that I presented no challenge to him at all. He held me as though I were no more than a chip off one of those wooden cabers he knew so well.

When Mac was out of the antechamber and back on solid ground, Niall carefully passed me back to him. In Mac's arms, I felt warm and loved. I pressed my face to his shirt and inhaled him. The man smelled so good, so manly, so . . . mmm.

My head was starting to spin and it wasn't strictly from Mac's closeness. It was possibly from lying upside down all that time.

"She's bleeding," Jane said in an accusing tone.

Mac gently touched my cheek. "You're

bleeding, Red."

"Am I? I guess so. And I'll be black and blue in a few places, too."

"Just a few?" Jane asked, then fumed. "Didn't I tell you to stay out of there until Niall came back?"

I tried to scowl but my face hurt too much. "I didn't go in there on purpose. I'm not a complete idiot, even though I looked like one a minute ago. Someone pushed me."

"What?" Mac almost hissed the word.

"Who pushed you?" Jane cried. "How?"

"I don't know." I rubbed my forehead. "I saw someone come into this hallway so I followed her. Or him."

"Why?" Jane demanded.

"Because I didn't recognize them. I should know everyone working here. And they didn't stop when I called out to them."

"She has a point," Mac murmured.

"Anyway, I came down here and didn't see anyone." I touched the top of my head, knowing I couldn't carry on a conversation much longer. "I looked at the bricks, felt a slight draft. Hard to describe, but it was like a waft of air. And then I heard someone behind me take a quick breath. And the next thing I knew, someone pushed me really hard and I went flying over the wall."

"I'm taking you to the hospital," Mac said.

Wouldn't that be the perfect end to a perfect day? "No. Please. I swear, I just need to rest. And maybe soak in a tub of Epsom salts. I'm kind of achy all over."

Jane touched my hand. "I'm calling Buddy and you're going to urgent care."

Buddy was an old school friend of ours who insisted that we now call him Dr. Bud.

"I don't have a concussion."

"Then why are you rubbing your forehead?" Jane pressed.

I frowned. A trick question? "Okay, maybe I have a headache and I'm a little dizzy, probably from lying upside down in there."

"Blood went rushing to her head," Mac explained, "and now she's leveling off."

"Urgent care clinic," Jane said.

"I'll take her," Mac said, leaving me out of the conversation.

"But even if I have a concussion I can still work," I insisted. "Or supervise, anyway. I can, you know, sit down and point at stuff."

Jane rolled her eyes. "Hurry, Mac."

"Yup. And I'm calling the police on the way." He started for the doorway, still carrying me in his arms. "Come on, champ."

Mac didn't pursue the subject on the drive to the urgent care clinic, letting me doze

194

instead. But how could I fall asleep when I had to listen to every word he said on the phone to Eric? He had the phone on hands-free as he reported the incident and made it more than clear that someone at the Gables was dangerous. Or worse, homicidal.

The chief's responses were peppered with curse words, especially when Mac revealed that someone had pushed me. Eric was clearly angry, but not at me, thank goodness. With that knowledge, I was able to doze off for the rest of the drive.

We were at urgent care for three hours. They ran a bunch of tests and did a brain scan. Dr. Bud — formerly Buddy — asked me a ton of questions guaranteed to give me a headache, but I knew it was important to answer them honestly.

"Yes, I have a headache," I said. "No nausea. Eyesight is good. No flashing lights. I was a little blurry for the first few minutes, but I'm fine now. Mostly I just have the headache. May I have some ibuprofen?"

"We need to put you in the hospital overnight, Shannon."

"But I don't want to."

"Don't act like a baby," he said.

I frowned. "I bet you don't talk like that to your other patients."

"That's because they don't act like a baby."

I smiled. "That's funny."

He pursed his lips. "Maybe you really are doing better if you're able to recognize my superior sense of humor."

"I do. You're really funny. So will you let me go home and sleep?"

"That's the problem," he said gently. "Someone needs to wake you up every two hours to check your vital signs."

"I know." I lay back on the pillow and looked up at Mac. "Maybe you'll do that for me?"

He glanced at Dr. Bud for a long silent moment, then looked down at me. "Yeah, I'll do that for you."

Dr. Bud let out a big sigh and frowned at Mac. "I'll agree to this as long as you promise to check on her every two hours and that you'll call me at the slightest sign of a problem."

"I promise."

Fifteen minutes later, Mac and I were halfway down the hall leading to the exit. As we passed one of the treatment rooms, a woman walked out with her arm in a splint.

It took me a few seconds to realize who it was. "Prudence? Prudence Baxter?"

"Yes? Who are you?"

Was she serious? "Don't you remember me from Hennessey House and from the protest demonstration up at the Gables?"

She squinted. "Oh, I guess you do look familiar."

"Yeah, you elbowed me. Hard to forget that moment."

She started to push past me. "I have to go."

"Why were you protesting?"

She looked offended. "That's none of your business."

"It's funny, because you were protesting one day and then sucking up to Dr. Fairchild the next. That seems like contradictory behavior to me. What do you think?"

"I think you're unforgivably rude." She sniffed with outrage.

"How did you hurt your arm?"

Now she huffed out a breath. "You clearly won't stop haranguing me until I tell you, so the fact is, I strained my arm."

"By elbowing me?"

"Certainly not!"

"Did you push me into those bricks?"

She blinked rapidly. "I — I have no idea what you're talking about."

And with that lie, she scurried down the hall and out the door.

197

"She's a troublemaker," I muttered on the way home.

Mac nodded. "I'll talk to Eric about her."

I fell asleep after that, but when we got home, Eric's police vehicle was already parked in front of my house.

Despite my protests, Mac wouldn't let me walk, so it took a few minutes to carry me inside and get me situated on the couch. Robbie and Tiger insisted on snuggling up to me and I was happy to let them. Mac brought me some ibuprofen and a glass of water for my headache.

My hero.

Eric sat down in the chair closest to my end of the couch.

I tried to straighten up. "Is Chloe in town yet?"

"She arrived about an hour ago. She's putting some things away and then she'll come over for a visit later today."

"Okay, good. I'll have time to sleep for a while." But I felt my shoulders relax at the news that Chloe was in town. "Hey, do you want coffee or . . . anything?"

"No, thanks," he said, reaching out to pat my hand. "Just relax."

"I'm okay, really."

Mac said, "I'm going to make some coffee anyway, if you want to change your mind."

"In that case," Eric said, "I wouldn't mind a cup."

"Coming up."

Mac left the room to make coffee and Eric sat and watched me for a minute. Finally he said, "Tell me how you got hurt."

I struggled to sit up straight because I needed to clear my head. I might've been feeling a little weak, but I didn't want to wallow.

"Okay," I began, "I saw a woman I didn't recognize and followed her into the back passageway. By the time I got into the hall, I didn't see her. I figured she was hiding in one of those rooms back there." I told him everything else, starting from the mishap with the ladder the night before and the falling bricks. It was slow going because it really did hurt to talk with my sore cheek. Leave it to me to land on my head and hurt my face. And everywhere else on my body. Sheesh. "Oh, and I guess it could've been a short man, but the person moved more like a woman."

"Possible short man," he murmured, and wrote it all down in his little notepad. "And you didn't hear anything?"

199

"I swear I didn't, and I didn't see any-thing, either. It's annoying. Whoever pushed me was able to get right up close without making a sound." I started to frown, but winced instead. "Stupid headache. Anyway, who in the world would do that? Who would sneak up on me and try to hurt me?"

Mac walked back into the room. "Do you want to take some guesses?"

I thought about it. "I don't really have any enemies, except for, you know, the mean girls." I didn't like mentioning Whitney's name when Eric was around because he worked with Tommy and hey, he actually liked Whitney. Go figure.

But Whitney would never do something like this, I thought. She wouldn't want to get her hands dirty. Besides, she and I had a very open enmity between us. She would've looked me in the eye before she pushed me.

"What about those protesters?" Mac said.

"I don't know any of the protesters. Why would they be angry with me?"

"You tripped that one guy."

"Yeah, but I can't picture him following me around, trying to kill me because of that." I shook my head. "The protesters know there are cops patrolling the grounds now, so I can't believe one of them would

200

take a chance and sneak inside our building to try to hurt someone."

"Depends on how desperate they are," Mac said. "Or how crazy."

Eric sat forward. "You've got to figure these protesters are completely opposed to what you're doing up there at the Gables."

"I know." I gave a short nod. "They want to burn it down."

"And you're an important part of the team that wants to rebuild it." He sat back in his chair.

"But I'm not the only one," I argued. "There are seven different buildings being remodeled. Each of them has a different contractor working there. I'm only in charge of one piece of it."

"Still, you want to bring it up from the ashes," Mac said. "Make it beautiful."

I smiled at him. "That's nice."

He shrugged. "Hey, I'm a writer. A word-smith."

I had to laugh, but then slowly sobered as he walked back into the kitchen. To Eric, I said, "Do you agree that their aim is to jeopardize our rehab project?"

"It's possible," Eric said. "By putting your life in jeopardy, they're putting the entire project in jeopardy."

"But why me in particular? Why not one

of the heads of the other crews? It seems like they're particularly concerned with Jane's wing. Maybe it's the hotel they want to stop."

Mac walked in and handed a cup of coffee to Eric.

"Thanks," the chief said, and took a sip.

I stared at both of them. "I don't think they care one way or another about me. I'm guessing they only attacked me because they want to destroy the project. Because, look, yesterday the attack was aimed at Rachel. Today it was me. So I probably shouldn't take it personally. But of course I do. And I want to find that woman that disappeared down the back hall." I frowned at the two men. "It could've been Prudence."

"Who?" Eric said.

"Prudence Baxter." Just saying her name made me rub my forehead. "She was one of the protesters and she's also got some connection to Dr. Fairchild. She's staying at Jane's B and B."

"So you do know one of the protesters," Eric said.

"I don't actually know her," I said. "I just saw her checking in at Jane's place and then I recognized her when the protesters showed up. And then we just saw her at the hospital with her arm in a sling."

202

Eric just nodded, jotting it all down in his notepad.

Mac sat next to me. "I really need you to be careful."

"Agreed," Eric said.

I gave them a weak smile. "I promise I'll be careful, but I want answers. And I really want to get inside that antechamber. I'm dying to see what's behind that door."

"You're starting to scare me," Eric grumbled. "Wait. I take that back. You *always* scare me."

Mac patted my hand. "Bet you'd rather we didn't tell Jane what you just said."

I winced. "I would appreciate it. She can be brutal."

He nodded. "Wouldn't want to get on her bad side."

I slept for two hours before being rudely awakened by Mac, who asked me what day it was and how many fingers he was holding up. I dozed off immediately after that, but woke up when the doorbell rang. Before I could drag myself up from the couch, the door opened and my younger sister Chloe walked in.

"Don't get up," she insisted. "Mac said I could come over to say hi and see how you're doing."

"You are always welcome," I murmured, as she wrapped me in a big, gentle hug. "I'm doing better now that you're here." I held her at arm's length, then smoothed a thick strand of blond hair away from her face. "Look how beautiful you are. I love you so much and I kind of hate you, too."

Chloe grinned. She had decided at sixteen that she wanted to be a blonde and it still really worked for her. I had always been perfectly happy with my curly red hair, even when it refused to be tamed. Despite the differences, we were clearly sisters. She was dressed in almost the same outfit as mine, except that her chic work boots had never seen a mud puddle or a slab of wet concrete. Her jeans were faded in all the best places, and her thick henley sweater was a shade of red rarely seen on a construction site. "What do you call that color?"

She glanced down. "Amaryllis."

"Oh, perfect." I had to smile. "It's really pretty. You look so darn cute and I'm totally dragging right now."

She was frowning at me. "And yet you still look good. Even with your face all scraped up. It's annoying."

I laughed again. "God, it's great to see you."

Robbie was so excited, he was practically

bouncing.

"Robbie thinks so, too."

"Hello, Robbie!" Chloe said, and patted her chair. The dog leaped up and Chloe scratched and patted him. "Such a good boy. What a handsome fellow."

Robbie let out another bark of joy.

Tiger was her usual demure self, winding her way in, out, and around Chloe's ankles. The cat gave my sister a couple of head bops to get her attention and as soon as Robbie jumped down, Chloe lifted the cat into her arms and snuggled.

Watching her play with my pets was making me feel all emotional and I knew I was headed for a crying jag, a sure sign that I was still in pain. It had been a crazy weird day.

"I've missed you," I said, watching the antics.

She pulled back and looked at me with suspicion. "Are you going to cry?"

"No. Maybe. Oh God."

"Okay, we need to sit and talk. But first, do you have any wine?"

"Are we related? Of course I have wine." I checked my wristwatch. It was almost five o'clock and I still felt punchy.

I led the way into the kitchen, which gave me a chance to pull myself together. Opening the freezer, I grabbed an ice cube and ran it over my forehead, across my cheeks, and around my neck. The cold would help wake me up.

"Okay, you want red or white?" I asked.

"Or pink. Uncle Pete did this amazing rosé of Pinot Noir that's fruit forward on the nose with a dry finish. It's so luscious, you'll swoon."

"Wow, way to sell it." She grinned. "It sounds great, but right now I kind of feel like white. We'll save the rosé until we can drink it together. You go sit down. I'll pour."

"Probably a good idea." I grabbed a bottle of water and hoped that I'd feel up to having a glass of wine later. Then we returned to the living room where I settled back on the couch.

"I want to hear about this accident," Chloe said when she sat back down. "Eric wasn't willing to tell me too much."

"You should bug him about that. He needs to spill the beans to you about everything. It's part of being a couple."

She grinned. "He will so buy into that. Not. Anyway, he did mention there was an accident at your construction site and you ended up with a concussion."

"Yeah. I got banged up a little. And by the way, it wasn't an accident." I gave her the quickie version while I sipped some water.

"Your cheek is scratched," she said, and leaned in close to touch the area with her finger.

"It's a little tender, but I'll be fine."

"Of course you will." But she gave me another concerned look and pulled Robbie back onto her lap. "Okay, if you want to doze off, go ahead. But meanwhile, tell me everything that's been going on. Tell me about the Gables. It's been years since I was up there."

So I got comfortable. Chloe sipped her wine.

It took me a while to recap because so much had happened in barely a week. I covered the highlights: showing Mac the Gables for the first time; spying the guy in the orange cap; Mac deciding to invest in the project; the protesters showing up; Rachel the gorgeous developer; the bucket of blood; me almost falling off the ladder; the brick wall that was no longer there; the arrogant Dr. Fairchild; and then me getting shoved into the pit of despair.

"Not that it's all about me," I quipped, trying to downplay things.

Her frown was intense. "And you really think someone pushed you?"

"Oh, absolutely," I said matter-of-factly.

"Shoved me right over the wall and down into the pit of hell."

"And you have no idea who did it?"

"I have some ideas," I said, thinking of Prudence, "but there's no proof and I can't figure out what her motive would be." And that was so frustrating I couldn't even explain how much. I really wanted to get some answers. "I mean, I saw this person sneaking into the back hallway, but then they disappeared. I figured they were gone. Or hiding in one of the rooms. I didn't expect them to pop out and shove me. I never saw it coming. Which makes me a fool."

"No, it doesn't. But it does kind of suck, kiddo."

"Yeah. While I was sleeping just now, I dreamed that the person was hiding in one of the rooms and was actually lying in wait for me. But that's even crazier, isn't it? I mean, I don't know these people."

"No, it's not crazy. But it was just a dream, right?"

"Yeah." It was just a dream, but it made me realize that I had to go back and check all those doors along that hall. I made a mental note to look into it first thing tomorrow. I wouldn't go alone, of course, but if there was a sign that someone had been hiding back there, I wanted to find out.

Chloe studied me. "You're plotting something."

"No, I'm not."

"And now you're lying, and not doing a very good job of it. Don't you know I can read your mind?"

"Cannot."

She laughed. "I knew you would say that."

I just rolled my eyes.

"I'm right," she insisted. "You're up to something. So that settles it. I was going to go shopping in Mendocino tomorrow but I've decided to stay here and follow you around the Gables like a puppy."

"I'd love that. I can show you around. And Jane will be happy to see you. We'll have fun."

"That's the plan." She stared for a long moment. "Seriously, I'm a little worried about you."

"I know." I nodded, accepting the reality of my situation. "But tomorrow you'll be with me. And look, I've got Mac and Niall and Jane looking out for me now. And all my crew. Wade and Carla, Sean and the guys."

"Sounds like you've got plenty of backup."

"I do. And by the way, Jane is turning into quite the little general. She says she'll be watching me like a hawk."

"Good." Chloe took another sip of her wine. "You clearly need supervision."

"Thanks. Take her side."

"I'll take anyone's side who will promise to keep you safe."

My eyes misted and I sniffed. "I love you."

She scowled. "Stop it. There's no crying in construction."

I had to laugh. "How could I forget the golden rule? Okay, I promise it won't happen again."

"Good." She sat back and swirled the wine in her glass. "I'm really looking forward to seeing the Gables."

"It's beautiful. And it's going to be even better when we're finished." I folded my legs under me. "Did you drive over here in Eric's car?"

"No, he dropped me off. He'll pick me up around six."

"Do you want to stay for dinner?" I rubbed the side of my head. "Guess I'm still kind of out of it."

"I can see that." Her look of concern made me feel guilty.

"I'm really okay," I said breezily. "I took some ibuprofen earlier and it always makes me sleepy."

"So you're in pain?"

210

"Well, yeah. Battered by a fallen wall of bricks." Then I waved her worries away. "Just some achy muscles and this puny scratch on my cheek. I'll be fine tomorrow."

"Let's not forget the concussion. And by the way, that puny scratch is turning black and blue."

"How attractive." I sipped my water. "Okay, enough about me. How's the show business?"

"Well, first of all, I love being on hiatus. But the show is great, better than ever," she said with a grin. "*Makeover Madness* is the number one show on the network and everyone is totally psyched."

"That's fantastic. And how's Diego?"

She grinned. "He's as hunkalicious as ever, as you once described him."

I held up my water bottle in a toast. "I cannot lie, he's a gorgeous guy."

She smiled. "We're having a great time together. The show is so much more easy-going than before."

"I'm so glad."

Last year the *Makeover Madness* crew had come to Lighthouse Cove to do a series of shows on Victorian houses. While they were in town, Chloe's producer was killed and we'd had to track down the murderer practically on camera. Afterward there had been rumors that the show might be canceled, but Chloe and Diego had made it work better than ever.

"Sounds like everything turned out okay."

"Better for some of us than others," she said frankly. "Especially in regard to my life." She gave a satisfied little smile. "Thanks in great part to you."

I shrugged. "All I did was introduce you to the chief of police."

"That's all it took." She sighed. "Every time I see him, he gets better looking."

"He is super-hunkalicious," I said, and we both laughed.

"Speaking of which, how's Mac?"

"He's wonderful. You'll see him if you stick around."

"I'll stay for a while, but Eric has informed me that he's planned a special evening for the two of us. So . . . maybe we can all get together tomorrow?"

"Sure. And I want to plan a dinner with Dad and Belinda and Uncle Pete and Mac and Jane and Niall and some of the girls." Belinda was my father's girlfriend — it still sounded odd to say that phrase — and she was Uncle Pete's winery manager. The three of them were tight friends.

"Sounds like a party," Chloe said. "Let me know when and what time, and what we can bring."

"I will. I should call Dad and check his schedule."

"I talked to him earlier and he promised to be available anytime we want to get together."

"Okay." Hey, when Chloe came to town we all wanted to spend as much time as possible with her. "I'll let you know."

The doorbell rang. "That'll be Mac." He had a key to my house, but he liked to ring the doorbell before walking in, just to let me know he was here. I jumped up to meet him at the door, then staggered backward.

"Whoa." Chloe firmly eased me back on the couch. "What happened? What's wrong?"

"Nothing's wrong. Sorry. I just stood up too fast and got a little dizzy."

She gave me that suspicious look yet again. "You stay. I'll get the door."

I closed my eyes and willed myself to shape up. I had hit my head and scratched all sorts of body parts. I needed to take it easy. Especially if I was going to get dizzy every time I stood up. So no wine for me at all tonight, and that was just sad.

Mac and Chloe talked quietly at the door for a minute, and then he followed her into the living room. "How's my girl?"

I smiled. "I'm great."

"Would you like some wine or a beer, Mac?" Chloe asked.

"I'll have a beer, thanks," he said, but didn't take his eyes off me.

Chloe walked into the kitchen and Mac sat down on the coffee table in front of me. He leaned in close, held up two fingers. "How many fingers?"

I sighed. "Two."

"Okay, what's going on?"

"I stood up too fast and got dizzy for a second. But I'm really doing a lot better. My headache is gone. Please don't worry."

After another long stare, he nodded. "Okay."

"Here's your beer, Mac," Chloe said.

"Thanks." Mac stood up and took the bottle, then sat down next to me on the couch. Robbie jumped up to sit with Mac, who obviously gave the best scrunches and belly rubs.

Chloe sat back down in her chair and Tiger quickly wandered over and pounced up to cuddle with her. It was heartwarming to see my animals so happy to be with the people I loved.

"We're ordering a pizza," Mac said. "You and Eric want to hang out?"

"I would love to some other night, but he

214

told me he's got something special planned."

Mac grinned. "We'll expect details tomorrow."

Chloe wiggled her eyebrows. "Naturally."

I narrowed my eyes. "I just hope he isn't planning on re-creating your first date."

Chloe threw back her head and laughed. "Spend the night in a jail cell? I don't think so."

When they first met, Eric had locked Chloe in jail for her own protection. And he had slept all night in the cell right next to her. Was it any wonder that she fell in love with him?

The doorbell rang again and Chloe dashed to the door. Eric strolled in and we all chatted for a few minutes. Then the two of them took off.

Mac sat back down and wrapped his arm around me. "I have something special planned for tonight, too."

"Really?" I smiled. "What do you have in mind?"

"You might've heard me mention pizza."

"I did."

"Okay, I thought we'd order a sausage and mushroom pizza and antipasto salad to be delivered. We'll watch some quality TV and fall asleep on the couch."

I rested my head on his shoulder. "I can't think of a better way to spend the evening."

Long after the pizza and salad were gone, Mac turned on the local news before going to bed.

I had been dozing on and off, but as the show was about to go to commercial, the anchorman said, "Coming up, an interview with the doctor who used to run the Gables insane asylum. You won't want to miss it."

"Oh!" I said. "I saw that doctor this morning. They set up this whole press conference thing out in front of Jane's building."

"Let's tape it," Mac said, and programmed the TV to record the rest of the show.

But we ended up watching the entire segment. We couldn't look away. It was just as disturbing as the first time I heard her speak, and it reminded me that I wanted to read Palmer's daughter's interviews with the protesters. But that wouldn't be happening tonight.

"So what did you think of Dr. Fairchild?" I asked as we locked up the house and got ready for bed.

"She sort of reminds me of Nurse Ratched," he said.

"From *One Flew over the Cuckoo's Nest*?"

"It's apropos, right?" he said. "She had all

216

those people's lives in her hands and she came across just as arrogant and mean as the movie character."

"Yeah, I can see that," I said. "But can she really be that bad?"

He frowned. "I think so. It was her arrogance that nailed it for me. There's even a touch of narcissism in there. It was all about her. When she mentioned her patients, it was only to say how much they owed her."

"That was a bit much."

"Yup, I smell a narcissist. But maybe I'm being unfair. Maybe she's a peach."

"Right. A peach." His reaction was exactly the same as what I'd felt about the good doctor. "I'm sure she's a fine, upstanding citizen."

He grinned. "So was Nurse Ratched."

I gave him a light punch as we climbed the stairs. "I remember seeing that movie when I was a little girl."

"A little girl?"

"Yeah. I think I was about eight when I first saw it. Chloe watched it with me."

His eyebrows shot up. "If you were eight, then Chloe was seven. I don't want to sound stuffy, but you two were way too young to be watching a film like that."

"Oh, for sure." I shrugged. "But after my mom died, Dad wasn't sure what to do with us so he would line up a bunch of videos for us to watch when we got home from school. Some of them were a lot worse for little kids than that one."

"I'm sorry," he said quickly. "Your dad must've gone through a hard time."

"It was rough," I admitted. "That's around the same time he decided to start bringing us to his construction sites."

He smiled. "And the rest is history."

"Right. We both loved being there, and we learned a lot. All the guys on the crew watched out for us and taught us stuff. It was definitely better than turning us into latchkey kids."

"Absolutely."

We climbed into bed and Mac pulled me close to him. And within seconds I was sound asleep.

Even in sleep, though, my mind was working, going over everything that had happened. And sometime in the night, I dreamed I was flying over a mountain of bricks. Happily, I woke up before I crashed and burned.

Still, climbing out of bed, I couldn't shake the feeling of being hurtled onto that pile of bricks, and for a long moment I could feel every ache and pain in my body.

The only way I would stop reliving the

nightmare was if I could finally get the answers I needed. Why had they bricked up that section of the hospital? I needed to discover once and for all what secrets were hidden behind the mysterious door.

I only hoped it wasn't a body.

CHAPTER TEN

After being awakened every two hours during the night to make sure I was still conscious and breathing, the only breakfast preparation I could handle was making a pot of coffee.

"I'll take care of the eggs and bacon and muffins," Mac said.

"My hero," I murmured, and enjoyed the sight of Mac cooking while Tiger and Robbie waited patiently at his feet in hopes of catching some little morsel of food he might drop.

That didn't happen, but Mac made it up to them by filling their food and water bowls and then slipping them each a little treat.

Once everything was put away and the kitchen gleamed, Mac went home to write and I took off for the Gables. I was anxious to explore the back hall and I knew of a few people who would insist on joining in. I was perfectly happy to make it a group activity.

Chloe had promised to meet me and I had just parked my truck when Eric pulled up in his police-issue SUV. Chloe leaned over and gave Eric a kiss, then jumped down from the passenger seat.

He looked directly at me as he lowered his car window. "How do you feel?"

"I'm great." I gave him a thumbs-up. "No worries."

His eyes narrowed and he stared hard at me. Then after a few long seconds he nodded. "Okay. I've got a meeting in town, but I'll be back later. I want you to show me where you got pushed."

"Okay," I said. "Anytime."

Chloe ran around to the driver's window and gave him another big kiss. I couldn't hear their conversation but after a moment Eric threw his head back and laughed.

I couldn't help but smile. He had really mellowed since meeting my sister and I couldn't have been happier.

Chloe slipped her arm through mine and we walked along the side of Building Seven. "Are you really feeling okay?"

"Except for being awakened too many times last night, I'm really fine."

"Good." She gazed up at the building. "I can't wait to see the inside."

But as we turned the corner and walked

across the front lawn, she stopped and stared. "I don't think I've ever been so close to this place. Remember how we used to have to park outside that old stone wall and then give each other a boost up in order to see anything?"

"Did you notice the wall is gone?"

"Yeah, I noticed first thing when we drove up the hill."

"So what do you think?" I spread my arms wide. "It's pretty impressive, right?"

She gazed at the row of beautiful Victorian structures that went on and on across the ridge of the hill. "It's so big. It's fantastic." She whirled around. "And this view is incredible."

"Thank you! My crew gave me a hard time for wanting to admire that view."

"Well, they're wrong," Chloe assured me.

"Just one more reason why I love you. Now, let's go inside." We headed for the front door, but then I stopped her. "You should be prepared. It's pretty skanky in there."

"Remember who you're talking to. I grew up on the same construction sites you did."

"Yeah, but now you're all Hollywood and this is really nasty."

She grinned. "But not for long, right?"

I gave a firm nod. "Right."

222

"And besides," she said with a casual shrug. "We've been in plenty of funky homes before, so no big deal."

I held up both hands in mock surrender. "You be the judge."

An hour later, after Chloe had greeted and chatted with all of my crew guys and checked out most of the first floor, we walked up the stairs to the second floor.

"Okay," she said, wrinkling her nose. "It's definitely skanky up here."

"I did warn you," I said. "But give it a chance. We're only just getting started on this level. The floors haven't even been swept yet."

"But that stairway is glorious." She turned to look in every direction. "The whole place is going to be stunning. I would love to bring the show back here next year to film when it's all finished. In fact" — she pulled out her cell phone — "I'd better take a few 'before' photos to do a compare and contrast."

"I would love it if you brought the show here. Your fans would love it, too."

"Oh, for sure. A place like this would be a new level of awesomeness for *Makeover Madness*." She pressed her hand over her mouth. "Sorry. Was that tacky?"

I realized she was referring to the *Madness* part of the show title. "Don't worry about it. That's the name of your show."

"It just feels a little insensitive, given where we are and what this place used to be."

"I know what you mean. I've talked to my guys about it because we'll all probably run into some visitors who used to be patients here. So yeah, we need to be sensitive to the people around us."

In the spacious hallway we passed the two utility tables I had asked to have set up on this floor. On one of the tables, the ubiquitous gallon-sized bottles of bleach sat alongside one large bottle of vinegar and ten large spray bottles for spot cleaning.

"Glad to see you're ready to attack mold and mildew whenever you find it."

I flexed my arm muscles. "We are the mold warriors."

Even though the ceiling lights were on, there were light trees in place to illuminate the area even more. At the far end was a large picture window but it was still covered in the usual blue film so there wasn't a lot of light coming through.

I shook my head. "We're really going to have to open some windows all throughout this place. Not just to enjoy the view but for basic breathing purposes. I seem to remember reading that Dr. Jones believed in allowing fresh air to filter through the wards."

"It would sure help blow the stink out," Chloe said.

"That's so well put," I said, grinning. "At first I thought that having a breeze come through would be detrimental because, you know, it would blow all the paint flakes and scrapings around. But we really need some fresh air in here."

"You do. Either way, you'll need to wear masks and goggles. But the happy trade-off is clean air."

"Yeah." I sighed, knowing that some of my guys would rather suck in the toxic particles than wear those restrictive masks. I would have to talk to Wade and Carla about it.

Several of my guys were already at work up here, their ladders fully extended as they scraped paint off the tops of the walls and the ceiling. Sure enough, large flakes of paint and bits of plaster drifted in the air and would eventually settle on the floor.

"We should be wearing masks right now," I realized. "These particles can be awful if you get them in your nose or mouth."

"We don't have to stay long," Chloe said. "I just wanted to see what was going on up here." Glancing around, she absently picked up one of the empty spray bottles and twirled it around her fingers. "I know you have a long way to go, but it's obvious to me that by this time next year, Jane will have a fabulous, elegant, and very unusual five-star hotel to show off to the world."

"It's going to be amazing."

She stared up at the ceilings. "All this space is fantastic, isn't it?"

I smiled. "It really is." I refrained from breaking into my research riff on the theory of tall ceilings as therapy.

She used her phone to snap a few more photos, then slipped it into her pocket. "Eric should be here any minute, so let's go down and meet him. Then we can check out your pit of bricks, or whatever you call it."

"Pit of despair. Brick hellhole. Pit of hell. Take your pick."

"Sounds very colorful," she said with a laugh as we headed downstairs.

When we reached the first floor we saw Jane walking our way. "There you are," she said, and ran to give Chloe a hug. "How are you?"

"Couldn't be better," Chloe said. "I absolutely love this place. Or I will, once you're farther along."

"Thanks, Chloe." Jane looked at me.

"How are you feeling?"

"Much better, thanks."

"I'm glad." But then her sweet expression morphed into anger. "Did you watch the news last night?"

"The segment about the Gables? Yeah."

Jane huffed out a breath. "I recognized that doctor who worked here. She was my mother's doctor."

My mouth fell open. "You're kidding."

"No." She pounded her fist against her palm. "You know, I always suspected that she was cruel to my mom. And after seeing her on the news last night, I totally believe it. I've never met a colder human being."

"Jane, are you sure?" I touched her arm. "Did you ever witness her doing anything specific?"

"Well, yeah." But she screwed up her lips in frustration. "Okay, for one thing, she made it clear that she didn't like the patients' families to visit."

Chloe frowned. "That doesn't make sense."

"No, it doesn't," I said. "I should think she'd be supportive of family visits."

"But she wasn't." Jane's eyes sparked with fury. "I remember this one time we were sitting out on the lawn and I was braiding my mom's hair. That witch came over and told my mother — right in front of me! — that having me visit her was disruptive to my mother's well-being."

"That's horrible," Chloe said.

"And you know, she was speaking real softly so that nobody else could hear. But Uncle Jesse was right behind her and he laid into her."

"Good," Chloe said. "What happened?"

"The woman gave him a look that could've peeled skin. She finally turned and stomped off."

I wanted to cheer. "If Jesse were still with us, I would give him a big hug. He was right and I'm glad he stood up to her."

"For someone like her, in a position of authority, to say that?" Chloe shook her head. "Your mother must've been really upset."

"She was, and I think that's why I remember it so vividly," Jane said. "Because right before Uncle Jesse and I left that day, Mom started crying. Maybe it didn't have anything to do with the doctor's warning. Maybe she just wanted to come home. But seeing her cry like that? It really shook me up. I cried, too, all the way home." She winced. "Poor Uncle Jesse had to deal with two sobbing females that day."

I gave her arm a gentle squeeze. "I'm so

sorry." There didn't seem to be much I could say since I'd had the same impression of Dr. Fairchild. Still, I wanted to say something that might help. "Maybe the doctor was overwhelmed by having so many really sick people to deal with."

Jane glowered. "That's no excuse."

"You're absolutely right," I said, holding up my hands. What was the point of being a Pollyanna with my friends when the truth was right there for all of us to see? "She's obviously just as smug as she always was."

"*Smug* is such a good word," Jane fumed. "How dare she tell a fragile mother that her daughter shouldn't visit her? It was just so painful."

"It's downright malicious," Chloe said. "There's no excuse for it."

Chloe said, "Is there anything we can do for you, Jane?"

"No." She rubbed her arms to get rid of the chill she must've felt. "Until I saw her on TV, I was hoping she was dead."

"She's very much alive," I murmured. "And still arrogant."

Jane bared her teeth angrily. "I hope she never shows her face around here."

I frowned. "But she was right here yesterday, talking to reporters."

"Here?" She gaped at me. "I saw the

interview but I didn't realize where it was. She was here?"

"Yeah, out in front of our building." It was my turn to frown. "You didn't see her."

"No." She scowled. "And that's probably a good thing. I might've shoved her right off the roof."

"Wow," Chloe whispered. "I've never seen Jane so riled up before."

Jane had just hurried off toward the foyer to meet one of her vendors, and the two of us stood there frowning at her back.

"I haven't, either," I admitted. "But I don't blame her for being upset. That was such an awful time for her."

We walked more slowly in the same direction Jane had gone. Eric would be meeting us outside the front door.

Chloe was still worried. "Do you think that doctor will come around here again? She sounds like a tyrant."

"I was here for her speech yesterday and she was clearly on a power trip." I grimaced. "Actually, I couldn't figure out why she was here to 'answer questions.' Her day is done. This isn't a hospital anymore. I wonder if she thought she'd be able to recapture that feeling of power by coming around here."

"So you saw her in person and then you

watched her on the news last night?"

I shrugged. "Mac wanted to see the interview and I wanted to see it again. Afterward, he said she reminded him of Nurse Ratched. Do you remember that character?"

"Of course. I had nightmares after we watched that movie. She was scary."

I wrapped my arm around her shoulder. "You know we were too young to be watching it."

"No kidding. Oh, there's Eric." Her voice rose as the hunky police chief walked toward us. She ran to meet him and he caught her and kissed her soundly.

I stood by the doorway grinning. But then I saw Mac turn the corner and walk into view. And I went running.

He wrapped me in his arms and gave me a warm kiss.

"Best thing in the world," he murmured, hugging me closely. "How are you feeling?"

"My muscles are a little achy, but my head is clear. No headache, no dizziness."

"Good." He kissed me again.

"I didn't know you'd be coming here today."

"I was talking to Eric and he mentioned that he was headed over here, so I thought, what a good idea."

"I'm so glad." I glanced at my sister and

Eric, and I realized how lucky we all were to be so happy. And despite that, I still needed to ask Mac my question about the future. This wasn't the time, but soon. "Hey, did you finish your chapter?"

"Uh, not yet. Am I in trouble?"

"Not with me," I said. "But if your editor finds out . . ."

"Please don't tell her," he begged. "I promise I'll make it up to her."

"You'd better. She's pretty tough." His editor was a pussycat.

He grabbed my hand. "Let's do this."

Eric came up beside us and said, "You lead the way, Shannon."

"Okay."

We traipsed down the hallway and through the passageway under the staircase. When we reached the back hall, I saw Niall standing near the brick wall with two of his guys. Everywhere along the wall were stacks of bricks four and five rows deep.

"Wow, you got a lot done," I said, as we approached.

"I knew you wanted to get to that door, so we're clearing the way. Have a bit more to go."

I patted his massive shoulder. "I really appreciate it." And nodded at the two helpers. "Thanks a lot, guys."

232

"It was a good morning's workout," one of them said with a grin.

"Aye," Niall said. "No need for a gym membership, working for me."

Everyone chuckled, and then the two helpers went back to work, pulling bricks from the antechamber and piling them into stacks. It was slow going.

At that moment I realized that Chloe had never met Niall. "Chloe, this is Niall, my fantastic stonemason."

"Hi, Niall," she said. "You had just started working for my sister when I was in town doing my TV show."

"Yes, I was told we just missed each other." He shook her hand. "Lovely to meet you, Chloe."

"He's also engaged to Jane," I added.

"That's wonderful," Chloe said with a bright smile, then gave me a look that said, *I'll need the full story.*

And I gave her a look that said, *Later.*

I switched my gaze to Eric. "While they clear away more of the brick, we can look inside these rooms for any signs of life." I indicated the eight doors on the other side of the hallway.

Eric nodded. "So you think your attacker might've been hiding in one of them."

I didn't like the idea, but had to keep it

233

real. "It's possible. And I don't know how they could've sneaked up on me otherwise."

"Then let's check 'em out," Mac said.

He and Eric headed for the first door down the hall on the left and Chloe went with them.

I started to follow, then stopped and pulled out my cell phone. "I'm going to give Jane a quick call to let her know we're doing this. Otherwise, she might smother me in my bed."

Mac turned back, looking amused. "Really?"

I frowned. "She's not having a good day."

We were about to start on the first door when Jane jogged down the hall. "I'm here."

Niall looked up from his work. "And what a lovely treat it is to see you."

I watched her melt on the spot, then walk over and wrap her arms around him.

"I'm a sweaty mess, love," he murmured.

She shook her head. "I don't care." After a long moment, she stepped back. Glancing around, she met my gaze. "I'm fine."

I didn't need an explanation, just nodded. "Okay."

I knew she wasn't really fine, but she was doing all right for now. And we would talk about it again. Especially if the dreaded Dr. Fairchild showed up anywhere on the Gables property.

Niall's cell phone buzzed and he answered, spoke quietly for a moment, then ended the call. "I've got to go out to another site, but I'll be back." He gave Jane a smacking kiss and jogged off.

"Let's do this," Mac said, nodding toward the first door.

Each of the first four rooms was big enough to hold four patients — or four nurses, or staff, or whoever had been assigned to this area back in the day. But there hadn't been anyone inside them for decades. They were musty and dusty and the cobwebs had cobwebs hanging off them.

I refused to believe that they might've housed patients in these rooms because they were interior rooms with no windows. According to Dr. Jones's philosophy, that was a no-no. I would insist on installing a really powerful air conditioning and air filter system if Jane planned to use these rooms at all, but I knew they wouldn't become guest rooms. Maybe meeting rooms. Jane would agree.

"I'm sorry it's so filthy in these rooms," Jane said, holding her hand over her mouth. "I'm afraid to breathe too deeply."

"It's not your fault, Jane." I gave a quick glance around the room. "There's nothing in here. Let's take a quick break in the hall and breathe in some cleaner air before we check out the next one."

"Good idea," Chloe said.

"You all can take a break," Eric said. "I'll keep going."

Mac nodded. "I'm good to go, too."

"We'll just be a minute," I said.

Jane leaned against the wall.

"You okay?"

"Yeah." She smiled weakly. "My sinuses are about to rebel. There's no way these rooms can be turned into guest rooms. I'll use them for supplies or something."

"Regardless, we should all be wearing masks at all times," I said. "It's my fault. I didn't think to bring some with me."

"Not your fault," she said, repeating my words as she patted my back. "Let's just get the rest of the rooms done and then check out your hidden doorway."

"Good plan. But if you feel like waiting out here, we'll only be another couple of minutes. There's nothing in these rooms."

"But I still want to see them and figure out what to do with them eventually." She pushed off the wall and followed me to the next room. Mac and Eric were already inside exploring.

I walked in, saw their expressions, and

knew. "You found something."

"Don't touch anything," Eric warned.

"Over there." Mac pointed to the far corner.

I moved closer to get a better look, and frowned. "It looks like a yoga mat. A little thicker, maybe."

"They're doing yoga in here?" Jane said.

Chloe chuckled. "I doubt it, but I love that image."

"Probably used the mat to sleep on," Mac explained.

"You think so?" Jane said.

"Yeah." Eric nudged something with his foot. From here it looked like a crumpled-up wrapper. "Someone ate dinner in here."

"Is that recent?" I asked.

"Yes." He used his pen to lift it close enough to smell it. "You can still get a whiff of barbecue sauce."

"Eww," Jane muttered.

I cringed in agreement. "Too bad you can't go around sniffing everyone's breath."

Mac chuckled. "Yeah, do a breathalyzer test for barbecue sauce."

"They've probably brushed their teeth by now," Chloe said with a grin.

Along one wall was a skinny door that probably opened to a closet. "Did you look inside there?"

"Don't touch it," Eric warned. "Need Leo to dust for fingerprints."

I met Mac's gaze and knew he wanted to whip that door open and look inside as much as I did. I figured Eric wanted to do it even more, especially if it held any clues to the identity of whoever was haunting our project.

"Somebody was living in here," I said, glancing around.

Eric frowned. "For a few days at least."

I walked over to the door leading out to the hallway. "This was the perfect room to hide in because, look, it's right across from the brick wall." I walked out and straight over to the short wall. I looked around but didn't see Niall.

"The former brick wall," Jane corrected.

"Yeah." I turned back to Eric. "All they had to do was walk a few feet and shove me right over it."

Eric already had his phone out and was calling the police dispatcher. "Hi, Ginny. Send Garcia and Payton up to the Gables. Tell them to meet inside the main hall of Building Seven." He listened for a few seconds. "Good. Thanks. Oh, and get Leo up here, will you?" he added. "We've got ourselves a suspicious situation."

He finished the call and glanced at the

rest of us. "I'll be closing off this hallway to give Leo room to work."

I pressed my hands together. "Would you mind if we just take a quick little peek at the hidden doorway before you kick us out of here?"

"Please, Eric," Jane said. "I think we'll all go insane if we don't find out what's behind that door."

At the word *insane*, Chloe gave me a quick look. I raised my shoulders in a shrug. What could I say? Words like that — *insane, loony, crazy* — were ingrained in our language and they were usually harmless, unless they were being used to hurt or insult someone. I would have to keep that in mind and mention it again to Wade and Carla. I wouldn't want any of our people to accidentally hurt the feelings of someone who had once spent time here.

With Chloe giving Eric another pleading look, he relented. "Make it quick."

"All right!" I glanced around, then leaned and peered over the short wall. Seeing complete darkness down there gave me a chill, but I shook it off. I realized that the light tree had been turned off and moved farther down the hall. I pulled my cell phone out and aimed the flashlight into the antechamber. "It's still full of bricks," I announced, my disappointment obvious.

"Niall said he'd be back," Jane said, "but I'm going to call him to find out what the situation is."

She made the call, talked for a minute, then hung up. "He and his boys were called to an emergency," she explained. "A retaining wall fell over up on Coral Ridge Road. It trapped a carful of kids and their mother."

"That's terrible." My feeling of disappointment over the bricks vanished. I would never want to interfere with a rescue mission. "Is anyone injured?"

"They're fine," Jane said. "Just can't get out of the car."

"Okay, that's better than being injured," I said.

"And, Shannon, he said to let you know that he'll make sure the bricks are cleared up first thing in the morning."

"Wonderful," I said.

"He might need to borrow one of your men to get it done."

"He can have two of them."

"Okay, that's settled," Jane said.

Eric made a sweeping gesture. "Then let's get you all out of here."

"Excuse me! Excuse me!"

We all turned at the sound of a woman shouting at us. She stood at the open door

240

to the passageway.

"Oh my God, it's her," I whispered.

"Nurse Ratched in the flesh," Mac murmured.

"What are you people doing in here?" she demanded, her arms folded tightly across her chest.

"No," Jane said, pointing at her. "The question is, what are *you* doing here?"

"I . . . I'm allowed to be here. This is my hospital." She stared at the walls and the ceiling. "This is a very important part of my history."

"I don't give a hoot about your history," Jane said, walking boldly toward the woman who had once made her mother cry. "This is *my* place now and you're trespassing." She glanced over her shoulder. "And that man right there is the chief of police, so you're going to want to move your butt on out of here or I'll have you arrested."

"H-how dare you!" Fairchild sputtered.

"Oh, I dare," Jane said with deadly intent, both hands fisted on her hips. "So unless you want to spend a few nights in the slammer, beat it."

The doctor's cheeks were red with rage, but Jane didn't back down. "Go. Now."

Fairchild huffed once, then spun around and ran down the passageway and out to the main hall.

"I'll make sure she leaves," Mac said, and jogged after her to take care of it.

I spent the next few hours scraping walls in Jane's new reception office, just to be able to say I'd gotten some actual work done.

Chloe had taken off after deciding it would cheer me up if she organized a party that evening, the one I had meant to throw for her. She phoned my father to make sure he and Uncle Pete were available — they were, and so was Belinda — and then she called all of my girlfriends and invited them over.

By the time I got home, she had everything ready.

"This is so nice of you," I said.

She grinned. "Since the party's at your place and everyone has offered to bring food and drinks, I barely had to lift a finger."

I smiled at her. "Well then, you can help me clean the house."

"Your house is always clean," she said with a laugh. But she jumped into action and we got everything done in record time.

By seven o'clock the house was filled with people. The dining room table was overflowing with delicious-smelling hot casseroles, appealing cold salads, healthy crudité platters, three serving plates filled with meats and cheeses, and two baskets of breads and rolls. Condiments, utensils, and paper plates were set up on one end.

The kitchen island was the headquarters for all the drinks. A few dozen bottles of wine were set out, along with glasses and plastic cups. A large galvanized steel tub filled with ice sat on the floor below and held a few dozen bottles of fizzy water, soft drinks, and beer.

Desserts lined the kitchen counter, including three dozen cupcakes from Marigold, a small mountain of cookies from Lizzie, and a beautiful lemon cheesecake that Emily brought from her tea shop. The freezer was filled with every flavor of ice cream imaginable.

Most of the wine was courtesy of Dad and Uncle Pete, who brought more than a case from Pete's vineyard. Belinda, the winery manager and my father's girlfriend, brought me a very special bottle of their newest Pinot Noir. She knew that was my favorite. "Tuck that away somewhere and drink it on a special occasion."

I gave her a hug. "Thank you."

"You're welcome. Let me know what you think of it."

"I sure will. But I already know it'll be

fantastic."

"I don't want to sway you, but yeah, it's pretty darn awesome."

If I had to call someone my "best" friend, it would be Jane. But really I had four other besties besides her, and they were all here tonight. I loved having all of us together. For one thing, they all loved Chloe and always included her in their plans whenever she was in town.

My friend Lizzie spent an hour monopolizing Chloe's time, talking about Chloe's design book she had written. "It's gone into its sixth printing," Lizzie gushed. "That's almost unheard of these days. I'm just so proud of you. I hand sell it to everyone who comes into the shop."

"I love you the best, Lizzie," Chloe whispered, beaming with pleasure as she gave her a quick hug. "Don't tell the others."

"I won't. They get so jealous."

Lizzie owned Paper Moon, the book and paper store on the town square, with her adorable husband Hal. They were the only ones in our gang who had children, and those kids were growing up way too fast.

"Marisa's starting high school," Lizzie moaned when Chloe asked about them. "Thankfully, Taz is still my darling son, but he won't be for long. I'm waiting for him to

244

grow fangs."

Lizzie sighed, then grabbed my arm. "Hey, speaking of fangs, I saw Dr. Fairchild on the news the other night."

"Oh, yeah?" I said casually, but then caught the "fang" comment and homed in. "Have you met her?"

"Oh, have I ever."

Lizzie and I had both grown up in Lighthouse Cove, so between the two of us — or three of us, if I included Jane — we knew everyone who lived within twenty miles of town. "Spill."

"She came into the store."

I blinked. "Today?"

"No. It was the day before she showed up on TV. She came in to ask us to order a bunch of copies of her book."

"She wrote a book?"

"Yes. A memoir. And she insisted that everyone in town was going to want to buy a copy."

"Really?"

Mac came up from behind and wrapped his arm around my waist. "Hey, Lizzie. What's going on?"

I turned and looked at him. "Dr. Fairchild came into Lizzie's bookstore. She wrote a book."

"Did she?" he said. "Good for her."

"Lizzie was just telling me about it." I did a quick recap for him.

Lizzie took a sip of white wine. "She told me that if I knew what was good for our business, we would stock up now and get ready to cash in big-time. She said the news about the Gables project would turn her book into a blockbuster bestseller, and if we weren't willing to take advantage of her generous offer, there were plenty of other bookstores that would."

I frowned. "This is starting to sound a little pushy."

"Oh, yeah." She grabbed a cashew and popped it into her mouth. "It was more than pushy. It was borderline threatening. Like, buy my book or the puppy gets it."

Mac laughed. "What did you tell her?"

"I asked her if she would be paying cash or credit for the books."

"Ooh, ouch," Mac said, grinning.

I swirled my wine. "I take it she didn't like that."

"Uh, no. She fully expected us to buy at least fifty copies of her book and then hand-sell it to our customers. And she was furious that we weren't more excited about it."

"Did you see the book?" Mac asked.

"Sure did." She took another sip of wine. "You know me, Shannon. I'm a voracious

246

reader. I read practically everything that comes into the store. So of course I asked to see a copy of her book. And she handed me a bunch of loose pages stapled to a piece of cardboard. She had printed the title on the cardboard. That's when I realized that she also wanted me to *publish* her book."

"That's awfully naïve," Mac admitted. "She came across as sharp and savvy during that interview. I'm surprised."

"Naïve, yet entitled. A scary combination." I looked back at Lizzie. "So what did you do?"

"She was so angry when I turned her down that I had to call for Hal to come out to the front counter." Lizzie shook her head. "She finally stormed out of the shop. And then we saw her that night on TV." She twirled her finger next to her ear in the universal sign language for "whackadoodle."

I nodded slowly, then glanced up at Mac. "It sounds like she came to town looking to score big off the Gables renovation."

"She's delusional," he said.

I grabbed Lizzie's arm. "Do me a favor and don't mention this to Jane."

"Why not?"

I told her about the connection between the good doctor and Jane's mother.

"Oh, hell, I wish I'd known that." She

scowled. "I would've kicked her out of the store as soon as she walked in."

"Do you still have the book?" I asked.

Lizzie's smile was sly. "Of course. I flipped through it after she left." She grabbed my arm. "Shannon, it's filled with scribbles about experiments and trials she ran, and research stuff. But it doesn't make a lot of sense. First of all, it's just not interesting, and that's the kiss of death, right there. But also, it's got a kind of Unabomber vibe. Like she hid out in a yurt in the forest scrawling this stuff." She shook her head. "Takes all kinds, I guess."

I had to laugh. "I can just see her in a yurt."

"I know, right?" Lizzie rolled her eyes.

A few minutes later, Niall walked into the party with Jane.

"I'm so glad you guys could make it," I said to Jane, as Niall poured her a glass of wine and helped himself to a beer.

"Sorry we're late but Niall had to finish up some work," she explained.

"Aye, Shannon," he said as he popped open the beer bottle. "I was able to get back to the Gables this afternoon and my men and I cleared the rest of the bricks away. You'll be able to get to the antechamber door whenever you're ready to do it."

"For real?" I grabbed his arm and gave him a side hug. "Oh, thank you, Niall. I really appreciate you doing that."

" 'Tis not a problem. I know you're anxious."

"I guess I am." Anxious? How about desperate? Or maybe obsessed? I wasn't sure why, but I was dying to see what was so important about that door that someone had gone to the trouble of building a brick wall to hide its secrets. And why they had tried to hurt me to keep me from finding out.

And I thought again of Dr. Fairchild walking into the back hall and demanding to know what we were doing there. As though we were invading her territory. What nerve!

But nobody needed to hear any more of my annoyance tonight. Instead I smiled and asked, "How did your rescue effort go?"

"It went off well." Niall took a quick drink of his beer. "We cleared away most of the rocks and mud in almost no time at all. And everyone inside the minivan was able to get out without much fuss."

"Sounds like a happy ending."

"Ah well, the car will need some body work and a couple of runs through the car wash. And the property owners will have to build a new retaining wall. But otherwise, a happy ending indeed."

"I'm glad." I raised my glass in a toast. "Thanks to you, I'll be checking out that antechamber first thing tomorrow."

"I'll be there to meet you," Niall said. "And Jane has an interest in coming along as well."

"I know she does. And Mac will want to be there, too." I glanced around the room. Eric and Chloe would be there as well, I thought, since they'd been there earlier today. And I figured it might be smart to tell Wade and Carla to meet us there, too. The three of us would have to take notes and talk to Jane about her plans for that space — once we could actually see it.

With all those people showing up in the back hallway tomorrow, it was starting to sound like another party. I wouldn't be bringing champagne — yet. But there would be a celebration of sorts, because we'd be discovering a whole new section of Jane's hotel. It would be exciting to finally see what was behind that darn door. I just hoped it would be worth all the pain and trouble we'd gone through to get there. And not just a brand-new variety of pain and trouble.

CHAPTER ELEVEN

The first thing I saw when I drove up to the Gables the next morning was the large group of protesters carrying signs and marching in a wide circle out on the lawn. *Again?* I thought. This couldn't be good.

They were gathered within a few yards of the driveway that led around to the back parking lot. It was a little too close for comfort as I drove past. I could see the signs clearly and they were sending the same basic message as the ones from the other day: BURN IT DOWN! THE GABLES MUST DIE!

The difference in today's march was that their leader was quietly calling out the damning phrases while the rest of the group was repeating them — not so quietly, but not as shrill or as frenzied as they had been the other day. At least, not yet.

I drove slowly, trying to pick out any familiar faces from Monday's violent protest. I counted at least thirty protesters, which was more than I'd seen on Monday.

I didn't see Prudence, but I did spot Orange Cap, or rather, Ricky Patterson. It was almost a relief to see him. Like seeing an old friend — or frenemy, more precisely.

Maybe the group had considered that first day such a success that they had been able to encourage others to show up today. Marching and demonstrating this close to the driveway was a problem, though. I wondered if they were trying to discourage the arriving workers from staying and working on the Gables project.

If that was their goal, it wasn't working, because there were a lot more cars parked back here today than I'd seen before. And along with all of the workers' trucks and vans, I noticed two police vehicles.

"Ah," I murmured. So that was the reason they were marching so politely this morning.

I locked my truck and set the alarm before rounding the building and walking to the steps that led up to Jane's entryway. From here at the opposite end of the Gables, I could see the group marching but could barely hear their shouts and cries.

Even from this far away I could pick out the bright orange baseball cap on Ricky

Patterson's head. I didn't see Carrot Head, aka Judson Killian, anywhere. I wondered if the bucket-of-blood guy would show up later. And if he did, I really didn't want to see him.

Just as I was about to turn away and walk inside, I noticed Rachel Powers standing on the steps in front of the central building, also known as Building One. She was watching the protesters, too, and didn't notice me.

All of a sudden I saw her lift her arm and wave it once, then continue gazing in the direction of the protesters.

I scanned the area to see who she might be waving at. Because let's face it, I'm nosy.

But all I saw were the protesters, who were all waving their signs and fists enthusiastically, so it was hard to say if any one person was waving back at Rachel. Or maybe they were taunting her. Maybe Rachel had been waving at a driver in one of the cars that was arriving for the day. Or, what the heck, maybe she was waving at a family of raccoons up in the hills.

I rolled my eyes at my ridiculous imagination. The protesters were waving their signs. Rachel had raised her arm. The two actions had nothing to do with each other. I was creating conspiracy theories out of nothing.

It was crazy and pointless to try to connect the developer of this project with the protesters who wanted to tear it down just because a few people were waving their arms.

I shook my head. "Just walk away, girl." And that was what I did, pulling the door open and stepping inside. I strolled down the hall saying good morning to everyone as I headed for the back hallway. As soon as I got through the passage under the stairs I saw Mac and Jane standing near the antechamber.

"Hi, Jane," I said, and then gave Mac a quick kiss. "Hi, you."

He gave me a kiss back. "Hi, you, too."

And that was when my phone rang. "Oh, it's Chloe," I said, and answered the call. "Hi. Are you on your way?"

"Not quite yet," Chloe said. "Eric had something important come up so he asked me to call and give you a message."

"What's up?"

Chloe took a deep breath. "He said, and I quote, tell your sister not to take one damn step over that wall until I get there."

"You're kidding," I said, insulted, but not surprised.

"Nope. Not kidding. Apparently he spoke to Leo late last night. They got some results on the fingerprints they found in that room off the back hallway."

"Hold on. I'm putting you on speaker so Jane and Mac can hear." I did a quick recap for them and put the phone on speaker. "Go ahead, Chloe. Whose prints are they?"

She gave me a dry laugh. "Are you serious? You really think he told me anything about that?"

"But he loves you," I said lamely.

"Yes, he does, and he knows me well. Knows that I would run right over and tell you everything at the first opportunity."

"While that may be true — and I love you for it — it's so not fair."

"Yeah, I know," she said. "I'll beat him up later. Anyway, he'll swing by and pick me up in about a half hour and we'll be up there right after that."

"Okay. Thanks for calling."

We finished the call and I looked at Jane. "You got the gist of that, right? Eric has forbidden us to check out the hidden door."

"That's downright authoritarian of him," she said, only half-kidding.

Mac hid a smile. "Well, he is the authority around these parts."

"But it's *my* hotel."

I sighed and patted her back. "But it's his jail cell."

Mac just laughed and Jane managed a reluctant smile.

"But look," I said. "We can get some work done in the meantime."

"What do you have in mind?" Jane asked.

"I was thinking we could check out the wall outside your future registration office and decide how much we want to take down."

"Oh. That's a wonderful idea."

"That's something we could start work on next week." I gazed at Mac. "Do you want to join us?"

"Construction talk," Mac said. "Always a good time."

I grinned. He really was a good sport. "If you get bored you can always go wandering around."

He pressed his forehead to mine. "It's not as much fun without you."

"Aww," Jane said.

Did I look as happy as I felt? I leaned in and kissed him. "Love you," I whispered.

"Love you more."

"That's impossible," I said, and made silly smooching noises.

"All right, all right," Jane said, rolling her eyes as she walked away, leaving Mac and me laughing.

When we reached the foyer, I walked into

256

the front room and said to Mac, "This is where Jane's guests will check in. She wants a counter here" — I pointed — "with visitors' chairs on this side and three or four desks on that side for the front office crew. It'll be pretty and functional."

"It's a big room," Mac said. "That window is going to give you a great view."

"As soon as we can get rid of that blue paper," Jane said.

"I've discussed the subject of blue paper with my people," I said. "And we've decided to start removing it as we go along. We thought about keeping the paper to protect the glass, but basically, we need the light. And when we start painting, we'll have to hang tarps. And if we break anything, we'll replace it."

"Yay! I just can't wait to see the view when it's all done." She turned to Mac. "It's going to be wonderful."

I pulled out my little pink tape measure — instead of my big honking twenty-five-foot classic I had hooked to my tool belt — and handed it to Jane. "I thought we could take away about six feet of the wall and that would give you a nice big entryway for you and your guests."

She held it steady at the doorway while I pulled the tape out to six feet.

"What do you think? Do you want to take more?"

Jane looked at the tape and narrowed her eyes, trying to imagine that much of the wall gone. Then she nodded. "I think that's perfect. But isn't this a load-bearing wall?"

"Oh, definitely," I said. "But we're not taking away enough of the wall to make a difference. And on the off chance that we need to bolster it, we will."

Mac stared at the wall, frowning. "I have a question."

"Go ahead."

"You told me a while ago that contractors aren't allowed to make a lot of changes to these historical buildings. So is it really okay to take out part of this wall? It seems like a significant change."

I smiled. "Very good question."

He grinned. "Thanks, Professor. I've been dating this cute contractor and she knows a lot of stuff."

"Good to know," I said, laughing. "Okay, it's kind of a quirky rule, but for this specific project we're able to take out as much of this wall as we want." I held up my finger to make a point. "As long as the edges of the new wall are still rounded, just like the original."

I pointed to the doorway edge. "See how

258

it's rounded here? There are no sharp edges."

Mac stared at the rounded edge and back at me. "That's amazing. I never noticed it."

"It's subtle," Jane said, smiling. "The interior corners of the rooms are slightly rounded, too."

"The corners?" He walked around and checked out each of the four corners. "That's just bizarre. No sharp corners either, no sharp edges. What's that all about?"

"Just one more way of keeping people safe," I said. "Less chance of someone hurting themselves. Like Jane said, it's subtle, but important, I think."

"I love that detail," Mac said. "I need some pictures."

I watched him pull out his phone and stroll around taking pictures. It was fun to know that some of these ideas would end up in one of his books someday.

"It was another one of Dr. Jones's edicts," I explained. "I've told you most of them, so this was one more. Rounded corners and doorway edges. You know all the others, right?"

"Yeah, high ceilings and big windows."

"Right. And the window recommendations covered everything, right down to the size of the panes of glass in patient rooms."

"Seriously?" he asked, genuinely interested.

"Yeah. They wanted the windows to be large enough to allow a lot of light to come in, but the individual panes of glass are small, about ten to twelve inches."

"Ah." Mac nodded knowingly. "So patients wouldn't be tempted to go jumping out the window."

"To put it plainly, yes."

"So this wasn't a patient room," he said, gazing around and narrowing in on the big picture window that took up half the wall.

"No. This first floor was mainly administrative, so there was more leeway here."

"Huh." He snapped another few shots. "Okay. Any more window trivia you want to share?"

"Always," I said, chuckling. "So you've noticed the wide hallways."

"I have," he said. "And they're great."

"I think so, too." I idly picked up a scraper from the utility table and began to run it against the surface of the wall. "Well, every hallway was designed with large bay windows along the outer wall to allow in lots of sunlight and ventilation." I shook my head. "Ventilation was truly an obsession with these guys, not that that's a bad thing. And all of the patient rooms were located on one side of the hall, opposite the windows."

"Was that for safety reasons?"

"Actually, yes. These halls were called single-loaded corridors. According to my research, they designed it that way to improve the airflow."

"Really? They did it for ventilation?"

"That's what I found out. But there was also a more mundane, practical reason for the setup. With the patients' chairs lined up along the same wall as their rooms, the staff was better able to keep an eye on their patients."

"I get it. Instead of having to look back and forth on both sides of the halls, the nurses and staff could keep their backs to the exterior wall and basically see everyone under their charge."

I nodded. "Pretty much."

"Okay, so for historical purposes, you can't change the windows or the ceiling height or the airflow or a dozen other things. But you can take out this wall."

I smiled. "As long as we round the edges."

"Got it," he said. "So you're ensuring the doctor's architectural legacy."

"Exactly."

The front door flew open.

"We made it," Chloe said, breathless, her

cheeks red from running.

"You didn't have to run," I said. "Where's Eric?"

"He refused to run with me." She laughed. "But I had to, and it felt good. The air is so clear today and the view is awesome."

"Now that you're here, I'm going to call Niall," Jane said. "I'll have him meet us by the chamber."

"Where is he?"

"He's out back, behind the building," Jane said, "scoping out the patio and spa area."

Chloe beamed. "That's so cool. I can't wait to see what he has in mind for that space."

A few seconds later, Eric walked inside.

"I beat you," Chloe said, laughing.

He smiled, but then got serious. "It's not dignified for the chief of police to be running around. Unless I'm chasing a criminal."

"And you're always very dignified," she said primly, and leaned against him, kissing his chin.

"Okay," I said, breaking it up. "Let's go do this."

I led the way down the hall and into the passageway. Then I moved aside so Eric could go ahead of me. "You're in charge here, Chief."

"I'm not so sure about that sometimes," he muttered.

I grinned and followed him to the opening in the brick wall.

Mac was talking to Jane about something so Chloe came over and joined me. "Thanks for the fun party."

"This party right here? Or last night's?"

"Well, this one's going to be fun, but I was talking about last night."

I smiled at her. "But you did all the work."

She waved her hand. "It was nothing. Anyway, it was great to see everyone. And did I overhear Belinda inviting us out for a barrel tasting while I'm in town?"

"You did. We're supposed to call and let her know when we can do it."

"Awesome." She grabbed my hand and squeezed it. "I'm so happy."

"I can tell. And I'm so glad."

I heard the sound of heavy footsteps and turned to see Niall heading this way, carrying what looked like a pool ladder.

"I've cleared the chamber floor of bricks," he said, "but I haven't yet taken down this short wall. So I've found a ladder we can use to climb into the space."

He hooked the curved handrail over the top of the short wall. "I'll help you step up onto this small platform, and then you can turn and descend, same as you would a stepladder."

"That's so smart," I said.

Jane smiled. "Thank you, Niall."

"I can't have you scrabbling over the top and falling into the pit, now, can I?"

I gave him a tight-lipped smile. "I've already done that, thanks."

Mac rubbed my back in sympathy.

I glanced around. "Eric, do you want to go first?"

"No, Shannon," he said indulgently. "You go ahead. Your bruises entitle you to be first."

I exchanged a look with Jane to make sure she was cool with that and she signaled for me to go. "Okay, I'm going first."

"No flying in there," Chloe murmured.

I smiled at that, then held out my hand for Niall to hold steady. Stepping onto the little platform, I felt it wobble a bit, but Niall helped me turn around. I clutched the rail and made my way down the ladder and into the pit. Niall had moved the light tree close enough so that I could see most of the space. The floor, the walls, and the low, arched ceiling were covered in old brick.

"It's gorgeous in here," I said. "And it's also very tight quarters." It was more of a passageway than an actual chamber, I thought. Less than five feet wide and about ten feet long. I wasn't sure we would all fit down here, but we would find out soon enough.

Jane came down next, and then Eric.

"Watch your head," I said. "The ceiling's pretty low."

"Thanks for the warning," he said, and looked around. "I think we've reached capacity. Let's get that door opened and then all of you can take turns checking out the space." He glanced up at the others. "Okay with you guys?"

"Fine with me," Mac said, gazing down at us. "I'll take a turn once you've all seen enough."

"Do we have a key for this door?"

"I hope so." Jane tried each of the keys on the ring she'd been given, but none of them fit. Finally she grabbed the doorknob and tried to turn it. She pressed her shoulder against the door. "Big surprise, it's locked. Or stuck. I can't tell."

Eric reached for the doorknob to make sure. "It's locked, not stuck." He glanced at Jane. "Say the word and I'll break it down."

"Wait," I said in a near panic. "This door is too gorgeous to break. I'll find another way." I studied the door for a minute. It was made of old, thick wood, solid and rich.

Probably mahogany. It was rounded on top to fit the arched opening. There was a lovely inlaid herringbone panel running vertically down the center. Oh, man . . . I had to take a breath and remind myself that we were on a mission. "The hinges are on the other side, so we can't remove them. I have a wedging tool, but even if I slip it between the wood and the brick, it won't go anywhere. And it might chip the wood."

"So what should we do?" Jane asked.

I looked at her for a long moment. "Amanda can always repair the door."

"Okay." Jane nodded briskly. "Let's get in there. I'm so curious, I can't stand it."

"Me, too," I said. "I want to know what was so important that they had to erect a brick wall to hide it."

"And tried to kill you," Jane added quietly.

I suppressed a shiver, then glanced at Eric. "Go for it."

Jane and I pressed ourselves against the wall to give Eric enough room. He took three steps back, then charged at the door, slamming into it with his shoulder.

"Didn't even budge it," he said, disgusted as he stretched and adjusted his shoulder from the impact.

Niall said, "Would you like me to give it a try?"

Eric looked up at Niall, then back at the door, then back to Niall. "Yeah. But remember, I loosened it up for you."

We all laughed at that one.

"Let me get out first." Eric climbed up the ladder and over the wall. Then Niall climbed down.

Niall took up even more space than Eric had. Jane and I exchanged a look, then pressed ourselves even flatter against the wall. I shut my eyes, imagining wood and splinters flying when Niall charged into the door.

He moved back as far as the space would allow, which was only about a foot farther back than Eric had gone. He grunted loudly and then, as he charged for the door, he shouted out a phrase that could have come from a warrior in the movie *Braveheart.* It was boisterous, to say the least.

I heard the loud thud as he rammed the door. He hit it again and that was when we heard a splintering crack.

I opened my eyes. The door had broken away from the lock and was now open a few inches. I pushed it but it wouldn't go any farther. I gave Niall an appraising look. "You did it."

Jane reached out to touch his shoulder. "Are you hurt?"

"Ach, I barely felt it."

I had to laugh. "I am wildly impressed. You really are one big, strong man."

"Aye, it's true." He brushed his hands together, a task well done.

"What did you shout when you ran for the door?"

"It's the motto of the Rose Clan," he said. " 'Constant and True.' "

I just stared at him. Sometimes I thought maybe he had come from another time and definitely another place — and I was so glad he'd landed here.

"Well, shall we see what we can?" he said finally.

Niall's amazing feat had made me forget what I was doing here. "Oh, yeah. Let's check it out."

I took three steps to the door and tried to push it inward again, but it would only go so far. "It doesn't open all the way."

"I can pull it all the way off for you," Niall offered.

"If you can wrangle it out this way, I think that'll work."

"Aye." He grasped the top of the door with both hands and pulled.

I had to squeeze my eyes shut, but quickly opened them again. It was the last straw for the poor door. It fell off its one remaining hinge with another sharp crack and Niall yanked it into the antechamber. "I'll lay it down on its side against the wall."

"Thank you."

"We need more light in here," Jane said, trying to see into the formerly hidden room.

She grabbed for her phone as I pulled my mini-flashlight from my tool belt and aimed the beam through the doorway. "Are you kidding me?"

"No way!" Jane cried.

"What is it?" Mac called.

"It's another brick wall!"

I hung my head, feeling defeated. This interior brick wall stood back from the door about three feet and completely blocked any access to the room beyond.

"What the hell?" Eric's irritated voice floated down to us. "What are they hiding in there? Plutonium?"

"This is ridiculous," Jane said.

"It's like a stupid puzzle," I muttered irately.

Niall aimed his larger flashlight beam in every direction, but stopped when he got a look at the floor. "Shannon, it's no puzzle."

"Oh my God, no!" Jane cried, and turned to Niall, who grabbed her.

"Come here, love," he said. "You needn't look."

269

I, on the other hand, couldn't help but look. Then I shouted, "Eric, we need you down here. It's worse than plutonium."

Lying on the cold stone floor in front of the brick wall was a man's body. His orange hair stuck out from his head like an unruly mop. Up close I could see flecks of gray hair at his temples, making me think he was even older than I'd thought he was. I couldn't see any blood, but that didn't matter. Carrot Head, otherwise known as Judson Killian, was dead.

Eric immediately took over the scene. He hustled Jane, Niall, and me out of the antechamber as quickly as we could scurry up that ladder. Then he called his dispatch operator for the second day in a row, ordering squad cars and CSI to the Gables *stat.*

The rest of us huddled together in the hallway as if to protect ourselves from a cold wind. I felt bad for Judson Killian, though he hadn't seemed like the most fantastic human around. But I felt horrible for us, too. Jane's shiny new hotel had a body in it. And I, once again, was the murder magnet.

Eric asked us all to exit the back hallway completely, requesting that we wait outside on the front lawn.

"Wait, Shannon." Eric pulled me aside

and Mac stayed close by. "I want you to round up all of your crew and get them out of there, too." He glanced around. "Mac, can you help?"

"You bet," he said. "I can take the third floor."

"Okay," I said. "I don't think we've got anyone working up there yet, but it would great if you could make sure."

Mac and I took the stairway together and at the second level I took off running. Mac kept going up to three.

I jogged up and down the hall announcing to everyone who could hear me. "Whoever's working on this floor, I need you out of here immediately. Take your belongings with you, but leave the ladders and heavy equipment behind. We've got a police emergency."

"Hey, boss." Sean walked out of one of the rooms and joined me. "What the hell?"

I leaned in close. "We found a dead body downstairs."

"Aw, jeez, Shannon. Not again." He raked his fingers through his hair. We had been through this before, more than once or twice.

"Yeah, again," I said. "Can you make sure everyone leaves this floor right away? They can bring all their personal stuff, but leave everything else. We'll lock up the place and be able to get back in here in a day or so."

"You got it. See you downstairs." He turned and went running down the hall, stopping at every doorway to check for workers. I ran upstairs to find Mac.

"Anyone up here?" I asked when I reached the third floor and saw him walking toward me.

"Found four guys up here," he said. "They were just starting to sweep the floors. I've rounded them all up."

"Okay, thanks." I watched my four amigos come trudging down the hall with their backpacks and toolboxes.

"Thanks, guys," I said, and all of us went downstairs quickly. We met up with Eric on the first floor.

"I think we've got everyone out who was upstairs," I told him.

"Good. I'll have my officers make a final sweep, just in case." He nodded. "Thanks."

"Anything else?"

"Just have everyone wait outside. Don't let anyone leave. I'll station two of my guys out there as soon as they arrive, just to make sure everyone sticks around."

"Okay."

He continued, "Tell your people that I'll be out to talk to the whole group as soon as

I've met with Leo."

I could hear the sound of sirens in the distance.

"And, Shannon, I'm sorry, but we're going to search everyone's belongings." Eric winced as if he hated having to say it. But this wasn't the first time we'd been through this.

"What are you looking for? How was he killed?"

Eric scowled at my questions, but then relented. "I can't be sure until the medical examiner comes. There were no visible signs of attack. That's all I can say."

"So maybe he was poisoned? Or someone gave him an injection of something?"

"We're finished discussing this."

"Okay, okay. But you know my crew would never do anything to hurt this guy." I sighed and gave a halfhearted shrug. "But if you feel it's a must to search everyone, then okay. I understand. But none of them were responsible for killing this guy." I shook my head, then held up both hands. "I'll go tell the guys."

He scowled. "I'd rather you didn't tell them anything specific."

"How can I tell them anything specific when you won't tell me anything specific?"

He just gave me a look.

273

"No problem," I said, holding up my hands in surrender. "I'll just tell the guys to stick around."

"That works. Just keep everyone here for now."

I gave him a salute. "Will do."

Mac and I started for the front door, and then I turned around. "Hey, Chief. Chloe said you found fingerprints in that other room. Were they Carrot Head's? Sorry. I mean, were they Judson Killian's?"

He simply glared at me and said nothing. I smiled innocently. I had been the recipient of that glare on more than one occasion so I wasn't exactly intimidated. Still, it was always a bit unnerving, for sure. Finally he simply shook his head and continued walking in the other direction.

"Guess we better get out of here," I murmured.

"Yeah," Mac said, but he was grinning as he threw his arm around my shoulders. "Told you I wouldn't be bored. It's always an adventure with you."

I shook my head. "I can't believe this is happening again. And more important, why?"

"Just the way things roll in your world."

I snorted politely. "Thanks for that."

When we got to the front door, he took

hold of my arm to stop me from going outside. "I've got to ask you something. Why did you want to get into that room so badly? Did you have some kind of, you know, a premonition about it?"

I sighed. "Not really a premonition. I just had a bad feeling about it, especially after studying the blueprints. Why had that entire wall been bricked up? What were they hiding?"

"Whoever *they* were," Mac muttered.

"Right," I said, feeling morose. "We have no idea who *they* are. And we still don't know what's behind that second brick wall!"

We walked outside and I relayed Eric's instructions to Wade and Carla. Then I said, "Do you mind letting everyone know? Mac and I need to take a little walk to clear our heads."

Carla squeezed my arm sympathetically. "No problem, boss."

"We'll take care of it," Wade said.

"Thanks."

Mac took my hand and we crossed the grass until we reached the rows of neatly pruned hedges that lined the hard-packed dirt pathway, away from my crew who had gathered closer to the building.

"So now one of the protesters is dead," Mac mused as we strolled along the path.

275

"Who killed him? Another protester? A former patient? The doctor? Her weird sidekick?"

"And who is he? Who is Carrot Head? Why is he here?" I wondered out loud. I wasn't used to calling the guy by his real name, Judson Killian, but I would have to try to do it. He deserved to have some dignity in death, as well as in my own mind.

Mac sighed heavily. "We have to consider the possibility that if some of the protesters are former Gables patients, they may be dealing with some serious issues."

"I've thought about that." I knew what he was intimating and I didn't really want to consider it.

We stopped to watch three black-and-white police cars come zooming up the hill, sirens blasting. They didn't bother parking in the back but drove right up on the grass and came to a stop a safe distance away from the crowd.

A minute later a black van pulled up and parked nearby. Leo Stringer jumped down from the driver's seat, carrying his heavy-duty silver briefcase with all of his forensics tools and CSI goodies inside. Lilah O'Neil climbed down from the passenger seat, carrying a smaller version of the same briefcase. As far as I knew, her kit contained, among other things, all the equipment necessary for taking fingerprints. Leo and Lilah went running across the grass to the front door and disappeared inside.

Two minutes after that, another SUV pulled up and Tommy Gallagher hopped out. He saw me and waved before walking quickly into Building Seven.

"Full police presence," Mac murmured.

"They're going to shut us down." It made me feel like cursing the universe, but I managed to keep it together. Instead of feeling sorry for myself, I would feel sorry for poor Judson Killian.

"It'll just be for a day or two," Mac reasoned.

"I hope you're right. But I guess that will depend on what they find."

We walked in silence along the edge of the grass for a few minutes. The birds hadn't gotten the dismal message that a murder had happened here because they continued their chirping and chattering and flittering from tree to tree. The sky above was blue and the sun was shining, but the air was cool. I noticed some gray clouds gathering over the water. Would there be a storm tonight?

"He couldn't have been in there too long," I said.

"No," Mac said, knowing exactly what I was referring to. And wasn't it lovely to be able to have a meeting of the minds with a special person like Mac? Even if our minds were meeting over the latest murder victim I'd found. "No more than twenty-four hours."

"Probably less." I thought about it for a moment. "Wait. We saw him on Monday when he was hurling fake blood at Rachel Powers. He was taken to police headquarters and was released later that day. Eric said he lawyered up, remember? I don't remember seeing him after that." I had to take a breath. "Is it possible he could've been dead all this time?"

"But Shannon, he couldn't have been inside that room the whole time."

"That's right." My head was starting to spin, but in a good way. "Because Niall hadn't moved all the bricks out of the way yet."

"And there's a brick wall on the other side of the door. So there was no way anyone could even get close to that space behind the door before last night."

"Let alone open the door and drag a dead body inside. Thanks to all those bricks."

"Niall only just finished the job last night," Mac said. "That's why he and Jane were late getting to the party."

"So whoever killed Judson had to have hauled him into the room sometime after that."

Mac picked up a small stone and tossed it as high as he could. It went over the eucalyptus trees and landed in the distance.

"Nice throw," I said.

The movement seemed to center him. "This is one of those things I do when I can't figure out how to structure a scene. Take a walk, hunt for seashells, toss stones into the water. Mostly, I just need to move around, change the scenery. It all helps."

"What do you do with the seashells?"

He smiled. "Sometimes I'll keep one or two and leave the rest on the beach."

I took a moment to watch the leaves dancing in the breeze, then looked back at him. "Have you structured this scene yet?"

"I'm getting there." He knew which scene I was talking about. He brushed my hair away from my face. "You are, too, I think."

"I've got fragments," I said, frowning. "Not the whole picture."

"Let's put them all together."

"Okay." I took a breath and let it out. Mac and I had done this very thing before and I thought we made a heck of a team. "Just theorizing here, but I see two possible scenarios happening last night. One, Judson met someone in that hidden room and was killed on the spot. Or two, he was murdered somewhere else and his killer moved him to the hidden room."

"Judson wasn't a big guy, but his killer would still have to be really strong to move him."

"Oh, yeah," I said. "That would take some serious maneuvering. First carrying the body over the wall and down into the antechamber, then getting the hidden door opened and putting him in there."

Mac nodded. "If Judson wasn't killed on the spot, then it had to have happened nearby. Logistically speaking."

I gazed at Mac. "Like, maybe inside one of those rooms along the back hallway?"

"It's possible. The police had already searched all of those rooms, so the killer might've felt safe using one of them." He frowned. "That's if the killer even knew the police had been there."

"Right. And all those rooms were un-locked." I scowled. "And by the way, we still don't know whose fingerprints Leo found. Eric wouldn't share."

He chuckled. "He's stubborn that way. But look, the door to the hidden room was locked, so the killer must've had the keys to that lock."

"Jane has a set of keys to this place," I said. "But who else does?"

"Rachel does," Mac said thoughtfully. "She unlocked a few doors while we were touring around the place."

I thought for a second. "I wonder if Dr. Fairchild still has a set of keys."

Mac just stared at me.

We had been staring at each other a lot lately, probably because things kept happening around here that continued to blow our minds.

"Oh, man, that doctor," he said grimly. "You've got to wonder why she came back here."

"To sell her book?" I said.

"Yeah, maybe."

"Or to reclaim her power?"

Mac's eyes lit up. "Very possible. And to make sure the Gables reputation wasn't sullied."

"That makes sense," I said. "The reputation of the Gables would reflect on her. At least, she would think so."

"If I were writing this book," Mac said after a moment, "I'd bring the doctor back to the scene so she could make sure her secrets weren't being revealed. Like, maybe she didn't want anyone getting near those brick walls."

I considered that. "So she's returning to the scene of the crime."

Mac grinned. "It's always a winner."

Chapter Twelve

I gazed at Mac. "Sometimes I'm awestruck by our combined brilliance."

He laughed out loud. "I think what we have is what's technically called a Vulcan mind meld."

I had to laugh. "And the brilliance keeps on coming."

"Thank you." He bowed. "Thank you very much."

"I think we're getting a little punchy."

"We're allowed."

He grabbed my hand and we continued walking. And talking.

I plucked an odd-looking leaf off a bush as we passed it. "So obviously, Judson must've had a connection to the Gables. And he was part of the online protest group whose other members are also connected to the Gables."

"He's old enough to have been a patient," Mac said.

"Or he could've been on staff." I stared up at the trees, my mind wandering. "I wonder if he knew Jane's mother."

Mac squeezed my hand. "Shannon, you can't possibly think this has anything to do with Jane's mother."

It was like being yanked out of a dream. "What? No! Not at all. It was just a random thought. I get them all the time." I gave my arms a quick rubbing. "God, I'm giving myself chills. But no, there's no way Jane's mom could be connected to any of this ugliness."

After a few long seconds, Mac said, "I don't think you ever told me why Jane decided to build her hotel in this wing of the Gables."

I had to take a breath. "This building housed the women's nonviolent ward. It's where her mother stayed when she was a patient here."

He nodded slowly. "Okay. That's heavy."

"I know. But it makes Jane happy to think she's turning it into a brighter place for her mom."

"She's amazing," he murmured. We walked a little farther, and then Mac said, "Let's sit down for a few minutes."

"Okay."

"How about right here on the grass? We've

even got a patch of shade."

"Perfect."

He knew I was still upset with myself and I could tell he wanted to comfort me. It was working. We settled down on the grass and I leaned back and closed my eyes. As I'd told Wade and Carla, I tried to clear my head.

After a few minutes, I opened my eyes and gazed at Mac. "I've got my tablet with me. How about if we look up that chat group? I want to see who some of these people are."

"Let's do it."

I pulled my tablet from my bag. We were on the far end of the lawn and I gauged the distance. "I think we're close enough to the building that I can connect through the Gables Wi-Fi."

"They've already wired this place for Wi-Fi?" Mac nodded slowly. "Pretty smart."

"Jane told me that all of the lessees insisted on it. It makes sense, right?"

"Absolutely." He paused, then asked, "Do you know what you're looking for?"

"Names. Comments. Rants." I shook my head. "I guess I got a little off track when I veered toward Jane's mother."

Mac smiled. "Hey, everything gets a green light." He took hold of my hand. "No right or wrong track. And no judgment."

"I'm judging myself."

"Don't. It's entirely possible that Judson Killian really did know Jane's mom. It doesn't mean there's a deeper, darker connection to it." He stretched his long legs out on the grass. "We're just playing the Scooby-Doo game, tossing ideas around, remember? It's just you and me."

Was it any wonder I was in love with him? Even when I was being paranoid and a little bit judgmental, mostly about myself, he was being just . . . totally cool. A real superhero. I bet he'd look great in a cape.

I smiled at him. "This is good."

"Yeah? You okay?"

"I'm great." I managed a short laugh. "It was just weird to consider, even for a minute, that Jane's mother could have a connection to what's happening now."

"It's not totally far-fetched."

"Yeah, but it's unrealistic and I'm grasping at straws and dreaming of conspiracies, just to make sense of things. Sorry."

"Dead bodies can do that to you."

"No kidding." I swiped my tablet to open it. "Hey, speaking of connections, I've got one."

"Good. Do we know the name of the chat group?"

"No. I'm going to try a search linking

286

Judson Killian and the Gables. We'll see what comes up."

He moved closer so he could look over my shoulder.

"Wow, it worked," I said. "It links to a website called Burn It Down."

"That's just charming," he said dryly. "But it sounds right."

"It's not much more than a message board."

"Guess they were going old-school."

"But they do have a member list." I began to scan the names.

"Do they actually use their real names?"

"Not on the postings, but they must've had to log on with real names or e-mail info in the beginning. Probably wanted to verify that everyone had some link to the Gables. On the board itself they use their online names. Killian goes by the name Red Menace."

"Ah. Red hair," he murmured. "Clever."

"Isn't it?"

"Do you see Ricky Patterson on there?"

I continued to scan the list. "Here he is. Giants Number One Fan. All one word with a hashtag, you know."

"I get it."

"His baseball cap should've been a dead giveaway."

Mac grinned. "You think so?"

I stared at the screen. "There's about two hundred names on this list. That's a lot of disgruntled folks. I wonder if they're all ex-Gables people."

"If they are, we can probably guess why they're disgruntled."

"Yeah. Nurse Ratched."

"But barely ten percent of them showed up Monday," Mac estimated. "And a few more than that came back today."

"I'm going to go back a few weeks on the message board to see what they were planning for the groundbreaking ceremony. If there's any talk about violence or destroying property, I'll pass it on to Eric." I glanced at Mac. "Chances are, he's already got this info, but we still need to keep up with what's happening. Right?"

Mac grinned. "Oh, absolutely."

"It's not really snooping, is it?"

"Of course not. We're . . . helpers."

I gave him a thumbs-up. "Exactly." I looked back to the screen and searched a few pages until I found a thread called "Find RP." There were plenty of comments on the thread but they were innocuous. I showed it to Mac. "What do you think this means?"

"RP?" he said. "Let me think. Real People?

Raw Potatoes? Yeah, no, probably not." He looked at me at the same moment that I figured it out.

"Rachel Powers." We said it together.

"So she was a target from the first," he guessed.

"If that really is what RP stands for, then yes."

"Wait. Here comes Eric," Mac murmured.

I closed the tablet and watched Eric walk out to the front steps. It gave me a little tingle of pride to see my crew people come to order at Eric's entrance. And seeing them reminded me that I hadn't even checked to make sure they were all present and accounted for. I had to hope that Wade and Carla were more on the ball than I was. I silently excused myself for being ditzy. After all, it wasn't every day that I found a dead body. To be honest, though, it seemed to be happening more and more lately.

Mac and I got up and walked over to the edge of the group.

"Is everyone here a member of Shannon's crew?" Eric asked the crowd.

I took a more careful look at the people who were here and recognized every single person. "They're all mine, Chief. Well, except for Chloe and Jane."

"That's affirmative, Chief," Wade said.

"We had twenty-three show up for work today and that's how many are out here now. They're all on our crew."

"Good. Thanks, Shannon. Wade."

"You bet," my foreman murmured.

Eric looked directly at me. "Shannon, you have contact information for everyone here? Can I get that from you?"

I exchanged a quick glance with Wade and we both nodded. "We'll e-mail it to you ASAP."

"All right. You're all free to go for now. And I'm sure you realize that we'll have to close down the building for a day or two to investigate."

I only hoped it wouldn't be more than two days.

"Jane and Shannon," he continued, giving a nod to each of us. "I'll inform you both immediately as soon as we've cleared the building and you can go back to work."

I was losing track of how many times I'd heard him say it, and that was depressing. But I just nodded back. "Sounds good, Chief."

"Thanks, Eric," Jane murmured.

Eric glanced around at everyone waiting. "Thank you all for your cooperation." He gave another brief nod and walked back into the building.

■ ■ ■ ■

I was pleased to realize that Eric had changed his mind about putting my guys through the indignity of searching their belongings. I appreciated that more than he knew. Most of these guys were like family to me and I didn't want anything to damage the good feelings we had for each other and for our local police.

I stayed and talked to my guys for a while and Mac took off for home to finish his writing for the day. He promised to come over later that afternoon to have a glass of wine and grill some salmon. I still had plenty of fish in my freezer from my dad's latest fishing trip with Uncle Pete.

"We'll continue our game when I get there," he said, and kissed me good-bye.

"I can't wait." And I couldn't contain my smile. Mac had introduced me to the Scooby-Doo game early in our relationship at a time when I was trying to solve the murder of a dear friend. It was something Mac liked to do when he was writing his books. He named it the Scooby-Doo game after the cartoon show he used to watch when he was young.

At some point in the show, Scooby and

the gang would sit around and figure out the suspects, the motives, how the crime was covered up, and what the friends could do to trick the bad guy into confessing. Mac told me it was basically a brainstorming session. With a dog.

The last of my guys left the Gables and I took a few minutes to talk to one of the cops I'd known since grammar school. Then I grabbed my tool belt and headed for the parking lot, taking my usual route around the side of Building Seven. I had a few hours to take care of business before Mac showed up for dinner, so I mentally made a list of things to do as I walked. I would stop at the market for groceries on the way home and then work on payroll, schedules, and other business stuff the rest of the afternoon.

I spotted my truck halfway across the lot. As I approached the driver's side, a man walked quickly from the other direction and I suddenly found myself staring at Ricky Patterson.

I took one step backward. "What do you want?"

He lifted his bony shoulders in a shrug and said, "Heard you found the body."

He wore his orange baseball cap backward today and I wondered briefly if he owned any other caps. It was none of my business and I didn't really care. It was just one of those idle thoughts that passed through my head when I found myself facing someone who might be dangerous.

"That's right, I did," was all I said.

The day had turned warm so Ricky wore a thin white T-shirt with his navy hoodie tied around his waist. Marching around protesting could work up a sweat, I figured.

I almost jumped when I felt my phone begin to vibrate in my pocket. I recalled turning off the sound earlier while Eric was talking. I didn't want to answer it now in case it caused Ricky to react badly. At the last minute I pulled the phone out. "I've got a call," I said.

"Okay."

Just as I pressed the button, the call disappeared. But I saw that it was Mac. Darn it!

"I know your name," Ricky said.

"You do?"

"Yeah. Shannon. Shannon Hammer. You're building a hotel inside the Gables."

"That's right. I'm a contractor."

"Do you know who got dead?" he asked.

My eyes narrowed on him. "Do you?"

"Yeah." He was angry now. "It's my friend, Jud. Judson Killian."

I nodded. "That's right. And I'm sorry

your friend is dead."

"You saw him, right?"

"I did."

"Well, so how did he die?" Ricky demanded.

I took a deep breath, unsure how to handle this guy. Was he dangerous? Or did he just want information? "I'm not sure I can tell you." Because I didn't really know, I thought, but didn't mention it. And now I really wished I knew how Judson was killed.

"Why not?" He was almost whining. "The cops won't tell me anything."

"Did you ask them?"

"No." He gave another insolent shrug. "Why should I? I already know they won't tell me."

I was beginning to realize that even though Ricky was somewhere in his midthirties, he wasn't awfully sharp. I tried to tell myself that this was the guy who had terrorized a bunch of people the other day. The guy the police had hauled down to headquarters, albeit briefly. But even so, he came across as vulnerable and innocent.

So I tried to explain myself as simply as possible. "I'm just not sure I can trust you with the information, Ricky."

He nodded vigorously. "Yes, you can. You can trust me."

"But your protest march on Monday turned violent and your friend Jud attacked that woman on stage."

His forehead furrowed in a deep frown. "She wasn't hurt."

"She was frightened and that's not okay." I kept my voice soft and even. "Throwing blood on someone is the same as hurting them."

"It wasn't real blood."

"I know. But it frightened her very badly. And it was disruptive and scary for everyone else."

He shrugged again. It seemed to be his signature move. "He didn't mean to hit her with the juice. He got bumped. You saw it, right?"

"Yeah, I saw the lady bump into him."

"That's right, so that messed it up. But Jud said it would be okay. It was part of the plan."

"You have a plan?"

"It's nothing." His lips clamped shut.

"Ricky," I said quietly. "Did you kill Jud?"

His mouth dropped open and his eyes widened. "No! I didn't do it. Why would I? He was my best friend. I owe him. He saved my life."

"Really? How did he do that?"

Again Ricky pressed his lips together in a

stubborn line, then finally blew out a breath. "He stopped them from hurting me."

He sounded like a child. And I suddenly had a dozen questions for him, but I held back. "Can you tell me who was hurting you?"

"No."

"Please?"

He scuffed his shoes against the blacktop pavement and kicked a small stone a few feet. "I was only twelve years old and I couldn't fight back. Judson came to my rescue."

"Was he a patient at the hospital?"

"No, he worked there. He was an orderly."

So I was right in guessing that Judson Killian was on staff. Fascinating.

"How did he rescue you?" I asked.

"I told you, they were hurting me."

"What were they doing to hurt you?" And who were *they*? I wanted to ask. But not yet.

"It was electrical," he mumbled.

Electrical? Good grief. "What do you mean? You were electrocuted? On purpose?"

"The shock machine." Another shrug. "Supposed to make you happier. Quieter. She said I'm unruly, so it calmed me down. But now, I don't know, I forget stuff sometimes."

What in the world? The hospital was performing electroshock therapy on a twelve-year old? Was he making this up? "But you said you weren't a patient here."

"I wasn't. But I lived here for a while before I went to live with my dad."

I took a stab in the dark. "Did Dr. Fairchild perform the therapy?"

His eyes clouded and he scowled. "Yeah."

"Was she your doctor?"

His lips curved downward and I thought he might start to cry.

I asked him again, more gently this time. "Ricky, was Dr. Fairchild your doctor?"

"No. She was my mother."

Whoa!

What in the world? It took me a few more seconds to recover from the shock of that revelation. I took some deep breaths to slow down my heart, which was surely racing. I gazed up at the sky, bright blue, and over at the trees wafting in the breeze. Okay.

Meanwhile, Ricky had wrapped his arms protectively around his middle. I couldn't blame him. He was just a kid when he lived at the Gables. Why would his own mother perform the same techniques they used on adults? But then, I had to remind myself who his mother was. Dr. Lorraine Fairchild had used her own twelve-year-old son as a human guinea pig in her experiments in torture. Maybe that was too harsh, but I didn't care. It was sickening, no matter how you termed it.

I was about to broach the question of him coming with me to the police station, when I got another shock.

Mac Sullivan.

I watched him pull his big, shiny SUV into the lot and drive straight toward me. He stopped his car directly across from my truck and stared. I held up one finger, hoping to hold him off for a few seconds. Again, I didn't want to scare Ricky away.

I needed to do this right.

"Ricky, have you ever seen a Jake Slater movie?"

"Yeah," he said with enthusiasm. "Jake Slater is cool."

"Well, the man who writes those movies and all the Jake Slater books is here. Right now."

"What? Where? No way." His face lit up like a kid at his first rock concert.

"Would you like to meet him?"

"Maybe. I think so." He suddenly sounded shy.

I smiled. "You'll like him. He's a good guy. His name is Mac and he's just like Jake Slater. He takes care of people. He can protect you."

"He's just like Jake?" He said it reverently. "Is he a Navy SEAL?"

"Yes, he is."

Ricky glanced around. "Where is he?"

"He's right here." I breathed a quick sigh of relief and waved Mac over. Mac climbed out of his car and strolled toward us.

"He's kind of big," Ricky murmured.

"Yes. He's big and strong and he's just the best guy you'd ever want to meet."

"He looks like Jake," he whispered. "What'd you say his name was?"

"Mac."

"Hi." Mac kept his eyes on me as he walked straight to me and took hold of my hand. "Tried to call you."

"Sorry."

Scoping out the situation, Mac glanced at Ricky, then back at me. "How're we doing?"

"We're good," I said. "Mac, this is Ricky. He's a big fan of Jake Slater."

"Hey, Ricky, good to meet you." Mac stuck out his hand and Ricky shook it a bit warily.

"Nice to meet you, too," he said. "Jake Slater is really cool." Then he looked at me. "Is he your boyfriend?"

I wasn't sure if he meant Mac or Jake Slater, but either way, it made me smile.

"Yes, he is."

Ricky stared at Mac for a long moment. "You're the one who knocked me down."

"Yeah. I was trying to stop you. Sorry if I hurt you."

"It's okay, I forgive you."

"And I forgive you," Mac said.

Ricky grinned and stuck out his hand. "Shake."

Mac laughed and shook his hand. "All right."

It was just that simple, I thought, and very sweet. I turned to Mac. "Ricky was telling me about something that happened to him and I'm hoping he'll tell you, too. Because I think we can help him." I looked at Ricky. "What do you think, Ricky?"

"I'm not sure."

"Do you mind if I tell him what you said?"

Ricky's mouth twisted as he tried to figure out the right thing to do. Another shrug. "Okay."

"Thanks." I looked at Mac. "Ricky was waiting by my truck when I got out here because he wanted to ask me about the dead body we found today." I glanced at Ricky. "Right?"

"Yeah."

"He told me that the man who was killed, Judson Killian, was his best friend. Jud was an orderly many years ago at the Gables and worked with Dr. Fairchild."

"Yeah, and she was really mean," Ricky interjected.

Mac nodded. "I hear you."

"Ricky became best friends with Jud when he saved Ricky from being hurt by someone at the hospital." I glanced at Ricky to make sure he was still okay with all of this. It seemed he was, so I continued. "They were trying to give Ricky electroshock therapy."

"I was unruly," Ricky said, glowering.

"He was twelve," I said.

Mac snorted at that. "Let me tell you something, Ricky. If a twelve-year-old kid *isn't* being unruly, there's probably something wrong with him. So what was the big deal?"

"She didn't like it," Ricky grumbled.

Mac glanced at me, then looked straight at Ricky. "I'd say she's the one with the problem."

Ricky looked positively thrilled with Mac's take on the subject. "Yeah."

I turned to Mac. "As you might've figured out, 'she' was Dr. Fairchild."

"Yeah, I got that." He glanced back at Ricky. "That totally sucks, man."

Ricky grinned at Mac's colorful word choice. "Yeah, it sucks."

Mac frowned. "You were awfully young to be living in this place and going to a doctor who wanted to give you electroshock therapy."

I gave Ricky a look, and he answered by staring at the ground. I wrapped my arm through Mac's and held him firmly. "Mac, Dr. Fairchild is Ricky's mother."

"What?" He almost roared out the word but managed to hold it down to a mere shout. He sucked in a breath, let it out slowly, and said to Ricky, "Sorry, pal, but I was not expecting to hear that."

He smiled again. "You got mad."

"I sure did."

"I like you," Ricky said.

"Hey." Mac grinned. "I like you, too."

I could tell his words were genuine, but I could guarantee he didn't feel any of that same warmth for Ricky's horrible mother. And I was right there with him.

"Ricky," I said, ready to change the subject. "Lately, do you ever sneak inside the Gables and hide?"

"No." He made a face. "I hate it in there."

"I saw you up here the week before the groundbreaking ceremony." I watched his expression for a sign that he was going to lie. "Do you remember seeing Mac and me walking on the grass?"

302

"I remember." He scowled. "I didn't want you to see me."

"What were you doing up here?"

"I was looking for Jud. He went inside to find something."

"So Jud was going inside the Gables, even before the groundbreaking?"

Ricky stared at the ground. "Maybe."

"Did Jud live in there?"

"Sometimes."

I frowned. "Didn't he have a place to live?"

"Yeah, he has a place. But he was looking for information."

Information? What information? I sighed inwardly. Whatever information he was trying to find, it was probably what killed him. Whether he found what he was looking for or not. "Ricky, I'm really sorry to talk about this, but I need to tell you that we discovered Jud's body in the space behind the heavy door inside that pretty brick passageway. Do you know the place I'm talking about?"

"Yeah." He nodded briskly. "We called it the Passage. Before they put up all the brick walls, we used to go through the Passage to get to the Baths."

"There's a bathroom behind that wall?"

He laughed out loud. "No, not a bathroom. The Baths. If you get sent to the Baths, you get really quiet."

"Why is that?"

"Because the water's so cold, you can't talk anymore. It's ice-cold."

I glanced at Mac and grimaced. *Ice-cold baths?* Ugh. "Ricky, did you ever go in the Baths?"

"Once, when I was being unruly."

I had to take a few deep breaths, exhale slowly, and try to calm down. Because I really wanted to kill this guy's mother.

"When did you leave the Gables, Ricky?" Mac asked, changing the subject again, thank goodness.

"It was a little while after the shock therapy. Jud sneaked into town and called my dad and a few weeks later he came and picked me up. He had a court order and everything. Dad got there right after Regina died."

"Who's Regina?"

He smiled. "We called her Reggie. She was pretty. Her daddy sent money to keep the hospital open."

Was this the wealthy benefactor who kept the place open well into the 1990s? "Do you remember Reggie's last name?"

"Pomeroy." He smiled. "I remember because I like to say it. Pomeroy."

"Do you know how Reggie died?" Mac asked.

Ricky frowned. "The newspapers said that she killed herself. But Jud was pretty sure she died in the Baths."

Mac offered to drive Ricky home and I hoped he would be able to pry more information out of him on a man-to-man level. He promised Ricky that they would take a quick detour into the drive-through at Goody Burger on the way. It turned out that Ricky had been staying with Jud, who had a small apartment over by the high school.

Meanwhile, I stopped at the market for veggies and a few other items, along with pet food and paper products. My luck ran out when I got to the checkout line and had the misfortune of running into Whitney Reid Gallagher. I was *this close* to escaping unscathed, I thought. But it was not to be.

"Well, if it isn't Miss Dirty Boots," Whitney said, and did her usual snotty perusal of my outfit, from my work boots all the way up to my mop of curly red hair. Talk about *unruly,* I thought. But Mac seemed to like my curls just fine, so Whitney could kiss my butt splicer.

"Well," I said in the same haughty tone, "if it isn't the formerly rich princess turned —"

"Shut up!" She whipped around to make

sure no one had heard me.

"Hey, I'm just here trading quips with the townies." It was amazing to see that she was still trying to pass herself off as the pampered daughter of her tycoon father who was swindled out of his fortune last year.

Now Whitney was forced to live on her adorable husband's salary as the assistant police chief and the pin money she made pretending to be an interior decorator. But she still stuck her nose in the air whenever I saw her. Still called me "townie" at every opportunity — which was why I had just called her that. And she still went grocery shopping in her usual uniform of sequined halter top, shiny black spandex jeggings, and black patent leather Christian Louboutin stiletto death heels. Comfy.

"I'm glad I ran into you," I said, realizing I really did have something to talk to her about. "I wanted to ask how you know Ricky Patterson."

Her lip curled. "Why is that any of your business?"

"Because I met him today and he was saying lots of nice things about you." When in doubt, flatter the woman, I thought. Worked every time.

"Oh." She waved her hand breezily. "His mother was a dear friend of my father. In case you don't know, Dr. Fairchild was a very important woman around here for many years and when my family used to visit here — years before we had the bad luck to actually move here — Daddy was on the board of directors of the Gables. It was a very prestigious institution once upon a time. So naturally Ricky and I were friends." She studied her manicure. "Now, of course, it's become so tacky, I hear they've even leased a space to your little friend Jane."

Sometimes I just had to stare at her in disbelief. Was anyone really that shallow and stupid?

Yes, Whitney was all that.

"Well, I'd love to stay and chat," I said, "but I'm already bored. Buh-bye." I stepped up to the clerk, paid for my groceries, and escaped out the door.

I raced to my truck and I confess I might've burned a little rubber in my rush to get away from that woman.

What did it say about me that I would've rather dealt with a murder than talk to Whitney?

CHAPTER THIRTEEN

Mac walked into my house at four o'clock carrying a bottle of chilled white wine and a bouquet of yellow roses and multicolored peonies. How could I not love him?

"I saw these and thought of you," he said, handing me the bouquet and kissing me soundly.

"You're so sweet." I kissed him back. "They're beautiful. Thank you."

He gave me another kiss. "You're more beautiful than any flower," he murmured.

"Wow, thank you." I breathed in the scent of roses and peonies. "I love you for thinking of me."

"Can't seem to think of much else," he muttered, and leaned back against the counter. "You look good, Shannon."

I blinked in surprise. "Thank you, Mac." I couldn't help but smile as I touched his cheek and kissed him again. "So do you."

"Yeah, I'm a rock star."

"Ricky certainly thinks so." I grinned. "And I do, too."

After another long moment of mutual admiration, we both began to laugh. It was definitely not the right time to bring up the "relationship" question. I was happy just to live in the moment for now.

"We need a drink."

I was still smiling as I stooped down to pull a vase from one of the cupboards under the island. "I'll put these in water."

"And I'll open the wine."

"Perfect."

Robbie, meanwhile, was practically shaking with excitement, waiting for us to play with him.

Mac took a step toward the wine bottle, then stopped. "But first, I'd better give this little guy some attention."

I laughed. "Because he's so calm and dignified and not starving for affection at all."

"Poor neglected critter." Mac sat down and gave the side of his leg a pat. Robbie hurled himself up onto Mac's lap, then rolled over to get his belly rubbed. "Who's a good boy?" Mac said as he gave the little cutie a brisk rub and some scratches behind his ears. "You a good boy? Yes, you are. Yes, you are."

I stopped to enjoy the two of them, then watched Tiger saunter in. Aloof and totally cool, she stared at them for a moment, then started batting at Mac's shoelaces.

"You have made their lives complete," I said, and put the vase of flowers on the island so I could admire them while we got dinner ready.

After a few minutes, Robbie finally jumped down and Mac moved on to open the bottle of wine. After pouring it into two glasses, he handed me one. "Let's toast to something great."

"How about, to us," I said. "So brilliant and only slightly punchy."

He chuckled. "Don't think I've ever heard a better toast."

We clinked glasses and took a sip.

"Isn't that nice?" I said, savoring the rich flavor.

He grinned. "I'm sure you noticed it's from your uncle's winery."

"I noticed." I smiled and took another quick sip. "I love the earth tones he captured."

His eyebrows lifted. "Pete told me this one barely touched the barrel, so you really get that great mellow mineral taste in every sip."

I nodded. "It really comes through."

A buzzer went off so I set my glass down

and walked over to the stove. "The rice is done and it can rest on the stove for now. We can start the grill whenever you're ready, but I would love to sit and relax for a little while if you don't mind."

"Not at all. I think we both deserve that."

I would've suggested the back patio, but the March weather tended to turn cool in the late afternoons. Instead we took our glasses out to the living room and sat on the couch together. I turned on some music and for a few minutes we just chilled out and enjoyed the peace. After a day like the one we'd had, we needed it.

Finally I had to ask, "How did it go with Ricky?"

Mac took a deep breath and let it out. "I want to kill his mother, but other than that, it was an interesting trip home."

"As soon as you left, I thought of so many things I wanted to ask him."

"Like what?"

"Oh, you know, does he think his own mother would try to kill him?"

He frowned at me. "Are you worried about that?"

"Yeah. Aren't you? You've seen her. She's scary." The chilled wine was causing condensation to form on our glasses, so I opened the drawer in the end table and brought out two coasters. "She seems to lack maternal empathy, for sure."

Mac nodded. "She's got all the warmth of a black widow."

"I'd say that's putting it mildly."

"It's kind of a giveaway," Mac said. "When a mom wants to electrocute her unruly twelve-year-old child."

I still couldn't wrap my head around that one. "Isn't that sickening?" I shook my head in dismay. "Okay, so maybe she wouldn't kill her own kid, but I'd like to ask Ricky if he thinks his mother killed Judson."

"Good question," Mac said. "And important, too. She's definitely on our suspect list."

"And speaking of suspects, guess who I ran into in the market? You won't guess so I'll tell you. It was Whitney. And I asked her how she knows Ricky. Remember they were talking together at the pub?"

He grimaced. "I wish I'd remembered that. I would've asked him about her. But you're just kidding about Whitney being a suspect, right?"

"She's always on my dream suspect list, but I guess she doesn't qualify for this one. Darn it." I took a quick sip of wine, then let him in on what Whitney had told me about her father and the doctor being good friends and board members. "So Ricky and Whitney have known each other for years. That's why they were talking at the pub."

Mac gave a low whistle. "There's a lot of weird connections weaving their way through this case."

"Sure are." I thought about it for a moment. "I wonder if Whitney's father knew what kind of torment the good doctor was putting her son through."

"I doubt it."

"Me, too. She's had a lot of people fooled for a long time."

We sat in silence for a long minute and then Mac said, "Speaking of the pub, Ricky said he might walk there tonight. He said he wanted to be around other people."

"I guess that's a healthy attitude to have." I sipped my wine. "That reminds me. Chloe texted me earlier to say that she and Eric were going to the pub for dinner. She asked if we wanted to join them, but I felt like eating healthier tonight. But if you'd like to walk down there later for a nightcap and to say hello, I'm up for it."

"I wouldn't mind saying hello to them and checking up on Ricky. He's an interesting guy." Frowning a little, Mac looked down into his wineglass. "I want to call him a kid because he seems so young, but he's not.

313

Guess how old he is."

"I was thinking he must be about thirty-four."

Mac chuckled. "You nailed it. He was ten years old when his parents divorced and his mother got custody. She moved him to the Gables to live with her."

"What a nightmare for him." I shook my head. "Imagine being a child living at a mental facility. It had to be awful even before the electroshock incident. And his father got him back when he was twelve. So for two years Ricky lived there."

"Two years is a lifetime for a kid or for anyone when they're being abused." Mac scowled.

"She should be in jail."

"I agree one hundred percent."

"Believe it or not," I said, "I was about to ask him if he wanted to come to the police station with me and report his mother to Chief Jensen. You drove up just then so I wasn't able to. I doubt he would've gone with me, though."

"Maybe I'll bring it up when we see him again." He swirled his wine, took a sip, then said, "So, do you honestly think that Dr. Fairchild killed Judson?"

"Oh, yes," I said firmly. She was cold, ambitious, egotistical. She checked all of my boxes. "I honestly do."

"Just like that? I mean, we have no real clue to any of this."

"That's okay. I still think she did it. I think she's certifiable." I set my wineglass down on the coaster. "And you just know that Judson was trying to find some way to prove that Fairchild killed that girl, Reggie." I adjusted the pillows to sit up straighter. "Maybe Judson found the proof he was looking for, but even if he didn't, the doctor had to get rid of him."

"You've been giving this a lot of thought."

"I have. Am I wrong?" I tilted my head to get a better look at him. "What do you think?"

"Oh, I totally agree." He lifted his wineglass in a toast. "She did it."

"I'm glad to hear you say it."

"Who else would have a reason to kill him?"

"That's the big question." I thought about it for a second. "You know, it's really bugging me that we don't know how Jud died. Eric wouldn't tell me, and frankly, I'm not even sure he knows yet. But I didn't see any blood so I don't think it was a bullet or a knife wound."

"I couldn't get a very good look at the body, but from my vantage point, I didn't see any blood, either," he said. "That's what led us to think that he might've been killed somewhere else and moved."

I nodded. "Yes, but after talking to Ricky, I'm not so sure he was moved."

He sat forward to rest his elbows on his knees and glanced back at me. "What are you thinking?"

"The doctor and Judson used to work together closely. I think she could've lured him to that spot because it was a familiar place that they went to every day. The Baths." I shivered. "Ugh. The name alone gives me the creeps."

"I want to get in there and see these Baths."

"Right now my imagination is doing a fine job of picturing them." I thought of all the poor patients who were sentenced to be dunked in icy water. Hadn't they had enough problems to deal with without Dr. Fairchild's less-than-kind benevolence?

"I just remembered, what about Prudence? Who is she? She's cranky about everything, unless Dr. Fairchild tells her to do something. Then she can't wait to bow and scrape."

"They must've worked together," he said. "Let's ask Ricky when we see him." He drank some more wine, then set down his glass. "Okay. Now as an intellectual exercise, let's come up with three more suspects and three more motives."

"Seriously? Are you teaching a class?"

"No," he said with a grin. "But you're good at this. And besides, as much as we would hate it, the doctor might be innocent."

"That would be a total bummer. But okay." I mentally went through every possible suspect I could think of. "It's too bad we didn't get to know some of the other protesters."

"Yeah. They pretty much stayed in the background and let Ricky and Judson take the lead."

"And they were all pretty hostile to us until they saw Dr. Fairchild speaking. Then they just seemed sad and scared, like Ricky." I sat up straighter on the couch. "But until further notice, they're all suspects as far as I'm concerned. Even though I see no reason why they would kill their protest leader."

"I wonder if they'll keep coming around the Gables."

"Good question." I took my last sip of wine. "I need to get things ready for dinner. Let's talk in the kitchen."

"Let's go." He stood and picked up both wineglasses.

In the kitchen he poured us each a half glass of wine and filled two glasses with water.

"Thanks." I gulped down half of the water, then pulled out the medium frying pan and set it on the stove for the spinach I'd be sautéing when the fish was ready.

Mac sat at the kitchen table and played with a joyful Robbie while I emptied the dishwasher.

"Okay, I'm ready for my first suspect," I said.

Mac smiled, then nodded. "Go for it."

"That would be Ricky."

"Haven't we eliminated him?"

"Well, yeah. But he was actually our main suspect until we got to know him a little better."

He held up his hands. "Hey, for all we know, he could still be a stone-cold killer, just pulling the wool over our eyes."

"Always possible."

"So what's his motive?" Mac asked.

"Hmm." Even though I had considered him a suspect until a few hours ago, I had to give it some thought. "What if Jud was going to kick him out of his house because Ricky didn't have any money for rent?"

He groaned. "That's pitiful."

"I know," I said with a laugh. "But it's

318

real, right? Okay, how about this? Ricky is secretly still tight with his mother and she has promised to give him co-author credit on her new blockbuster novel about the Gables. Judson wants in on the deal but Ricky doesn't want to share. So . . ." I frowned. "Wow. This one started out really strong in my mind, but it's totally unraveling."

"I like it. Keep going." He grinned. "You have a real flair for the absurd."

I choked out a laugh. "That is not a compliment."

"No. Sorry," Mac said unrepentantly. "So let's come up with another suspect."

"It's your turn to name one."

"Okay." Mac seemed to ponder the possibilities, then said, "Rachel Powers."

My eyes widened. "Oh, yes. A dark horse. Excellent. What's her motive?"

"She was having an affair with Judson," Mac said, "and he threw blood all over her."

I rolled my eyes. "That's just cheap."

He laughed. "I know. Okay, let me think about this. She really needs to have a good motive."

"Why is she involved with this property?" I asked.

Mac shrugged. "She's a key member of the development company."

"But what else do we know about her?" I wondered, then added, "She's beautiful. But I suppose we need to dig deeper."

Mac frowned. "She knows everything there is to know about the Gables."

"That's . . . interesting." I gazed at Mac. "What are you thinking?"

He shrugged and gave his wine a swirl. "She's a little . . . neurotic. The day she gave me the tour, I saw her get all hyper and then kind of freak out and have a meltdown. It wasn't quite that dramatic, but she can definitely swing up and down."

"Sort of a drama queen?"

"Yeah." He shrugged. "Not a reason to suspect her, but hey, we're just playing a game, right?"

I must've been getting a little neurotic myself because I was suddenly starting to feel sorry for the woman. And that was after feeling a tiny bit jealous of her that first day. "She did get blood thrown all over her so I can't fault her for being dramatic."

"It was fake blood."

I shook my head. "Ricky said the same thing, and the fact that it was fake doesn't matter. It was still traumatic."

He held up his hand in semi-surrender. "I'll give you that. But even before the bucket-of-blood incident, when she gave me the tour, she had a few drama queen moments."

"But I thought you said she was savvy and knowledgeable about the whole project."

"Oh, she was, definitely. That's why I jumped on board. Well, that, and the fact that you and Jane were involved in the project."

"So what did she flip out over?"

"Well, when she saw that the lock on Jane's building had been tampered with, she got really angry."

I pressed my hand to his leg. "Mac. Hold on. The lock was tampered with? You didn't tell me that."

He winced. "Sorry. There was so much going on, I guess I forgot."

"No worries. But that's not like you."

"I know." He brought my hand up to his lips and kissed my knuckles. "Because I tell you everything."

I broke into a big smile. "Stop trying to distract me."

He raised his eyebrows. "Is it working?"

"Of course it's working."

"Good to know. The thing is, as soon as Rachel's freak-out was over, she called Jane and told her about the broken lock. And Jane calmed her down, said it wasn't a problem, no worries. You know how Jane is."

"Yeah. And it probably wasn't much of problem because none of our stuff was in there yet. Certainly nothing worth stealing." But still, I wondered why Jane didn't mention it to me. I would have to ask her next time I saw her.

"No doubt the lock was broken by Judson," he said.

"Probably. Ricky was concerned that Jud was trying to find something incriminating. That's why Ricky was sneaking around the day we first went up to the Gables and saw him."

Mac stared pensively as he swirled his wine. "The tampered lock takes on a whole new meaning."

"Sure does. And so does Rachel's freak-out."

"Do you think she was more angry or more worried?"

"Can't say for sure," he said.

"Maybe we need to get to know her." I thought about it for a few seconds. "She was probably under a lot of stress with the upcoming groundbreaking. And she was meeting a very important investor, don't forget."

"Extremely important," he said, chuckling.

I gazed at him, my eyes narrowing. "Do you think there might be some deeper connection between Rachel and the Gables? I mean, maybe she and Judson were really working together. And she flipped out over the lock because now she realized that he had gone inside the place without her." I frowned. "Or is that lame, too?"

He considered it. "Not so lame. But more important, I like the idea that she might have a deeper connection to all of this."

"Me, too." I rubbed my stomach. "I think I'm ready to start dinner."

"Good idea. I'm getting hungry."

While Mac fired up the grill, I set the dining room table. Then I freshened Tiger's and Robbie's water bowls and gave them each a treat for being so well behaved and adorable.

"The grill will take ten minutes to heat up," Mac said when he walked back into the kitchen.

"Okay. I just remembered something. I don't know if it's relevant, but when I was talking to Ricky, he indicated that throwing the blood was part of a plan."

"Part of a plan," Mac murmured. "What plan? Was she the target or not?"

"I think they hoped it looked that way, but Ricky said that Judson was aiming for something else and he got bumped."

"He got bumped," Mac mused.

"Oh my God," I said, my eyes growing wide at the realization. "He got bumped by Prudence."

Mac just stared at me in numb silence.

"Prudence," I repeated. "Dr. Fairchild's right-hand girl."

Mac frowned. "She bumped into Judson and the blood went all over Rachel."

"She bumped Judson and now he's dead," I whispered.

"And she's the same person who walked out of urgent care wearing an arm brace after you were shoved over that brick wall."

"I was shoved pretty hard. Is that enough to require an arm brace?"

"It's possible," Mac said. "She could've wrenched her elbow."

"So that's a whole bunch of coincidences."

"No such thing," he said through gritted teeth. "She's next up on my suspect list."

"Mine, too." I sipped my wine and thought about it. "We need to ask Ricky about her. If she knows Fairchild well enough to carry her purse right after taking part in the protest, she's tangled up in this."

"I'll talk to Ricky tonight at the pub."

"Okay, I'm about to go off on another tangent."

"Go for it."

"Do you think Rachel and Judson were in cahoots against the doctor?"

Mac sat down at the kitchen table. "That's a stretch. But it's possible."

"I know." I lifted my shoulders lightly. "But that's what we're doing here, right?"

"For sure. But, except for Ricky mentioning a plan, we don't know anything about Rachel."

"She's the developer of the Gables. How did she get that job?"

"You think she's connected to the hospital?"

I grabbed the salt and pepper shakers. "What if she is, Mac? What if it's true that she and Judson had a *plan*? If that much is true, wouldn't that indicate that they had a history together?"

He exhaled heavily. "We're working with a lot of suppositions."

I smiled. "We're just playing a game."

He laughed. "I know, I know. But I keep forgetting the game part because we seem to be getting into it pretty deeply."

"I know. I love it."

He put his elbow on the table and held his chin in his hand. "Okay, Ace, I want to hear where you're going with this."

"Well, I'm just spitballing here, right?"

"I love when you talk in sports metaphors."

I had to laugh. "So, do you remember that the message board talked about RP? And of course we figured that had to refer to Rachel Powers, right?"

"I think that's a sure thing," he said, then picked up the platter of fish. "Hold that thought. I'm putting these on the grill."

He walked outside and Robbie toddled through the doggie door to join him because he recognized that grilling was a job for the men of the house.

A minute later, I grabbed my down vest off the back of the chair and joined them outside. The air was cold and clean and the fish on the grill smelled like heaven.

"I was about to come inside," Mac said.

"I felt like changing my environment, for a few minutes anyway."

"Well, have a seat. We can hold hands."

"What a lovely idea."

We sat on the chaise longue, held hands, and gazed up at the sky. It was early enough that there was still a touch of blue on the horizon and the stars were just beginning to show themselves.

"Nice," Mac said. "You've got a beautiful place here, Irish."

"I love it," I said with a sigh. "Wouldn't

want to live anywhere else."

"It's pretty special," he agreed.

We fell into a comfortable silence and just relaxed for a while. Less than ten minutes later, we brought the fish in and let it rest on the table.

I heated up the frying pan and added a touch of olive oil, then dropped the fresh spinach leaves into the pan and tossed them until they were all coated in oil. I turned off the heat and put the lid on to let the leaves steam. "This will be ready in a minute."

"Great."

Sure enough, a minute later, I tossed the steamed leaves with a touch of salt and pepper. Grabbing two plates from the cupboard, I filled them with salmon, rice, and spinach.

"This fish smells so good," he said. "Everything does."

"And it's all so healthy," I said.

"Probably a good idea after pigging out at the party last night."

Mac refilled our wineglasses and while we ate, we picked up our conversation where we left off.

"When last we met," Mac intoned, "we were talking about the message board referencing someone with the initials *RP.*"

"Right. We knew that it referred to Rachel

Powers." I held up my finger to make a point. "But the actual wording of the message said *Find RP.* So I'm going to make a giant leap and propose that what it really meant was that the group was supposed to find her in order to connect with her and possibly receive instructions from her."

He put his fork down and reached for his wineglass. "You're right. That's a giant leap right into covert operations land."

"Well, they don't have to be part of an international spy ring, but as far as the Gables is concerned, it feels really sneaky and secretive."

"And just what are these instructions she will be giving them?"

I shrugged, then gave him a shy smile. "I don't know. How about *Kill Dr. Fairchild?*"

"Definitely a leap of giant proportions," he said, laughing. "I like a woman with ambitious ideas."

"Well then, hang on to your hat. There's something else we should consider."

"I'm afraid to ask."

I grinned. "Don't be afraid. The thing is, there's someone else whose name has the initials *RP.*"

He thought about it and then stared at me. "Ricky Patterson. Coincidence?"

"I know what you think of coincidences."

"I don't like them."

"Me, either. It's all so weird, isn't it? Oh, and I have one more little twist to add."

"Yeah? Well, don't hold back. You're on a roll."

"The girl that Ricky Patterson thought was so pretty. The one who died. Do you remember her name?"

"Oh, man." He raked his fingers through his hair. "Oh, man. Regina Pomeroy. They called her Reggie." Mac pushed his chair back, rounded the table, and kissed me thoroughly. "You are awesome. This is freaking great." And he kissed me again.

I practically giggled, and then he slowed down and gave me a dozen kisses on my lips and all over my face and down my neck. The man truly did love to play the Scooby-Doo game.

"It might not mean anything," I warned, when I could manage to speak in full sentences again.

"True, and then, it might mean everything." He swung back around and sat down.

"So what do we do now?" I asked, and took a bite of fish. "By the way, you cooked this salmon perfectly. It's tender and flavorful. Really delicious."

"It's not bad," he admitted. "Everything is

329

good. I love spinach. Have I ever told you that?"

"You might've mentioned it."

"Okay, so what next?" He sipped his wine as he pondered our next step. "I think we need to ask Ricky about Reggie."

"Yes. And we need to ask him if he knew Rachel Powers back when he was living at the Gables."

He stared at the ceiling. "How old would you say Rachel is?"

"Maybe about forty," I guessed.

"That's close to Judson's age."

"What about Prudence?"

"Mid to late fifties, I'd guess." He took a forkful of rice, piled it onto a bit of salmon, and ate it in one bite. Then he stared at me. "I wonder if we could find an old obituary for Regina Pomeroy."

I shrugged. "Why not? She came from a very wealthy family. I'm pretty sure it was her father who single-handedly supported the Gables for the last ten years of its existence."

"I'll look into it," Mac said. "That's what I do all day. Research. I'm a mastermind at the Google."

"I'm so impressed." I took my last bite of spinach. "Think we should call Eric about this?"

330

He thought about it. "Not yet. It's all making perfect sense to us, but we might be completely delusional."

"That's entirely possible," I said. "But still."

"Still," he repeated. "I think we're getting close to finding some answers, but we're not there yet. So far, all we have are all these segmented parts and I'd rather not bring Eric into it until we're ready to show him the whole big picture."

"Okay, then let's round up more segments. I'd really love it if you can find that obituary for Reggie Pomeroy."

"And while I'm working on that, you're going to look into Rachel Powers's background."

"I can do that, even if I'm not a mastermind."

"Few are," he said with a grin. "And in our spare time, we should check out some of the other protesters. They all must have some connection with the Gables."

"Okay." I took the last bite of salmon and put down my fork. "How about if we clean up and then walk to the pub?"

"Sounds good," Mac said, picking up his empty plate. "It's time we had another chat with Ricky Patterson."

CHAPTER FOURTEEN

A half hour later Mac and I walked into the pub and found Eric and Chloe in a primo booth over by the window.

"Hey, you made it," Chloe said with a wide grin. "Kind of late, but whatever. You want to join us?"

"We've already had dinner," I explained. "We decided to take a walk and see if you were still here."

"We're still here." She patted the seat next to her. "Want to sit down?"

"Sure."

Mac and I exchanged a glance and he said, "You go ahead and sit down. I want to talk to someone over at the bar."

I looked over toward the bar and saw Ricky sitting alone on the far side. "Okay. I'll be here."

I smiled at Chloe and Eric and scooted into the booth. "How's it going, Chief?"

"Couldn't be better. You?"

"Fantastic."

"Great. Oh, hey," Eric said, gazing over my shoulder. "There's Tommy." He turned to Chloe. "Mind if I go talk to him for a minute or two?"

"Not at all," Chloe said, and the two of them kissed before he slid out of the booth and disappeared.

"I'm not going to turn around and look," I said, "but is what's-her-name here with Tommy?"

Chloe leaned over to see past me. "Oh, yeah. She's here."

I grimaced. "What a treat."

"Yeah." Chloe smiled tightly. "She's going to be trouble."

"For you? Why?"

"Well, Eric wanted them to join us for dinner tonight and I had to break the news that as far as I'm concerned, she is lower than the green jaws of hell."

I laughed. "What'd he say?"

"He carefully explained that Tommy is a good friend and a good cop. I said that I could tolerate Tommy, except to point out that he was a spineless worm who chose Whitney over my sister."

"Oh dear. What did Eric say to that?"

"He said, and I quote, 'But Whitney was pregnant. What else could Tommy do?'"

She shook her head, still stunned. "Men, I swear. So I just looked at him for a good long minute until he started to squirm."

"I refuse to believe that Chief Jensen has ever squirmed."

"Oh, he squirmed," she assured me. "So finally I explained that what came first was the cheating. So yes, I still blame Tommy for being a cheating jerk. And even though I can't blame Whitney entirely for getting pregnant, because, you know, it takes two to tango, I do blame her for being so evil and torturing Shannon over her relationship with Tommy."

"Wow." I nodded slowly. "What did Eric say?"

"He said — and again I quote, 'Okay, I get what you're saying.' "

"Did you say anything after that?"

She smiled. "I didn't have to."

"I love you, sis."

"I'm a lovable girl."

I laughed and squeezed her arm affectionately. "But look. If it's going to screw up your relationship with Eric, you go ahead and hang out with them. I won't give you too much grief."

"Seriously?" She took a deep breath. "From the minute Whitney Reid moved here she looked down her nose at us. She called me a townie from day one. She made your life a living hell. She still does. I will never 'hang out' with her, no matter what Eric wants."

I took a deep breath. "You are the absolute best."

"I know." She smiled. "But here's the thing. As soon as we got our table here and sat down, she came over and started flirting with Eric. Her husband's boss! While I'm sitting here. The woman is just a horrible human being."

"What did Eric do?"

"Since we had already had our conversation about Whitney, he looked her in the eye and said, 'I'm trying to enjoy a quiet meal with Chloe.' And then he turned away from her and gazed adoringly into my eyes."

"Aww." I pressed my hand to my heart. "He's a sweetheart. What did Whitney do?"

"She walked away, strutting like a stripper. You know what I mean. It was sad."

"She defines the word *tacky.*"

"I wanted to smack her. I probably will at some point," Chloe admitted. "She's just so gross and obvious about it. Frankly, I don't know what sweet Tommy ever saw in her."

"She's desperate," I said with a shrug. "She's always been desperate. That's why she glommed onto Tommy and now it's worse. She's lost all her money and she's trying to keep it a secret. Basically, all she has left is her looks."

"Not for long if she keeps wearing all that pancake makeup. Stuff clogs your pores and ruins your skin."

"Please don't tell her."

She laughed. "What makes you think she would listen to me?"

"Oh, you're right. She wouldn't listen to you." I leaned in close. "You're just a townie."

She laughed. "God, I hated that."

"I know. I did, too."

"But you stayed."

"I was always happy here. Except for one long year of misery, after Tommy pulled that number with Whitney. That was not a happy time." I shrugged again. "Never mind. It's all better now."

Chloe leaned over to get another look. "Why does she dress like a Las Vegas show-girl? No offense to showgirls everywhere, but the sequins? Ay caramba."

I had to laugh at that. When we were growing up, our dad used to say it whenever we got into trouble. I started to turn around, then stopped. "Don't tell me. She's wearing the sequin top."

"Yeah. And the pleather pants."

336

"What a townie," I muttered.

Chloe threw back her head and laughed. "Such an insult!"

"Sorry." I waved away the bad vibes. "Let's change the subject."

"Please." She smirked. "Even though that was kind of fun."

I laughed. "Okay." Grateful to not have to think about Whitney, I asked, "How's it going at Eric's house? Are you happy? Having fun?"

"I'm so happy," she said softly. "We're having a blast. Have you seen his house?"

"Yeah, he bought the old Merrick place and fixed it up really nicely."

"It's beautiful. He's got the prettiest little garden and we sit out there and have our morning coffee."

I squeezed her hand. "I'm so happy for you."

"I'm happy, too. Of course, Eric's bummed that he caught a murder case while I'm here. But I'm dating a cop. It comes with the territory. Besides, I should be used to it, right?"

"Yeah, you should." The last time Chloe visited, there was a murder case and she was not only the main suspect, but also the potential victim of a vicious killer.

"Okay, tricky question," I said. "Do you

337

think you'll marry him?"

"Oh, absolutely."

My eyes widened. "Really?"

She glared at me. "But not if you cry."

I sniffled, but managed to hold back the tears. Still, I was so happy at the thought of Chloe maybe moving back to town at some point. She could do her show from here as easily as Hollywood. "It's not just about your situation. I've been doing that a lot lately."

"Why?"

"This job at the Gables isn't helping with my moods. It's so weird to be working in that place with all those sad and creepy vibes. So much emotional baggage was left behind. I know that sounds stupid."

"No. I get it."

"And somehow I keep hurting myself. Almost fell off a ladder, then got shoved into the pit of despair and hit my head." I absently touched my cheek. "Pain is never a good thing."

"No, it's not. You have to stop that."

I smiled. "I'll do my best."

"So how's Mac?" she asked, sitting back against the booth.

"He's wonderful."

"Well, then, let me return the favor and ask if you think you'll marry him."

I couldn't say anything for a few excruciating seconds.

"Earth to Shannon, what's going on?"

"I . . . I don't know."

"You don't know?" She turned in the booth and looked directly at me. "Shannon, you guys have been together for like, two years, right? What's the deal?"

I was beginning to feel a touch of déjà vu. Hadn't I had almost the same conversation with Jane just last week? I couldn't get into it again, even with my own darling sister. "Let's just say I love him and we're happy. And we'll see what comes next."

Luckily I was saved by Eric's return.

"We'll talk later," Chloe murmured.

Knowing my sister, I was sure she wouldn't forget about this. And so I would absolutely have to ask Mac about the future and what our plans would be, just as soon as we pinned down a vicious killer.

"I'd better go find Mac," I said.

Chloe squeezed my hand. "I love you, sis."

"I love you back." I turned around to look for Mac.

"He's over on the other side of the bar," Eric said, pointing. "Talking to the protester we interrogated the other day."

"Thanks, Eric." But he had an expectant look on his face so I said, "Yeah, Ricky

Patterson. I met him in the parking lot earlier today and we talked for a few minutes. Then Mac joined in."

Eric's eyes narrowed in on me. "Something going on there, Shannon?"

"Nothing's going on. He's turning out to be a really nice guy." I sighed a little. "He's got a few problems, but he's not dangerous. I think."

He sighed. "Just . . . be careful there."

I flashed him a big smile. "I will. Thanks, Eric."

"Oh, and we'll be finished working in the Gables and have it opened up for you on Monday."

"That's great! Thanks, Chief." I winked at Chloe. "See you later, sis."

She blew me a kiss. I reached out and caught it in my hand and grinned all the way over to the bar. I managed to avoid coming face-to-face with the dreaded Whitney, so it was a win-win all the way around.

As I walked up to Mac, I heard him say to Ricky, "Are you sure we can't give you a ride home?"

"No, I'm good, man. I'm going to finish my drink. Besides, it's only three blocks and I like to walk." He glanced beyond Mac's shoulder. "Hey. Hi, Shannon."

"Hi, Ricky."

"Okay, man," Mac said. "Be careful. See you around." The two men went through an elaborate handshaking-fist-bump routine before Mac said good night and grabbed my hand. We both waved to Chloe and Eric and then walked out of the pub.

"Let's go get my car," he said immediately, and walked quickly across the street.

As we headed toward my house on Blueberry Lane a half block away, I asked, "What's up? What did he tell you?"

"I'll tell you the gist of it, but first I want to get my car and bring it over here. We're going to follow him home."

"You think he's in trouble?"

"My gut says yes." He tucked my arm through his and we turned left onto Blueberry. "Ricky told me that he was walking here earlier and as he crossed the street right in front of the pub, he heard a screech of tires. He ran for the sidewalk and barely missed getting hit by a car. He brushed it off as an accident."

"If he really believed it was an accident, he wouldn't have bothered telling you about it."

He smiled down at me. "You're pretty smart."

I gave a short laugh. "Gee, thanks. You're not bad yourself."

"I'm a mastermind, remember?"

I shook my head, laughing. We passed another couple of houses before we crossed the street to my house. "You know, maybe we should've told Eric about Ricky's situation while we were in there."

"I thought about it," he said. "But frankly, I didn't want Ricky to see me talking to the chief of police. He might think I was betraying his trust."

"That would be stupid of him, and yet I get your point."

"So we'll follow him tonight, make sure he gets into his house safely, and then Monday . . ."

"Monday?" I prompted.

His smile lit up his face. "There's a shortcut into the Baths, and he's going to show it to us."

"Oh my God, are you kidding? That's super cool!" I squeezed his arm.

"Thought you might say that."

But a second later, I winced. "It's cool and yet really creepy at the same time."

He chuckled. "Thought you'd say that, too."

"Both can be true," I insisted as I sat down in his car. "Something tells me that the Baths were one more way for Dr. Fairchild's sadistic side to show itself. It was a way of hurting people."

"I happen to agree with you," he murmured, slamming the car door. "Even if it was accepted practice back then, I'll bet she enjoyed herself a little too much, forcing people to soak in that icy water."

"But still, I think it's important that we see the Baths. Be a witness, you know? And then tear them down, destroy them, and replace them with something beautiful, as Jane would say."

"That's a really good plan." He leaned over and kissed me, then started the engine.

A minute later, Mac found a parking place a few cars down from the pub, facing the front door. From here, we would be able to see whenever Ricky left.

We weren't parked for more than five minutes when I saw Dr. Fairchild stroll past the pub with Prudence Baxter.

"Do you see what I see?"

"Yeah. They've stopped to look in the window."

"Think they're looking for Ricky?"

"Yes." Mac practically snarled the word.

After another minute, the two women walked away, heading toward the pier.

"That's just weird," I muttered.

"Yeah. They've got something going on."

After another twenty minutes, we saw

343

Ricky walking out of the pub. He looked both ways before he stepped off the sidewalk.

"Guess he learned his lesson," Mac murmured.

Ricky walked through the neighborhood I'd always lived in, past modest Victorian cottages and the occasional "Grand Dame" mansion. He passed the little group of shops — the convenience store that still carried comic books and an amazing selection of penny candies; the barbershop my father still goes to; my dry cleaners; and our favorite Chinese restaurant — a block from the high school. Kids could stock up on candy or get a haircut after school and their moms would pick them up and then stop for takeout.

I noticed that at each corner Ricky would again look both ways before he took a step into the street. At the third corner he turned left and walked one more block.

Mac pulled into an empty space and we watched Ricky climb the stairs to a second-floor apartment across from my old high school. The building was typical of others around town: two stories, four units, with an indoor staircase between.

Would someone be lying in wait for him at the top of the stairs? I wondered and worried for a full minute before a light finally went on upstairs. And still we waited another few minutes.

"I think it's safe to leave." Mac pulled out his phone and dialed a number, then pressed the speaker. "But it doesn't hurt to check, just in case."

"Hello?"

"Hey, Ricky," Mac said. "It's Mac. Just checking that you got home safely."

"Aw, thanks man. I'm good. Safe and sound. But it's weird not to have Jud here."

"I'm sorry, man," Mac said. "But I'm glad you're safe. So listen, I heard from Chief Jensen that the Gables will be back open on Monday, so I'll give you a call and we can figure out where to meet and do that thing we talked about."

"You got it. Thanks, Mac."

"No problem. Call me anytime. And have a good weekend."

As we drove away, I looked at Mac. We could do nothing about the unanswered mysteries at the Gables but wait until Monday.

On Friday morning, I had a meeting with Wade and Carla to look back over the week and reconfigure our schedules and our crew. We also assigned some of our guys to help

345

out at three of our other construction sites around town. Then I got in my truck and drove around myself, just to make sure my crews had everything they needed. That night Mac and I walked up to the town square and stopped in at some of our favorite places. It was always good to get out and see people. At the bookstore, we chatted with Lizzie and Hal and she showed us the bizarre handmade book that Dr. Fairchild had foisted on her. Sure enough, it was stapled together with the title printed on a piece of cardboard. We walked out shaking our heads.

When we strolled into the Crafts and Quilts shop, my friend Marigold ran over and grabbed my hand. "I'm so happy to see you. I wanted to show you what a dear old friend sent me from back east."

"Okay."

"It's in the back." Mac and I followed her to a well-lit office where she opened a box and took out a large piece of folded cloth. "This is an exceptional example of a quilt made by a woman who was a patient in one of the old asylums back in the Victorian age. I don't want to open it all the way, but you can see the quality."

"Oh wow. It's beautiful, Marigold."

"Do you think Jane would want to hang it

on a wall in her new hotel?"

"Are you kidding? I think she would be thrilled." I opened up one part of a side panel. "Oh, these little figures are so charming."

"There are only a few of these types of quilts around today," she explained. "The original asylum quilt is one of a kind and considered priceless. But apparently it became quite common for women to gather for a quilting bee when they were stuck in these asylums for years at a time."

"That's one way to pass the time," I murmured.

"Yes." She held up a small section of the quilt. "These figures depict the dozens of friends and nurses and cooks and helpers the women got to know while they were patients, along with the plants and flowers and trees and little animals they saw every day."

"It's a piece of art," Mac said. "It probably belongs in a museum."

"Probably," Marigold said with a smile, "but I would love to have Jane hang it, if she wants to."

"You know she will," I assured her.

We talked for a few more minutes and then Mac and I left to have dinner at Bella Rossa, my uncle Pete's Italian restaurant on the square.

And after a craze-filled week, we were perfectly happy to go to bed early that night.

Saturday morning I spent two hours delving into the world of Rachel Powers and the Gables Development Company. I figured there had to be a parent company that owned the Gables Development Company, but I couldn't find anything about it online. And when I called the company's number I got a recording.

"Because it's Saturday, knucklehead," I muttered.

In the meantime, I checked out the company website. It was slick and professional with beautifully detailed sketches and photographs of the property and the buildings. It featured a lot of information, history, and fun facts about the Gables.

I learned that the company also planned a second Gables phase during which they would begin to renovate the three buildings at the opposite end from Jane's hotel — Buildings Two, Three, and Four. They intended to build twenty luxury condominiums for those who could afford it.

I had to shake my head at the idea of luxury condos. But why not? After all, we were going to transform this end of the

348

Gables into a five-star hotel. Life was funny, for sure.

Rachel's biography on the website was extensive and impressive; she had attended several private schools in the San Francisco area and one private day school outside Mendocino. She went to Stanford University and Yale Law School, where she graduated summa cum laude and magna cum laude, respectively. She belonged to several professional societies and was a member of numerous business organizations. Her family still lived in Mendocino.

It listed her skills, qualities, and interests: *Self-starter; highly motivated; skilled negotiator. Rachel enjoys tennis, golf, and surfing. She performs in her local theater, plays piano and guitar, and sings in her church choir.*

The woman was a serious overachiever and clearly brilliant. And beautiful, with great taste in clothes. With all of us working at the Gables for the next year, I didn't see why we couldn't be friendly. I just hoped she wasn't quite as big a drama queen as Mac seemed to think she was.

Mac showed up Saturday afternoon and we took a walk over to the Lighthouse Pier, where we nibbled on fried clams at one of our favorite food stands. We left the pier and strolled along the boardwalk, holding hands and window shopping. Then we trudged through the wide stretch of clean white sand to the water's edge, where we sat and skimmed small stones along the calm surface of the water. It was silly and fun and we deliberately avoided talking about anything serious like murder and torture and all that awful stuff.

It would all be there waiting for me when I went back to work on Monday. And with that in mind, I asked Mac to check in on Ricky. He made the call and reported that Ricky was fine, to my relief. Maybe I was being super paranoid, but who could blame me after discovering the body of his best friend?

Back at the house, Mac helped me gather veggies from my garden for a dinner salad and then I started a big batch of tomato sauce for pasta.

Mac sat at the kitchen table with his laptop and read through my notes and the copies I had made of Rachel's résumé, along with some of the obscure historical facts about the Gables that despite my meticulous research on the place, I had never heard of before that morning.

With Mac working nearby and me prepping dinner, it felt so ridiculously comfortable and homey that I wanted to keep the picture of it in my mind forever. I thought it might be the perfect time to bring up my vague question about our future, but would I be rocking the boat? Spoiling the comfy vibe? And just as I was about to bite the bullet and bring up the subject, Mac came over, put his arm around my waist, and leaned over to test the pasta sauce. I was pitifully grateful for the distraction.

"That's fantastic," he said, then gave me a kiss on the cheek and went back to his computer. "So I tracked down Regina Pomeroy's obituary."

"Did you? That's great. Where did you find it?" I waved the question away. "Never mind, Google mastermind. So what does it say?"

"Among other things, it says that Regina graduated from the Wildwood Day School."

"That sounds vaguely familiar."

He grinned. "That's because it's the same private day school outside Mendocino that Rachel Powers graduated from."

"What are the chances?" I turned the burner down and put a lid over the sauce. I walked over and sat down next to Mac. "What else did you find?"

"I was able to find Regina's obituary right away. Her family's local mortuary in Mendocino published it, even though she didn't die in the city."

"No, she died at the Gables," I said.

"That's right. Also, apparently the news of her death wasn't disclosed to the family for nearly two weeks."

My jaw dropped, but as I thought about it, I said, "I'm shocked, but not surprised. Fairchild tried to cover it up."

"Probably to give herself time to come up with a plausible alternate reason for her death."

"And more important, to keep the funds coming in for as long as possible. Because you know that as soon as Fairchild told the family about Reggie's death, her father's checks would stop coming in." I let that sink in. "Did they publish her photograph with the obituary?"

"They might've published it in a newsletter or something," he said, flipping through pages. "But it hasn't shown up online. Not even on Google Images."

"I would really love to see a picture of her. We might be able to tell if she's related to Rachel."

Mac looked me in the eye. "Or Ricky."

"Oh my God." I cringed at the thought. "If she was related to Ricky, it would mean she's Dr. Fairchild's daughter."

We paused a minute to digest that creepy

possibility. Because it would also mean that the doctor had killed her own daughter. But we were getting ahead of ourselves.

"Let's take it one step at a time," Mac said. "I've got one more website to try." He tapped at the keyboard with lightning-fast fingers, then murmured, "Here we go."

"Where are we?"

He grinned at me, but didn't answer. Just went back to staring at the screen. There was more tapping, and then he groaned.

"What?"

"They want my e-mail address." He shrugged. "Oh well, I'll never be lonely. This website will hound me till I'm dead. Fine, I'll just enter a brand-new e-mail address so I'll know it's from them whenever they send me something." He continued tapping keys and a minute later, he stopped. But the muttering continued as he scrolled. "Okay. Okay. Whatever."

I smiled. "Where are you?"

He looked up at me. "I think I've found the answer to one of our questions."

"Which answer? Which question? How'd you find it?"

"Hang on." He tapped the keyboard a few more times. "Okay, I finally found this high school yearbook website. You can look up any school, any year, and see every page of the yearbook for that year along with photos of all the students."

I squeezed his arm. "That was brilliant, Mac."

He tapped his head. "Mastermind."

I had to smile. He looked so boyish and eager and excited.

"But like I said, the trade-off is that they'll be sending me junk e-mail until I'm dead. But okay," he continued, "you wondered if Rachel had a deeper connection to the Gables."

"Right." I watched his expression. "So? Did you find a connection?"

"That would be yes."

"Really?"

He turned the computer around to show me the photo of a pretty, teenaged girl with a bright smile and a blond Farrah Fawcett hairstyle.

"Oh, it's Rachel." I smiled. "Gosh, she's so young."

"Yes, she is," he said. "Except this isn't Rachel. It's Regina Pomeroy."

My eyes boggled and I had to take a closer look at the photograph. Then I stared back at Mac. "Rachel and Regina look like exactly the same person."

"But they're not the same person," Mac said. "They're twin sisters."

Chapter Fifteen

We tossed around a dozen different scenarios having to do with the Gables and murder and connections and twins. We sat down to enjoy an incredible dinner of spaghetti and meatballs and a fabulous Chianti and tried to talk about happy things, but that didn't work. We were still tossing around possibilities and ideas and theories until midnight when we were finally able to fall asleep.

Mac and I woke up Sunday morning knowing there was nothing we could do about that thunderbolt of information we'd collected but simply wait until Monday. It wasn't easy. I could hardly wait until we could get back into the Gables.

Mac tried calling Rachel to set up a meeting, but the call went straight to her voice mail. He frowned when he ended the call. "I have no other way to get in touch with her."

"Do you think she's safe?"

"I hope so."

I let out a pensive breath. "I'm going to go with the theory that she's fine and dandy but simply isn't answering her telephone on a Sunday morning."

"Okay, we'll go with that," Mac decided. "And Ricky's doing fine, too. I talked to him a little while ago when you were on the phone with Chloe."

"I'm glad you called him." I folded up the last of the kitchen towels from the load of laundry I'd done. "So we're free to let it all go for now. You ready?"

"Absolutely," he said. "I can't wait."

Ten minutes later we were in Mac's car and he was starting the engine. "I'm looking forward to the barrel tasting."

I grinned at him. "It's almost as fun as solving a murder."

"Oh, for sure."

We drove south and then east for almost an hour until we reached the Bella Rossa Winery. In Italian, the words meant *beautiful redhead*. Uncle Pete had named the winery for me and Chloe when we were two little red-haired girls. But now that Chloe was a blonde, I teased her that the name was all about me.

It wouldn't be wrong to say that the Anderson Valley was hard to find. You definitely had to want to go there because they didn't make it easy. It was miles away from both the coast highway and the more heavily traveled Highway 101. And while the other more popular wine country regions like Napa and Sonoma were mere minutes from anywhere in the Bay Area, the Anderson Valley was downright obscure. It could be reached by way of a narrow, often treacherous, winding two-lane highway that meandered through forests and hills. Once you arrived, though, it was a little piece of heaven. Rustic and rural, it still had that small-town charm that the other more populated regions had lost.

Uncle Pete's winery had expanded from the one-room shack of a tasting room to a gorgeous modern glass-walled building that offered stunning views of the vineyards and hills beyond.

The afternoon air was cold and clear, with an unobstructed view of the big blue sky above and the surrounding evergreen-clad mountains in the distance.

For the barrel tasting, we were a small party of seven. Mac and I, Chloe and Eric, my father, Uncle Pete, and Belinda McCoy, his winemaker and Dad's girlfriend.

Regular visitors were being taken care of by two of Uncle Pete's best wine tasting

357

helpers. That way, he and Belinda could join us in the barrel room.

The wines were wonderful and Belinda gave us all the most elaborate details of each wine and how it came to taste the way it did. She definitely proved that she knew what she was talking about when it came to wines. And since I had learned that she had worked for several years at Château Margaux in the Bordeaux region of France, I never doubted her.

Dad and Uncle Pete had taken Eric and Mac out to the vineyard to show off their newest plantings, so that left Belinda to entertain Chloe and me.

Belinda inserted the tube-shaped glass tool — otherwise known as a "wine thief" — into the barrel and siphoned out a generous serving of the delightful Bordeaux-inspired Cabernet Sauvignon she had been experimenting with since first coming to work at Uncle Pete's winery. She poured the dark liquid into Chloe's glass. Then she did the same for me.

"Let me know what you think."

We both tasted and let out little moans of joy. "It's wonderful," I said.

"You're a genius," Chloe effused, and took another sip.

"Thank you. So Chloe, are you planning

to move back here and live with Eric?"

Chloe began to choke and I slapped her back, laughing the whole time. When she could catch her breath, she said, "How much did my father pay you to ask me that?"

Belinda laughed. "Well, it was more like a bet. He bet me I wouldn't be able to get an answer out of you and I told him I would."

"How much?" I asked.

"One hundred dollars."

Chloe gave a little snort. "Easiest hundred you'll ever make. The answer is yes, I'll still work on my show, but I'll live here and commute. Our shooting schedule is conducive to that plan since our director lives in Taos and one of the producers commutes from Bend, Oregon."

"Well, that's handy."

"It is." Chloe took another sip of the Cabernet. "I'll be shipping my things over the next few months, and then we'll pick a weekend and Eric will fly down and drive with me back up the coast."

I grabbed my sister in a hug. "I'm so happy." But seconds later, I glared at her. "Why are you just telling me this?"

"Calm down," she said, laughing. "I didn't tell you before because you hit your head on a brick."

"That's no excuse," I grumbled. "And this is the second time I've been the last to know about someone's big relationship news."

"And also," Chloe continued undeterred. "Because Eric and I only worked out the details last night."

I narrowed my eyes. "Are you telling me the truth?"

She laughed again. "Yes."

"Okay." Then I pulled her in for another hug. "I'm really happy for you."

"I'm happy, too," Belinda said, and hugged us both. "And a hundred dollars richer."

We all laughed, and Belinda said, "I don't know why your father didn't just ask you himself."

Chloe grinned. "Because he's shy, and because I probably wouldn't have told him as much as I'm telling you."

"It's a Dad thing," I explained, grinning.

"What's a Dad thing?" my father asked as he strolled into the barrel room followed by Uncle Pete, Eric, and Mac.

"Oh, it's just girl talk," Chloe said. "But you owe Belinda one hundred dollars."

He blinked, then looked at Belinda, who just beamed at him. Then he looked at Chloe and I watched his eyes fill with tears. "My girl's coming home?"

"Yes, Daddy."

They threw their arms around each other while I tried to wipe away my own tears. Mac moved over and slipped his arm around my waist. "You'll tell me all about it on the way home?"

"Yes," I said, sniffling, but smiling.

A few minutes later, after we had all laughed away our tears and had another taste of a new Pinot Noir, Dad cornered me. "Walk with me."

"Okay."

He walked toward the open doorway and we stood on the terrace looking over the vineyards. "I've been wanting to talk to you ever since your party the other night."

"What's up?" I asked. His tone was more somber than it should've been. "Is something wrong?"

"I realize I should've said something to you a long time ago, but it never seemed like the right time." He gritted his teeth and blew out a breath.

I was starting to worry. He had been so happy a minute ago and now . . . "Dad, what is it?"

"It's about that place. The Gables."

"Oh." I smiled. "You should come up and visit the site, see what Jane's planning to do. You'll be impressed. It's going to be awesome, Dad."

"I know it will be. And I'll get up there one of these days."

"Good."

He stared out at the rows of grapevines. "Do you remember visiting the Gables with Jane when you were young?"

"Sure. Jane used to go every week with Jesse, but I only went up there three times. And then I didn't go anymore." I frowned, then shrugged. "I don't think I did anything wrong. I just figured it got too hard for Jesse to take both of us along for a visit. Things could get pretty emotional, you know?"

"Yeah, I know." He took a slow sip of his wine. "And you didn't do anything wrong. Once Grace got better and she was able to come back home, she drove over to visit me."

"That's right. You and Mom were friends with her."

He smiled at the memory. "Grace and your mother were very good friends. But this visit was long after your mother passed away."

Just hearing him say those words made me reach out and grab his hand. I had to work out the timeline in my head. My mother, Ella, died when I was ten and by the time Grace Hennessey was being treated at the Gables, I was closer to fourteen.

"I recall us sitting on the patio," Dad continued. "Jesse was there, too. And Grace looked great. She said she felt healthy and ready to get back to living. But a few minutes later she confessed that she knew she would end up back at the Gables one of these days." Dad gazed out at the hillside. "She was so much more fragile than we ever knew."

"When I was really young I thought she was a fairy princess. So ethereal and yeah, fragile."

"Yes." He reached for my hand. "She told me and Jesse that day that she didn't want you to visit her anymore."

In that moment, I knew what it meant to feel my heart drop. I gasped. I felt weak and had to press my hand to my chest. "Dad. Why?"

"She wouldn't tell me why exactly," he said, "but it wasn't about you, sweetheart. She was worried about something. She said that something was wrong at the Gables. One of the patients had died while she was there and nobody would talk about what happened. But she knew that the people in charge were bad. She used those words. 'They're bad.' "

"What did Jesse say?"

"He told her flat-out, he hoped she'd never have to go back, but if she did, he wouldn't stay away and he wouldn't keep Jane from visiting her."

"She went back, Dad," I said, still rubbing my chest, still hurting for Grace. And Jane, too. "If she knew something was wrong, why did she keep going back?"

"She was so ill during those years," he said. "Her nerves were so delicate. Sometimes I wondered if she might literally shatter from the internal chaos she was dealing with."

Dad's tone made it sound like everyone had suffered along with her. Of course they would. She had friends and family who loved her. They would feel her pain. "But ultimately she came home for good and never went back," I said. "It was great, especially for Jane. But how was she able to finally make it work?"

"Frankly, the drugs got better. Her doctors were getting a lot better at regulating her medications. I remember her telling us that she felt normal again." He chuckled. "And she always used to laugh at that word, *normal.* But she was so much better. Healthy again. Able to live a good life."

"I'm so glad."

"Yeah." He chuckled. "Way back, when

your mom was still with us, she and Grace were very close. Grace was a crackerjack. She threw wonderful parties and she loved to go sailing. She and your mother used to play baseball together. Do you remember?"

"I do," I said, grinning. "I remember you and Mom taking us to the park and I sat in the bleachers with Jane and Chloe and we had hot dogs. And you guys all played baseball and drank beer. I mostly remember seeing you laugh."

He grinned. "We all laughed a lot back then."

"I just remember being happy and having fun all the time." I shook my head. "God, I was so young. Just a kid. That was a long time ago."

He wrapped his arms around me and hugged me tight.

My mom died a few years after that, I thought. And then Jane's mom got sick. And everything changed. I took another breath, let it out in a huff, and reached for his hand. "I'm back to being happy, Dad. I even manage to have fun most of the time."

Belinda walked out to the terrace then and smiled at both of us.

"So do I, sweetheart," Dad said, reaching for Belinda. "So do I."

■ ■ ■ ■

Once we finally finished the barrel tasting, we were in serious need of a long walk through the vineyard and around the property. When we got back, the kitchen staff had fixed a beautiful late-afternoon lunch for us. Several pasta salads, a fresh green salad, a charcuterie platter, wonderful cheeses, and lots of chunky breads.

"I need to take another walk and then a nap," Chloe said, holding her stomach.

"This was so wonderful," I said, giving Belinda a big hug. With lots of hugs and promises of more get-togethers while Chloe was in town, we finally took off for home.

On the drive home, I told Mac everything my father and I had talked about.

"So Grace Hennessey knew something was wrong up there," he said. "Wow."

"Oh, yeah, she did. I know there were plenty of patients who died while they were at the Gables, but I still feel like she might've known this girl, Regina, who died. Grace would've been much older, but the timing does work."

"It's possible. But look, even if she didn't know Regina, she knew that something was rotten up there."

It was dark when we arrived back in Lighthouse Cove. Mac walked Robbie around the block while I refreshed the water bowls and got things ready to go back to work tomorrow. Mac and I talked a bit of strategy about how to approach Rachel with what we had found out yesterday through the obituaries and the high school yearbook page. Mac gave Ricky a call to make sure he was still safe and willing to meet us the next morning in front of Building Seven.

By ten o'clock we were ready for bed and I was sound asleep within minutes.

Monday arrived and I had to struggle to get out of bed. But once Mac reminded me of what the day might bring, I jumped into action and hurried off to take a shower, get dressed, and feed the pets. Downstairs, Mac made coffee and scrambled eggs and I took care of toasting two English muffins.

We took our separate cars since Mac intended to go home and get some writing done, once we had explored the Baths with Ricky. He also hoped to find Rachel and quiz her about Regina Pomeroy.

"I hope she can give us some answers to our questions," I said, as I locked the kitchen door and headed for the back gate.

"I'd just like to find out who she is exactly."

"Yeah, that would be nice," I said. "And she must have some clue about Dr. Fairchild. Oh, and maybe she knows more about the protesters than she's let on. I'm still wondering if more of them belong on our suspect list."

Mac just grinned. "See you there," he said, and gave me a kiss before climbing into his SUV and pulling out of the driveway.

I followed him up to the Gables and parked my truck next to his car.

I tucked my small purse under the driver's seat, then locked my door and set the alarm. I buckled my tool belt around my waist and slipped the car keys into one of the pockets. Then I hefted my toolbox out of my truck. "Let's go find Ricky."

The excitement I'd felt earlier faded and I had a deep sense of foreboding as we rounded the building and walked toward the front entry. But Ricky was standing there waiting for us and I was able to let go of the breath I was holding. At least he was safe.

We walked inside and down the hall. Along the way I greeted the few guys that were already at work this early. We made it through the passageway under the stairs and into the back hallway. The remnants of the brick wall remained the same. The broken door still lay against the wall of the ante-chamber. I couldn't look beyond there without picturing Judson Killian's body on the floor.

"Where are we going?" I asked.

Ricky pointed. "It's at the end of the hall."

I glanced at Mac. We had never made it this far down the hall so I had no idea where we would end up.

Ricky stopped and turned to a door on the right and I was certain I'd never noticed it before. It was shorter than the regular doors that lined the left side of the hall.

"Here we go." He pulled the door open to reveal an old stone staircase that spiraled down, well below the first floor. The walls and steps appeared to have been white-washed sometime in the last hundred years or so.

No wonder the door was different. It opened into another odd passageway, this one subterranean.

"I forgot there was a basement level." I hadn't paid much attention to it on the blueprints because Jane didn't plan to access it for the hotel. At least, not right away. She thought she might eventually use it for storage.

"Yeah, there's a bunch of stuff down here," Ricky said. "And there's also an underground route to get to the other buildings. It was used in case it was raining a lot."

Or in case someone wanted to sneak out of here and escape, I thought.

We started down the stairs. I was happy to cling to the iron railing that was attached to the outer wall, because the heavy stone stairs were very narrow and so steep that I imagined people fell in here all the time.

"It's similar to the circular stairway inside the old lighthouse," Mac murmured.

I nodded. "It was probably built around the same time."

We finally reached the bottom of the stairs and ended up in a long, tiled room that had clearly been an old bathroom. There were gated windows high up on the walls so there was plenty of light coming in. We could see everything — and what we saw made me want to strangle someone. How could they allow people to use these horrible facilities? I wondered.

The filthy, stained tiles were the least of the problems. I figured that some of that filth could be attributed to time and neglect. Along one wall was a long row of toilets. I counted twelve altogether. I couldn't call them stalls because there was no wall or door for privacy. Each toilet was separated by a thin, three-foot-high partition, but without a door. Everyone was forced to take care of their personal business in front of anyone who walked by.

It infuriated me at first, but I began to realize that this lack of privacy might've been for the patients' own protection. Still, I couldn't believe that the great Dr. Jones would've approved of this callous way of treating the most vulnerable members of our society.

Hey, at least build that partition a little higher, I thought.

"Did everyone use this bathroom area?" I asked Ricky.

"Anyone who came down here did. Yeah. Pretty much."

And now I had to wonder why anyone would come down here. But I guessed we were about to find out.

"It's over here," Ricky said when he reached the end of the room. "This way."

"It looks like a cupboard," I said, looking at the flimsy wooden door with the simple slide barrel bolt holding it closed.

He grinned. "Yeah. Cleverly disguised. They always had a nurse or someone standing here, so you couldn't just walk in without supervision. And you definitely couldn't walk *out,* either."

I paused, not sure I was ready for the next step.

Ricky slid the bolt out of its case, then jiggled the door handle. It opened and Ricky said, "After you."

I could feel and smell the humidity hanging in the thick air.

"Leave the door open," I said, looking at Mac.

He understood immediately. The last thing we wanted was to get stuck inside the Baths. He walked back to the other end of the long room and grabbed a chunk of broken plaster. Returning to the door, he set it on the floor. "There. Door stopper."

I sighed. "Thank you."

Before we walked in, I put my hand on Ricky's shoulder. "Ricky, are you going to be okay in there?"

I didn't want this to trigger any unpleasant memories for him.

"Sure, I'm cool. Let's go."

I'm glad he was cool because I was a little freaked-out over the whole situation. But I sucked it up and walked into another long narrow room. It was pitch-black.

"Can't see anything," I said. But I could

feel the chilly dampness. Pulling my mini-flashlight from my tool belt, I turned it on. I could vaguely make out a row of large bathtubs. They were old and grimy and rusted. Each tub was covered completely by a thick canvas cloth that appeared to be held in place by straps that wrapped around the bottom of the tub. The cloths were equally grimy with unspeakable stains all over them.

"What is that canvas cloth for?" I had a feeling I knew, but I had to ask.

"It keeps people from climbing out of the tubs. They've also got straps so you're completely trapped inside for as long as they want you to stay."

There was a good-sized hole on one end of each cloth. "And this big hole?" Again, I didn't want to ask, but had to know.

"Your head sticks out there so you can breathe," he said easily. "There's an extra strap that goes around your neck to hold your head up so you don't sink down and drown."

"Jeez Louise," I whispered.

I could hear the sound of running water but couldn't see well enough to tell where it was coming from.

"Do you hear that?"

"Is there another facility nearby that's using water?" Mac asked.

"It's something you hear," Ricky said with a shrug, then glanced around, frowning. "But these pipes were all replaced by the development company so they're usually pretty quiet. I'm not sure where that sound's coming from."

We continued to walk past the next tub and I shined the flashlight beam on each of them as we passed.

"Wait, what's that?" Ricky said, pointing farther down the row. "What the hell?"

"I can't see," I said, in spite of my flashlight beam.

He walked more quickly as he moved toward the far wall.

"Ricky, wait!" Mac shouted.

"Oh no! Oh God." He sounded like a panic-stricken kid. "I gotta get out of here."

"I was afraid of this," I said, grabbing Mac's arm. "He's freaking out."

I aimed the flashlight at Ricky, who was frozen on the spot, pointing and staring at the last bathtub.

"What is it?" Mac demanded, and walked faster. Water was making it slippery as we got closer to the far end.

And now I could make out a thick mane of pale hair draping out from the large hole in the canvas.

"Oh my God. Is it . . . is that Rachel?"

Ricky cried out. "No! It's . . . it's my mother." Then he whipped around and ran all the way back to the door we'd come in through.

"It's Dr. Fairchild," Mac muttered. He lifted up a heavy strand of wet platinum hair to find a pulse point in her neck. "She's dead."

CHAPTER SIXTEEN

I grabbed Mac's hand. "We have to call Eric."

"Okay. But let's get out of here first."

"Oh, definitely." No way did I want to be anywhere near the body of Dr. Fairchild. I hadn't liked the woman when she was alive and I really didn't want to spend time with her dead.

We moved carefully through the water that had dripped out of Fairchild's bathtub and onto the floor, and made it to the door at the end of the room through which Ricky had disappeared.

I was still shivering, but I would survive. It had to have been a lot worse — and a lot colder — for the poor folks who had been forced by Fairchild to sit in icy water for hours.

I would never say it out loud, but in my heart I wondered if Dr. Fairchild didn't end up getting the exact proper punishment for her crimes.

I knew Eric would disagree. Murder could never be a suitable alternative for justice. And he was right. Better to have the evil doctor be judged by a jury and forced to live the rest of her life in a cage.

But that was not to be. The woman was dead. Murdered. An entirely different jury had spoken, pronounced her guilty, and sentenced her to death. And whether Eric approved or not, I had to say I felt as if justice of a sort had been served.

And once again, we had no way of knowing how she died. Not yet, anyway.

We made it to the cupboard door and stepped into the long tiled bathroom, retracing our steps to the bottom of the treacherous spiral stone staircase.

We had to take it slowly and when we reached the door leading to the back hallway, I breathed a sigh of relief. "Made it. Let's call Eric."

But Mac came to a sudden stop in front of me, and I realized he was blocked by Ricky.

Mac put his hand on Ricky's shoulder. "Ricky, are you okay? Come on, bud. We need to move it on out of here and call the police."

But Ricky stayed right where he was and I

was getting a really bad feeling. I mean, I'd been getting bad feelings every day here at the Gables, but this was really bad. Especially when Ricky began to raise his arms in the air.

"What the heck is going on?" I whispered.

"Shhh." I heard Mac say it, but then I watched him raise his arms, too, and I wanted to scream. Someone was going to hurt him and I couldn't do anything about it.

I was still tucked inside the stairwell and couldn't see, but suddenly Ricky spoke and I got the gist of the situation.

"Hey, Rachel, that's not necessary," Ricky said, cajoling. "It's me. Ricky. You should put that gun down."

I thought I might pass out at the words, but I needed to think clearly. What could I do?

Rachel had a gun trained on Ricky. And Mac. Oh God.

"We understand what you're going through," Mac said carefully. "We want to help."

"You can't help me. Nobody can help me." Rachel sucked in a deep breath and I realized she had been crying. I hated that I knew what that sounded like. I'd been bursting into tears on a regular basis myself for the last week.

"It was supposed to be perfect," she moaned. "We were going to make it beautiful for everyone, but now it can never be anything but ugly."

"That's not true," Mac said, keeping his tone light. "We can make it work. You know Jane wants that, too. Her mom was stuck here for a while so she knows how ugly it was back then. But Jane's trying to give this place new life. And so are you."

"Jane knows," she murmured.

"That's right."

"Ricky," she said. "You know."

"Yeah, I know." His voice grew stronger. "My mom was an evil witch and she hurt people. She hurt me. I'm glad you put her in the Baths."

"She put me in the Baths," Rachel whispered, and I had a feeling she was starting to lose it. Or maybe she'd lost it a while ago, but she'd been able to put up a good front until recently.

"Hey, she put me in there, too." Ricky was back to cajoling, trying to relate. It was a good thing for him to do, but I wasn't sure it would work. The woman seemed pretty far gone. But Ricky kept trying. "Come on, Rachel. Put the gun down. Nobody here is going to hurt you."

"Judson was going to tell everyone about the doctor," she said. "He was going to find proof that she killed people. So she killed Judson." She sobbed as she said his name and I wondered if she had been in love with him.

"Why did he throw the blood at you?" Mac asked.

"He was supposed to throw it at the billboard," she explained. "It was symbolic."

I could see Mac nodding. "I understand."

"But that woman, Prudence," Ricky said. "She bumped into him and his aim was off."

"She was Fairchild's nurse," Rachel said. "She did everything the doctor told her to do."

"So you were working with the protesters?" Mac wondered. "You had a plan?"

"Our plan was to bring Dr. Fairchild here. Out in the open. We wanted her to face her enemies. Us."

"But then Prudence started to interfere," Ricky said.

"And then Fairchild killed Judson. I had to kill her."

"Of course you did," Mac reasoned.

"Judson was a good guy," Ricky said.

"And she killed him."

"She killed him," Ricky repeated the words.

"I had to kill her!" Rachel screamed. "She would've kept killing and getting away with it."

"I'm glad you killed her!" Ricky cried. "She told me she was going to put me back in a mental institution."

"When did she tell you that?" Mac demanded. "When did you talk to her?"

Ricky bowed his head. "She found me in the pub. She came in with her henchman."

"Prudence?"

"Yeah. She said I was still unruly and I needed to learn some discipline. She said she would give me a shot of something and calm me down. She liked to use needles."

Ricky's voice grew thinner and if I didn't know him, I might've thought he was twelve years old. He sounded so frightened.

I was pretty frightened myself. What a nightmare of a mother he'd had to live with.

Mac began to speak to her in his cool, calm voice and that was when I pulled my phone out and called Eric's direct line. I turned the sound way down and huddled behind the doorjamb.

When Eric answered, I whispered, "Back hallway. She has a gun. Hurry." Then I turned the sound all the way off so nobody would hear him if he started talking or if my phone rang. But hopefully Eric would be able to hear Rachel's voice. I held the phone up as close to the doorjamb as possible without being seen and hoped that Eric would get every word.

"Did she hurt your sister?" Mac asked. "Did she hurt Regina?"

"She killed my sister." Rachel sobbed. "She tried to make it look like a suicide. But my sister never would've killed herself. The doctor did it. She killed her. And it should've been me."

"Don't say that, Rachel," he said. "You're alive and that's a good thing. You'll be able to tell your story and everyone will know what the doctor did. You can spread the word about her. And you can tell them all the good things that your sister did. We need you to tell the world what happened here so that it never happens again."

"It should've been me," she repeated.

"Why do you say that?"

"I was sick," she murmured.

I realized what she meant just as Mac said, "Rachel, were you a patient here?"

"Yes." She sounded lost now. Maybe she was. "I was sick. My mind was cockeyed. I needed help. But the doctor didn't help me. She just hurt me."

"I'm sorry."

"My sister used to visit me and I would

382

tell her what they were doing to me. She believed me. And on one visit, she pulled me into the bathroom upstairs and she took off all of her pretty clothes and made me put them on. She combed my hair and made me look pretty like her. And then she put my hospital gown on herself. And she messed up her hair and she told me to go home with Daddy and get his doctor to give me the right medicine to make me feel better."

"Oh, sweetheart," Mac said. "So she stayed here and pretended to be you?"

"Yes. She said she wanted to verify all my stories so she could tell Daddy and he would fire the doctor and shut down this place. She wanted to get information on the doctor so they would believe her. So I got to go home."

"That must've made you happy."

"So happy," she murmured. "My sister said she wasn't worried because she knew that Daddy would come back right away and take her home. And then we could all be together again. But as soon as I got home, Daddy knew it was me." She smiled sadly. "He was the only one who could tell us apart. And then, maybe it was the shock of seeing me come home, or maybe because he was afraid that my sister was now stuck in this place, but he had a heart attack."

"I'm sorry," Mac murmured.

She nodded. "It was sudden and scary, but it turned out to be a mild one and he was only hospitalized for a few days, and then he rushed back to find my sister." Rachel sniffed and I knew there were tears in her eyes. "B-but she died before we could get there. I know Fairchild killed her because she could obviously tell that the two of us had traded places. The doctor probably thought that my sister was spying on her. And she was. And maybe Fairchild didn't mean to kill her but I know she had to be angry. And when she got angry, she got really mean."

"She put her in the bathtub," Ricky said. "Judson saw it. That's why he was looking for evidence."

"What kind of evidence?"

"I don't know," Ricky said. "Do you know, Rachel?"

She didn't speak and seemed to have drifted away to her own little world. But still, it all made perfect sense to me.

"DNA evidence," she said finally. "There was blood. She cut my sister's wrists."

"We can look for the evidence," Mac said.

"Really?"

"Yeah." Mac hesitated, then asked, "Is

384

your name Rachel?"

"I'm Reggie," she whispered.

Oh my God, I thought. This was Reggie.

That answered a lot of questions, but just now, I needed to get Mac and Ricky to safety. I could only hope that Eric was on the way.

I crouched down in hopes of sneaking a peek around Mac's legs to see what Rachel — Reggie — was doing without her seeing me.

She still had the gun trained on Ricky and Mac, but I didn't think she meant to kill them. She simply had run out of options, or so she thought.

And just then I saw Eric sneaking slowly down the carpeted hall and I knew I had to find a way to divert Reggie's attention.

I looked around and saw the stacks of glass windows leaning against the wall. Without another thought, I kicked out and watched half the stack crash on the floor.

Reggie jolted. Her gun hand went wild. The shot sounded like a small explosion and she screamed.

Mac dashed over and grabbed the gun and Eric raced to subdue Rachel.

I heard her moan. "Noooo!"

I ran to Mac, who grabbed me and whirled me around. "You saved the day."

"No, I think you did that. You and Ricky talked her down."

Reggie sagged against Eric, who was so kind and careful to hold her just gently enough to allow her to remain standing. The poor woman had to be exhausted and frightened to death.

"She didn't want to hurt us," Ricky insisted. "My mom was the one who hurt lots of people. Not just me. But Reggie, too."

"I know," Mac murmured.

"So Reggie, I mean, you know, Rachel. She didn't want to hurt us. She's a good person."

Mac nodded, glancing at me. "I think she was doing well with her medication all this time, but she must've been triggered when Dr. Fairchild came back to town."

"We were all triggered by that," Ricky admitted, his face pale and sweaty.

I recalled the faces of the protesters as they had huddled together, listening to the doctor's arrogant speech the other day. "I think you're right, Ricky."

Mac approached Eric. "I know you have to take her in, but I want to appear as a character witness whenever she goes before the judge."

"I'll let you know," he said. "Thanks to Shannon, I heard what she said. I'll be writing up a full report and you might want to see about getting her a good lawyer."

I gazed at Reggie, saw the calmness in her eyes. As if she had finally faced her demons and won. Turning to Eric, I said, "Something tells me she has a whole team of lawyers."

I knew that the woman had inherited her father's fortune and I wondered if maybe she'd been planning this moment for half of her life. Maybe this had all been part of her plan. I just hoped she would be able to keep the Gables project alive. Jane would need it for her own peace of mind, and in the long run, so would the protesters. I wanted to help her make this place whole again, to turn it into a sanctuary instead of a pit of despair. And the legacy of Dr. Jones would live on while Dr. Fairchild would fade away in infamy.

I was happy that Eric shut the whole place down for a few days while he processed the doctor's body and worked the crime scene.

I dispersed my guys to other work sites around town so they could keep busy and get paid. For myself, I couldn't concentrate, kept replaying Rachel and Reggie's sad story in my head. My two foremen were real troopers as always and picked up the slack, visiting the work sites and taking care of our crew. I found myself pacing around my house, fidgeting and worrying and wondering. I finally just walked out to the beach to clear my head.

I'd had mixed feelings about Rachel Powers, but now my heart was filled with so much sympathy for her and her sister, it would've made me cry if I hadn't vowed not to do that again. At least for a week or two.

After all my research on Dr. Jones and his philosophy of treating patients in all sorts of positive ways, it was sickening to see what Dr. Fairchild had turned the once-beautiful Gables hospital into. It had been a hellhole. A torture chamber. Maybe the protesters were right. Maybe they should've burned it down.

But no. I didn't really believe that. I wanted to do exactly what Jane had always dreamed of doing: turn the Gables into a good place. A peaceful spot on the hill overlooking the gorgeous blue ocean, surrounded by tall trees and lush gardens. And if there was any way that Reggie was able to keep the project alive, I would be right there to help those dreams come to fruition.

"I thought you might be out here."

I turned and smiled at Mac. "I'm so glad

you found me."

He sat down in the sand and wrapped his arms around me. We sat like that for a long time.

"That was rough," he said finally. "After the first minute, I never feared for my life. But I feared for hers."

"You thought she might turn the gun on herself?" Just saying those words made my blood freeze.

"She was suffering," he said. "So unhappy. And all because of that horrific excuse for a human." He shook his head. "I can't believe Fairchild actually held the title of doctor. What a travesty."

"I know." I leaned into him and just kept breathing. "I spoke to Jane a little while ago and told her everything. She said she's glad she won't ever have to see that doctor again."

"So am I," Mac admitted.

"I asked Jane if she remembered ever seeing Prudence when she used to visit her mom."

"What did she say?"

"She didn't remember her. Jane thinks maybe she was so focused on her mother, and also that awful doctor, that she didn't really see the faces of any of the others."

"Makes sense."

"And here's the bottom line. Jane told me that Prudence checked out sometime in the middle of the night and no one's seen her since." I shook my head. "She was so weird."

Mac nodded. "Ricky was saying he thought she probably just faded into the woodwork, which apparently was something she used to do on a regular basis."

"I'd like to find out if she was the one who pushed me, but we might never know."

"Probably not." He frowned. "I'd be happy never to see her again."

I sighed. "How's Ricky doing?"

"He'll be okay." Mac gave a firm nod, which I took to mean that he'd had a talk with Ricky and was feeling pretty good about his chances.

"I thought I might ask him if he'd like to work on my crew. Not sure he has any experience, but he could be a helper and maybe apprentice with one of the guys. I mean, if he wants to."

Mac looked at me. "You are amazing."

"So you think it's a good idea?"

"I think it's the best thing in the world." He leaned in and planted a kiss on my forehead.

"I just hope we'll be able to continue working on Jane's dream hotel."

"About that," he began. "I went with Eric

to the station and spoke to Reggie for a few minutes. She said that months ago, when she first worked out the plan with Judson to try to lure the doctor back to town, she called a meeting with her lawyers and the trustees of her family trust and instructed them all to continue with the Gables project."

"Really?"

"Apparently she had them put it in writing. So it's documented and it's budgeted and backed by a whole corporation."

"That's . . . wow, that's great." I felt my eyes tearing up and could only sigh. So much for my vow to remain dry-eyed. This had started to become a regular habit of mine and that was just wrong. It wasn't like me. As my sister had said, there's no crying in construction.

"Regina had a feeling that confronting the doctor — as she knew she would have to — wouldn't end well. But she was adamant that the Gables project continue in her sister's name."

"That is lovely."

"Yeah. She has a good heart. She just has, you know, problems."

I sighed. "I hope they'll take good care of her."

"We'll keep tabs on her."

"Good. I'm sure Jane will want to see how she's doing, too."

He paused for a few seconds, then said, "So I wanted to talk to you."

My heart plummeted. Those words never brought on good news. I cleared my throat. "What's up?"

"I'm thinking of moving."

I pressed my lips together. *Don't cry, you big baby,* I told myself, but then realized I was already crying. *You were waiting to have this talk with him, waiting to work out the future together. Maybe by thinking about it, I subtly pushed him into making a decision for himself. Was that crazy? Didn't matter. Now he was leaving. So this definitely did not turn out the way I planned. But God, why did it have to hurt so much?* "Is that right?" I said lightly. "When are you planning to make the move?"

"As soon as you say it's okay."

"Me? I don't want you to move."

"But I'm tired of living apart from you."

I stared at him. Slowly, I said, "I think I'm not thinking the same thing you're thinking. Tell me what you want to do."

He smiled. "I want to live with you. I want to be with you. Spend all my time with you. Is that clear enough?"

"Oh." I started to laugh. "Oh yeah. That's

crystal clear."

"How do you feel about that?"

"I feel . . . I feel so . . ." Happy? Joyful? Relieved? "I feel so ready to make that happen. I love you, Mac. I want to be with you, too."

He kissed me then, and all my doubts and foolish worries faded to dust. But then I frowned. "Your house is beautiful and you have the beach right there. But I really love my house and hate the thought of leaving it. But I will, for you. What were you thinking we might do?"

"As a matter of fact, I've been thinking about this for a while. You know the lighthouse was recently decommissioned so I don't have to worry about keeping it operational. I was thinking of turning the house and the lighthouse into a writers' retreat. I've done a lot of reading on the subject, because you know, I'm a writer."

"I knew that," I said, grinning.

"Right? And I'm a mastermind researcher. So I know that I should probably hire someone local to clean and cook and keep the place. So individual writers or a writers' group could come and stay for a week or a month, or whatever." He smiled. "And we could always use it as a vacation home when we want to get away from the hustle and bustle of Lighthouse Cove."

"Yeah, it can get hectic around here." I laughed. "But where would you write?"

He played with the bit of fringe on my denim jacket. "Well, you know I wrote my best work when I first moved here and was living in your garage apartment. Plenty of room. Great view. I was hoping you would let me rent one of them to use as an office."

I was taken aback. "You don't have to rent it, Mac. I'll give it to you for free."

He kissed me again. "You're making this too easy for me."

I touched his cheek. "It's the easiest decision I've ever had to make."

"I love you, Irish."

"Oh, Mac." I wrapped my arms around him. "I love you right back."

ACKNOWLEDGMENTS

I never dreamed that Shannon Hammer would someday be asked to transform a crumbling Victorian-era insane asylum into an elegant world-class hotel. But then I discovered Hotel Henry — formerly known as the Buffalo State Asylum for the Insane — and Shannon's newest project became crystal clear in my mind.

I spent two short days at Hotel Henry and I'm grateful for their hospitality and the truly wonderful cuisine of 100 Acres restaurant. I want to acknowledge the Richardson Olmsted Campus and the fascinating tours they offer. I'm grateful to them and to Professor Carla Yanni, author of *The Architecture of Madness*, for her extensive study of therapeutic design and the work of Dr. Thomas Story Kirkbride, who believed that "good architecture was essential for the comfort, security, and recovery of lunatics." While not the most sensitive or politically correct way of putting it, my fictional Dr. Jones nevertheless owes everything to both Dr. Kirkbride and Professor Yanni.

A very special thank-you to Mary Lou and Michael Debergalis, my Buffalo family, for first introducing me to Hotel Henry. It's been an adventure, for sure. And *muchas gracias* to the elusive genius Miri for her stunning photography and insights.

Thank you as always to my superagent, Christina Hogrebe, and everyone at JRA. I'm grateful every day for your guidance and support.

I am the luckiest writer in the world to work with senior editor Michelle Vega, who is just plain brilliant and always awesome, wonderful, cheerful, and kind.

To the amazing team at Berkley/PRH, including Jenn Snyder, Jessica Mangicaro, Elisha Katz, Dache Rogers, and everyone in marketing, publicity, and the art department: thank you all for making me shine and for making my books the envy of all the others on the bookshelf.

To my beloved plot partners, Jenn McKinlay and Paige Shelton, for your friendship, generosity, inspiration, talent, and empathy. May there always be road trips and bad breakfast choices.

To Jenel Looney, who basically makes my

life better every day.

To my brothers and sisters-in-law and my nieces and nephews for helping me get through a really tough year with love and laughter and, yes, a few tears. I love you all.

And as always, much love and thanks to my personal bartender, chef, and pool man, Don. I do it all for you.

ABOUT THE AUTHOR

New York Times bestselling author **Kate Carlisle** worked in television for many years before turning to writing. Inspired by the northern seaside towns of her native California, where Victorian mansions grace the craggy cliffs and historic lighthouses warn fishermen and smugglers alike, Kate was drawn to create the Fixer-Upper Mysteries, featuring small-town girl Shannon Hammer, a building contractor specializing in home restoration. Kate also writes the *New York Times* bestselling Bibliophile Mysteries, featuring Brooklyn Wainwright.

The employees of Thorndike Press hope you have enjoyed this Large Print book. All our Thorndike, Wheeler, and Kennebec Large Print titles are designed for easy reading, and all our books are made to last. Other Thorndike Press Large Print books are available at your library, through selected bookstores, or directly from us.

For information about titles, please call:

(800) 223-1244

or visit our website at:

gale.com/thorndike

To share your comments, please write:

Publisher
Thorndike Press
10 Water St., Suite 310
Waterville, ME 04901